CW01238827

UNDER DARKENING SKIES

Also by Hilary Jones

Frontline

Eye of the Storm

Hilary Jones

UNDER DARKENING SKIES

MLP

Copyright © Hilary Jones 2025

The right of Hilary Jones to be identified as the Author of the Work has been asserted by him in accordance with the Copyright, Designs and Patents Act 1988.

First published in 2025 by Mountain Leopard Press
An imprint of Headline Publishing Group Limited

1

Apart from any use permitted under UK copyright law, this publication may only be reproduced, stored, or transmitted, in any form, or by any means, with prior permission in writing of the publishers or, in the case of reprographic production, in accordance with the terms of licences issued by the Copyright Licensing Agency.

All characters in this publication are fictitious and any resemblance to real persons, living or dead, is purely coincidental.

Cataloguing in Publication Data is available from the British Library

Hardback ISBN 978 1 0354 2179 4
Trade Paperback ISBN 978 1 0354 2180 0

Typeset in 13.5/16pt Mrs Eaves OT by Six Red Marbles UK, Thetford, Norfolk

Printed and bound in Great Britain by Clays Ltd, Elcograf S.p.A.

FSC www.fsc.org
MIX
Paper | Supporting responsible forestry
FSC® C104740

Headline's policy is to use papers that are natural, renewable and recyclable products and made from wood grown in well-managed forests and other controlled sources. The logging and manufacturing processes are expected to conform to the environmental regulations of the country of origin.

Headline Publishing Group Limited
An Hachette UK Company
Carmelite House
50 Victoria Embankment
London EC4Y 0DZ

The authorised representative in the EEA is Hachette Ireland,
8 Castlecourt Centre, Dublin 15, D15 XTP3, Ireland (email: info@hbgi.ie)

www.headline.co.uk
www.hachette.co.uk

To the next generation. Bella, Luc, Lara, Amelia, Rafe and Eloise.

Prologue

St Mary's Hospital, Praed Street, London, 1928

Despite the fever, with her angelic, heart-shaped face and deep-blue eyes, five-year-old Ashlyn Roberts looked totally at peace. Usually bright and vivacious, with a ready smile and an infectious laugh, her parents adored her: the youngest of five children, she was the apple of their eye. Now, though, she lay in a crowded ward, recovering from a second operation on her left arm, a last-ditch effort to halt the infection that had been galloping upwards from the angry wound on the back of her hand. Four days earlier, she had been out playing hopscotch with her brothers and sisters and had taken a tumble, scraping her bare skin against a rusty metal drainpipe. Wrapped up in the excitement of the game, Ashlyn had hardly even noticed the graze. It was no more than a flesh wound at first, barely drawing blood.

Soon, though, a circle of redness had become visible around the scratch, and it felt a little sore. On the second day, thin red tendrils had begun to branch upwards from the graze, and the wound had swollen. Ashlyn's parents were far from wealthy, and, like so many people in their situation, did not qualify for any employee welfare insurance schemes, which would have entitled them to the services of a private doctor. So, her mother had tried to make do with poultices and antiseptics. That night, Ashlyn had become feverish, shaking uncontrollably with violent spasms. Despite their circumstances, her anxious parents had called for medical help. If necessary, they would sell their wedding rings to fund the treatment.

When the doctor arrived, he had taken one look at Ashlyn and arranged for her to be rushed around the corner to St Mary's Hospital. Dr William Burnett, the surgeon on duty, had immediately admitted her into his care.

'My arm hurts,' Ashlyn had said through her sobs. 'Mummy says you will make me better.'

Her desperate parents looked at the doctor imploringly. 'Ashlyn,' he said gently, 'the doctors here, and every one of these wonderful nurses, will do everything we can to make you better. But first, we need to get you into a nice comfortable bed on the ward with all the other children. I need you to be brave and say goodbye to your parents for now. I'll make sure you see them later.'

'It's OK, my love.' Mrs Roberts kissed her little girl on the forehead. 'We'll be right here beside you when you wake up.'

Will had already identified that gangrene was present; the odour was unmistakable. He had seen the disease many times before, during his time as a young stretcher-bearer on the Western Front. He had patiently and gently explained to Ashlyn's parents what needed to be done, and they had given permission for a surgery to save her life. Yet the operation had failed to stem the onward march of the microorganisms. Despite Ashlyn's high fever and rapidly developing anaemia, Will had had no other option but to perform an emergency second operation, this time at the shoulder.

He assessed his patient. Although her cheeks were flushed with fever, she was otherwise pale and fragile-looking. Her curly blonde locks were matted and her brow was spotted with beads of perspiration. The skin over her chest and limbs had turned blotchy and she was ice-cold to the touch. Will bent down and used a small glass pipette to administer a few drops of water into her parched mouth. He gently smoothed a thin layer of Vaseline over her dry, crusted lips. He was well-versed in the consequences of blood poisoning, and knew there was nothing else he could have done to prevent the poor young girl's life from ebbing away. He dreaded the thought of breaking the news to her parents; nothing short of a miracle could save her now. Retreating quietly from the bedside, he made his way back along the hospital corridor and up the stairs, towards the relatives' room at the rear of the building. How cruel that no matter how serious a child's condition, their loved ones were permitted to visit only once a week – and for a few snatched moments, at that. Though a man of great experience, Will still found it difficult to accept the loss of life, particularly when it came to the young. Though he tried to remain objective and detached, each and every loss proved harrowing and heartbreaking. Death was something that never became any easier to process, no matter how frequently he came upon it.

Normally, he would have been able to compartmentalise his feelings and balance his emotions with his important work. But not today. Not even the promise of a rare evening out with his wife was able to lift his spirits. He was in possession of front-row tickets for a production of *Good News* at a Haymarket theatre that evening, something with which he had been hoping to surprise her. Now, he had neither the inclination nor the stomach for it. He knew Grace would understand, though. As a frontline nurse, she had experienced similar situations herself.

Will handed the tickets to a pair of grateful staff nurses just going off duty, and received a generous peck on the cheek from each of them in return. As he watched the noisy pair hurry away down the corridor, he turned to peer in through the open door of the little room opposite, where a short man in a long white coat, who seemed totally absorbed in his work, had his back to him. Will knew the man to be rather shy and awkward, so he was not inclined to disturb him – and besides, he had a pressing engagement of his own.

*

Dr Alexander Fleming became vaguely aware of footsteps and excited women's voices in the corridor behind him, but he was too engrossed in his latest creation to trouble himself with investigating the commotion. He continued to carefully seed the different types of bacteria on to agar plates and watched them develop into multicoloured tapestries of varying textures. Growing slowly in the gelatinous, waxy material, the culture in front of him resembled a miniature version of Loch Lomond, blue waters surrounded by a forest of green. He could almost make out pine trees and pink heather. 'Astonishing!' he remarked.

Colonies of bacteria in the petri dish next to it resembled a replica of the islands of Skye, Mull, Islay, and Arran, surrounded by the wild Hebridean sea. Satisfied with his latest microbial portraits, Fleming placed the collection to one side and considered his recent observations.

He had returned from holiday that summer to discover that a colony growing on one of his discarded petri dishes had become contaminated by a mould. That in itself was not particularly surprising, since moulds and fungi were often known to find their way on to the agar dishes by chance, ruining otherwise pure cultures of microorganisms intended for study. No, what was interesting in this particular case was that there appeared to be no such bacteria growing anywhere near the mould. *No staphylococcal bacteria*, Fleming noted in his journal. There was exuberant growth on the agar elsewhere, but around the blue-green mould itself, there was only a transparent halo of bacterial cells – apparently, dead ones.

What had formerly been a well-grown colony is now a faint shadow of its former self.

Something about the mould appeared to be inhibiting the staphylococci, even killing them off. What was that something, Fleming wondered, and could it possibly be isolated, identified, and used as an antiseptic?

The most likely explanation is that the mould releases an enzyme, a naturally occurring cellular catalyst that digests the cell walls of the bacteria. Perhaps this enzyme might prove useful, he wrote.

Fleming's medical superior did not share his enthusiasm. Dr Almroth Wright, the highly qualified director of the Inoculation Department, who had previously developed a vaccine for typhoid, had seemed less than impressed when Fleming had brought his observation to his attention. Glaring at his colleague, he had dismissed the findings as unoriginal and insignificant.

As a lieutenant in the British Army, Fleming had witnessed first-hand the devastating consequences of wound infection sustained by soldiers on the battlefield. He would not be so easily dissuaded, and would continue to experiment with his precious microbes. 'After all, one sometimes finds what one is not looking for,' he told himself. His ingenuity and perseverance had already attained scientific recognition. Had he not designed a way of testing for syphilis using a mere drop or two of blood? Had he not also shown conclusively that in soldiers' uniforms uncontaminated by blood or pus, copious numbers of bacteria could be grown in the apparently clean material? A significant finding, which had helped explain why more than half the men who'd perished in the Great War had died from infection rather than from the wounds themselves.

The behaviour of microorganisms had occupied him since he had started working in the claustrophobic little laboratory, but now they consumed him. *Dr Almost Right*, as some people called him behind his back, might have had a monstrous ego, but he was not infallible, and Fleming resented his findings being so easily dismissed. A qualified doctor, he had never performed surgery, and had little hands-on contact or indeed anything much to do with patients at all, nor with the clinical goings-on in any of the wards. He was an awkward conversationalist and preferred his own company, finding it difficult to establish any kind of rapport with patients or colleagues. He was a bacteriologist by heart and his passion was simple: playing with microbes – and he was good at it. Consequently, although he had the results of a young patient's blood and swab tests in front of him, he had not visited the child's bedside and was unaware of her specific clinical condition. All he knew from the evidence before him was that whoever these samples belonged to was almost certainly going to die. Dismissing the thought instantly, he dropped his written findings into his out-tray, the contents of which the porter would soon collect and take down to the nurses' station on the children's ward.

Downstairs, leaning over a child's hospital bed surrounded by closed curtains, Dr Will Burnett closed little

Ashlyn Roberts' eyelids, drew the bedsheet over her face, and pronounced her 'life extinct'. He nodded to Matron to proceed with the laying out of the body and wondered again how he would be able to summon the courage to break such terrible news.

1

Mill Lane, Oxford, March 1937

Will Burnett woke up freezing and tried to extricate himself from the sleeping form of his wife. Trying hard not to wake Grace, he gently pulled his arm out from underneath her, though not gently enough, it seemed. She stirred and turned over, gazing at him with her beautiful blue eyes.

'Where do you think you're going?' she whispered. 'It's so cold in this room, and a girl needs to be kept warm!'

'That's Victorian dwellings for you. As for me, I've been doing my best. And making huge personal sacrifices in the process.'

'What sacrifices?'

'Well, I can't feel my left arm, for a start. It's as if it belongs to someone else.'

'Oh, do stop whining, dear.'

'Whining? I need this arm! It comes in very useful at work, I shall have you know!'

'Speaking of work,' said Grace, 'we'd better make a move. I can already hear the twins crashing about in the kitchen and if we don't get a wiggle on, we'll both be late!'

With the help of the man who had been so instrumental in offering Will his scholarship at St George's all those years ago, their son, Daniel, had secured a training post in psychiatry at

Maudsley Hospital in London, while his sister, Emily, had been perfectly happy to move to Oxford with her parents and explore her growing interest in engineering and aviation. A strange occupation for a girl, some thought, but Grace was secretly delighted as both she and Emily had always loved tinkering with engines.

'And in case you've already forgotten,' she added, 'we have half the extended family coming over for dinner tonight, and we have nothing prepared.'

'Damn. I *had* forgotten.'

'I told you yesterday!'

'Ah, that's right.' Will put his fingers to his temples in mock-reminiscence. 'It's all coming back to me, along with the feeling in my arm. I remember now – Jack is working locally over in Jericho, and Fitz is finally bringing Aunt Clara up on the train from London.'

'You're such a nincompoop.'

'I don't suppose Shauna will be coming, too?'

'Fitz hasn't said. But I can't remember the last time I even saw them together. If ever there was a marriage of convenience!'

'OK, so with Emily and Daniel both here as well, that will be seven of us. Eight, if your mother Dorothy finally decides she's up to it. I'll go to the outdoor market today for provisions. Do you want me to get a chicken from Kingswood farmhouse? I'll be passing there anyway.'

'Perfect. It'll be lovely to have us all around the same table again, catching up on the family gossip, won't it? It's been a while.'

'You bet. Oh, what about drinks?' asked Will, trying to rub away the pins and needles that were still pricking his arm with a vengeance.

'The cellar's well-stocked, Will. What self-respecting medical family would have it any other way?'

'Excellent. That's Jack catered for, then.'

'Never mind Jack. At the end of a busy week, I think we'll all be in need of some fortification!' Grace grabbed Will's elbow with both hands and squeezed it as hard as she could.

'Ow!' cried Will, rubbing the limb furiously. Now it was super-sensitive, the nerves jangling as the blood slowly flowed back to revive them.

2

Jericho Gardens, Oxford

The dilapidated row of pre-Victorian dwellings in Oxford's Jericho Gardens had, for decades, housed dozens of the poorest families. Now those houses stood cold and deserted, awaiting their fate. In moments, they would cease to exist.

Jack Burnett had found his calling in demolition, finding it so much more rewarding than construction. The tedious insistence of architects who rigidly adhered to technical plans and drawings was time-consuming, not to mention tiresome in the extreme. These people, he'd thought, these stuck-up graduates with their fancy degrees, who didn't have the foggiest idea of how to build anything themselves, and who never got their hands dirty. Well, as long as I get paid, he'd supposed. He could absorb their idealistic claptrap and their new-fangled ways, provided it was worth his while. After all, it was the client who was forking out, not him. If their unnecessary attention to detail and their cravings for amendments created delays and rework, who was he to argue?

With demolition, it was different. What might have taken years to build could be flattened and destroyed in a matter of hours, the devastation bringing with it an emotional outlet for Jack's unresolved anger and inner conflict. It was a form of catharsis. A painstakingly constructed dwelling, factory, or office block could be reduced to a heap of mangled steel and rubble in moments. It was noisy and messy, but it was quick, and effective.

In some ways, it was a bit like his relationships. So much easier to ruin and smash than to nurture and cherish. He was too impatient, really, to constantly revisit the same old project to refine and perfect it. He preferred something you could close the book on. It was the story of his life.

His relationship with Amandine was the nearest he had ever come to love. On the battlefields of Flanders, immediately after the Great War, their romance had blossomed at her father's farm. Despite his gruesome job, clearing the fields of discarded ordnance and the rotting corpses that were being unearthed, he had found a woman who had given him everything he had ever wanted. Unconditional love for the first time in his life, understanding, and a chance to marry and raise a family. She had also given free rein to his unconventional, unpredictable, and often selfish nature. Yet still, he had rejected that love, and Amandine had let him go. He was young, impetuous and restless. He had simply not been ready to put down roots. It was a decision he often regretted, but he allowed himself little time for recrimination or remorse. At least his war wounds were tolerable.

Demolition, though, had given him a purpose. It was as if his inner demons could be drowned out, along with the memories of the devastating explosions he had set off in the tunnels he had mined under the enemy trenches at Messines and La Boisselle. Now, as he watched the huge wrecking ball freefalling on to the roof of 28 Jericho Gardens, he felt a familiar sense of elation. It was the same intoxicating excitement he had experienced as a little boy, mischievously hurling a lump of coal through a neighbour's window or throwing a bicycle into the river.

Jack revelled in the thrill of it and assumed every hot-blooded young man would feel the same, which was why he had brought his nephew along with him this morning. Daniel had often asked what kind of work he did, and this project was an ideal opportunity to show him.

The huge, forged-steel sphere crashed through the tiles and slabs of masonry as if they were made of tissue paper. The crane hoisted the ball back up again on its steel chain, and, pivoting the boom to accelerate it towards its target, swung it to and fro like a pendulum until it was sent crashing through the walls of the little house and out the other side. It was rudimentary and capricious, and not a precision instrument by any means.

As Jack's eyes sparkled and his body tensed with the thrill of the devastation, Daniel regarded him with interest. He already knew quite a lot about his uncle's insalubrious past, and had often considered the differences between him and his own father. A pair of brothers, born just two years apart, yet so different in personality and outlook.

It was strange that Daniel's grandfather, Robbie, had reacted so differently to adversity than Jack, who had rather seemed to take to it. When Robbie's wife, Evie, had been taken from him in childbirth, he was pathologically bereaved. He had become withdrawn and depressed and had never recovered. He had survived the war, yet he had never been rehabilitated. Now, he languished in a residential home for the psychologically damaged and infirm. His son Jack, too, had witnessed terrible events, having tragically lost close friends, and suffered personally, but while Robbie would startle at sudden sounds and recoil from bright, flashing lights, Jack seemed to relish and embrace the unexpected. It seemed to give him focus and revive him, almost as though he lived for it.

Daniel looked over at the dust cloud rising from the wreckage of the collapsed building, the mangled iron rods jutting out from the rubble. Through the dust, he spotted his uncle gesticulating excitedly, and the quantity surveyor determining how many trucks it would take to clear the site. Two first-aiders were on standby in case anybody got hurt. There was also a policeman on hand for safety, to ensure onlookers kept their distance. It was people and personalities that piqued Daniel's interest, rather than places and buildings.

Jack glanced back to gauge his nephew's reaction to the demolition. He seemed to have been watching him instead of the unfolding scene. Daniel quickly averted his gaze, pretending he had not been staring. But Jack was fine with it. Daniel was a well-built lad, strong and athletic like his father, Will, but was also quiet, thoughtful, and curious. Better still, he rarely seemed to judge or criticise, unlike others Jack could think of. No, Daniel was a good lad. Jack felt relaxed and easy in his company, and was somehow calmer whenever his nephew was around.

3

Mill Lane

The coq au vin that Grace and Clara had prepared had been heartily devoured, with nothing left to waste. Even the residual juices at the bottom of the serving dish had been mopped up with slabs of heavily buttered home-made bread. Now eight of them sat around the dining-room table, enjoying an after-dinner drink and a family chat. In the end, Dorothy had finally declined the invitation to join them, in one of her familiar states of unnecessary anxiety – this time over the welfare of Rupert and Henry, another two of her offspring. Fitz, Grace's youngest sibling and MP for Southwark, had brought up to Oxford his newly appointed parliamentary assistant as well as Will's aunt Clara, and had selected from the larder a ten-year-old single malt whisky from Oban. Jack, the rest of the bottle in front of him, was carefully protecting it from the hands of others.

Kitty, Will's sister, was heading out to Spain. 'Kitty can look after herself,' said Fitz, trying to sound reassuring and to allay the fears of Will and Grace, who were going to take a lot more convincing. They both knew how unpredictable survival was in the theatre of war, and Kitty was still so young. Despite her adventurous nature and her passion for language and travel, they considered her rather too idealistic and naïve to recognise what might have been awaiting her in Spain, where a civil war had been underway for some months now.

'She'll be safe in the bosom of the Spanish Red Cross,' Fitz added, 'and besides, she has friends in Barcelona from the time she spent teaching there, as well as Thiago and Liese to hold her hand.'

Grace stared back at him. She had first-hand experience of what the fascists in Nazi Germany were capable of, and she had no reason to believe that those who had rebelled against the democratically elected People's Second Republic and marched into Spain would be any different. Yes, it was true that their friend Liese was travelling with Kitty, but how many lives did she have left?

Armed with forged papers, Liese had narrowly escaped Germany only six months earlier, smuggled across the Dutch border in a horsebox. Had she been detained, she would undoubtedly have been arrested and sent off to a concentration camp, just as her parents had been. She and Grace had been through a lot together. They were the same age, and both specialised in infectious diseases. Liese was smart, savvy and cautious, but hatred could make people do dangerous things.

'Liese knows what she is getting into,' Fitz continued. 'She hates the Nazis. That's why she has been helping Otto Schiff.'

'Otto Schiff?' asked Grace.

'He's the director of the Jewish refugee community. She's also been working with the immigration service at Bloomsbury House in London. She has been lobbying hard to accommodate as many German refugees as possible. She won't be taking any silly risks.' Fitz looked across the table towards his assistant, Stephen, for support. Fitzwilliam 'Fitz'

Tustin-Pennington was gaining something of a name for himself in parliament as a committed and passionate liberal who was not prepared to compromise his principles. As such, he had become something of a thorn in Prime Minister Stanley Baldwin's side – though secretly the PM rather admired him, what with his forthright approach and laconic sense of humour.

'But I fear she will, Fitz,' said Grace, cutting in. 'I know Liese, she's fearless. It's precisely because she harbours such animosity against the fascist military that she might not act rationally. I'm worried for her, but much more worried about Kitty, who I sense is going for the adventure of it.'

'I don't think so,' said Will. 'She is as antifascist as the rest of us. Anyway, we couldn't have stopped her. God knows, we tried hard enough. My little sister is just as impetuous and defiant as my wife.'

Grace raised her eyes to the ceiling, but grinned.

'And what with her fervour to support the suffragettes – and the liberal philosophies that you've instilled into her, Fitz . . . well, the Red Cross will only make her socialist leanings stronger.'

'Don't blame me for the recklessness of your sister,' Fitz retorted. 'The Red Cross is only allowed to operate in Spain because of its neutrality. There's no International Red Cross involved at present as it's an internal conflict, not an international one.' Stephen could sense Fitz becoming irritated, and nudged his foot under the table for reassurance.

'Fitzy, for a politician, you're so short-sighted sometimes,' said Grace. 'You've only got to look at what has already happened down there to realise the International Red Cross are bound to become involved. The appalling number of casualties and the atrocities on both sides could so easily spill over into a much wider conflict.'

Having patiently listened to the exchange in silence, Daniel diplomatically changed the subject to his grandfather Robbie, who he had been visiting regularly at the Maudsley Hospital, where he was being treated as an inpatient. Emily then brought the conversation round to her own favourite topic: flying. The human-powered aircraft *Pedaliante* had flown a full kilometre outside Milan the day before. But Will would not be distracted from his concerns about Kitty.

Fitz sighed. 'Look, Will, if I didn't have a dicky heart and could be of any use to the Republican cause, I'd be out there myself. As it is, I get breathless just arguing with Baldwin and Eden in parliament about their refusal to do anything. This Non-Intervention Agreement signed last August isn't worth the paper it's written on. Hitler and Mussolini are flagrantly ignoring it and are laughing in our faces.'

'Britain and France adhere to it for fear of being drawn into the conflict themselves,' said Will.

'They are making it worse, in my opinion,' continued Fitz. 'They closed the borders and banned arms sales to the government whilst Italy and Germany are sending men, transport and arms, tipping the scales in favour of the Nationalist rebels. They're even refusing to issue passports to people they suspect might be travelling to Spain, and are threatening to make volunteering illegal.'

Like the majority of the country, Will and Grace were sympathetic to the Republican cause, too. Will had come from a working-class background. His father had been a dockyard worker, his mother a seamstress. He had no time for the authoritarianism of the Army, and even less time for the church. He had fought discrimination and privilege to qualify as a doctor, and was all too aware that the health and social prospects of the poor and the less educated among his patients had been disadvantaged from the start.

Grace had come from an aristocratic background, an environment a world away from Will's own. Her beloved father, Arthur, had been a liberal who had only fought for king and country in the belief it would make the world a better and fairer place. He had treated the workers on his estate with decency and fair-mindedness. He'd considered them equals, and such egalitarianism had rubbed off on Grace. Her service in the Great War had demonstrated all too vividly the brutal realities of fascism, and she realised her father's liberalism was not dissimilar to the ideals of the Spanish anarchists who wanted equality and freedom from the aristocratic rule of wealthy landowners, and to run their farms and factories along communal lines.

'Why don't you just let her do what she wants?' said Jack, his words a little slurred now. 'We should all do what we want, shouldn't we, Fitzy? Shouldn't we, Stephen? Even if other people disapprove.' There was a clear insinuation in the question, but no malice.

Jack had been around the block a few times himself. 'Listen, Will, Kitty is my sister too, remember. We all take risks because we choose to. Sometimes we have to. You treat people with all sorts of contagious diseases, any of which you could catch tomorrow. Kitty is ten years older than we were when we enlisted. Leave her be.' He poured himself another large tumbler of whisky.

'I do admire her for going,' said Will after a long pause. 'Don't misunderstand me, Jack. I love her determination and spirit. We might not want to admit it, Grace, but I suppose he's right. We might have done the same at her age.'

'You both did,' said Clara, 'only in a different war and in a different country.'

'And you both survived, all right!' said Fitz, cheerfully.

'I supported Kitty and her decision,' Clara added. 'You might not thank me for saying it, but Kitty is a young woman who will not be caged, nor should she be. I've raised her as a mother would, and I hope I've done at least half as well as Evie would have done herself, had she lived. But if I know Kitty at all, she will flourish, and it will be the making of her. Although I will worry, I'm so very, very proud of her.'

The others were temporarily lost for words. They knew just how close Clara was to Kitty and how much they meant to each other. She was also wiser than the lot of them.

'Look at my poor brother, Robbie,' Clara continued. 'Think of your previous neighbours in Putney; that lovely little boy, Freddie, whose short life was snuffed out by diphtheria. The people in your hospital wards, Grace, dying of TB or typhoid, and the ones who can't be saved by surgery, Will. There are dangers everywhere you go. Yet we all need a purpose and a passion for life. I suspect that Kitty, just like the two of you, will always feel most alive in the presence of danger. I'm sorry, but there it is.'

'That makes me feel pretty lifeless by comparison, Clara,' mused Fitz.

'Rubbish,' she scoffed. 'It wasn't your fault the Army classed you as unfit for service. At least you tried. You have other talents, Fitzy. You have the power and voice to create political change. You have the ear of Baldwin, Attlee and Eden because you are reasoned and persuasive. You can probably do more than any of us individually. Your heart might be anatomically feeble, but at least it's in the right place.'

Everyone around the table turned to look at Fitz, who was feeling a little embarrassed by the generous tribute. 'On the left-hand side in the mid-clavicular line in the fifth intercostal space?'

'Very good,' said Will, laughing. 'That's exactly where it is. An honorary medical degree for that man.'

4

French–Spanish Border, March 1937

Kitty was not far from the snow-covered summit of the Cirque de Gavarnie in the French Pyrenees. Grabbing Thiago by the hand, she hauled him up the giant granite step to join the rest of their motley band, who had gathered around a broad, flat part of the path. Most of them sat catching their breath, hunched over ancient stones that had fallen from the peaks.

Kitty had known Thiago forever. Growing up, they had lived just a few doors away from each other in their little terraced houses in Chiswick, and had been in the same classes at school since they were four years old. Although she still adored him, she had long since outgrown him romantically, having once had a crush on him. Kitty knew Thiago was only here now because he wanted to come to the rescue of his grandparents, who were being persecuted by the fascist rebels. The two friends also shared the same political ideals. What they did not share was the same level of athleticism; Kitty's hard-earned gymnastic and sporting prowess left the slightly-built Thiago in the shade. He sat on his haunches with his hands on his hips, recovering from the climb.

They had left the hut just outside Gedre two days ago; the ascent in the freezing, driving sleet had been relentless and exhausting. Since the border with Spain was now closed, it was their only means of crossing it unofficially. When their guide, Florentino, had first pointed out the vast semicircle of rock in the distance that formed the Cirque, Kitty had wondered how on earth it could possibly be scaled. Crossing over it into Spain seemed unthinkable. Yet they had been expertly led this way and that, under the trees of the lower slopes and over rock scree and across turbulent streams until they had started to ascend like tiny figures on a giant staircase.

'Not bad for a girl,' teased Michael, grinning. Kitty regarded him levelly.

'And you're surprisingly sprightly for a man of such advanced years,' she shot back. The others all laughed. They had spent the previous few hours exhausted and breathless, and the light-hearted repartee was a welcome distraction from their fatigue. In truth, she had proved far nimbler and more surefooted than most of them. Michael had been a miner, but had been made redundant more than once, and had never fully recovered from, or been compensated for, the injuries he sustained in a pit collapse. Now an active trade union leader, his sympathies lay entirely with the Spanish Republic, and he was on his way to join the British Battalion to fight alongside them against the Nationalists.

The entire group of climbers seemed to share many common traits, from their backgrounds to their sensibilities. Like Michael, Frank had worked hard for a living, in the industrial factories and mills of northern England, struggling to earn a decent wage during the Great Depression.

Fraser reminded Kitty of her father. He, too, had fought in the Great War, a veteran of many brutal offensives, and seemed almost as quiet and withdrawn as Robbie. He appeared just as disillusioned and depressed, too, but his singular hatred of fascism seemed to drive him on regardless. Leonard, Kitty supposed, was what people would call an intellectual; a university academic who talked about the morality of the struggle and the repugnance of the Nazi ideal. A wiry, haunted-looking man, he had reluctantly asked for help on the latest part of the climb, and she wondered how he would ever cope when it came to the practical reality of warfare.

Manny was a Jewish refugee, like Kitty's friend Liese. They had many things in common, the worst of which was that everything had been taken from them in Germany, including the lives of their families.

Neil, a journalist, was in the habit of taking out his notebook and scribbling down whichever words came into his head whenever the group paused for a rest.

'Poetry?' Liese had asked.

'Well,' he had said, 'there is something inspirational about moments like this, a group of people thrown together in such an incredible place. Just look around you. Tell me you're not feeling inspired.'

Kitty looked beyond the people gathered about her; the scenery was magnificent. Behind the two young Frenchmen, who described themselves as communists working towards a better France, and Igor, the Russian who admitted to holding no particular political views and merely seemed interested in killing as many of 'the enemy' as possible, the snow on top of the Pic du Marboré and the Pic de la Munia glistened red in the approaching sunset. It was a wonderful moment, yet when it was time for the sun to set behind the distant ridges, the temperature would drop dramatically and the night would be long and bitterly cold.

'How are your knees, Michael?' Liese asked gently.

'Aching like hell. The damage was done years ago. Crouched down at the coalface on my hands and knees for as long as I can remember. Shoulders and back are buggered, too. But I can cope with that. It's my lungs that hold me back. Going uphill is a challenge, all right. Full of dust, I suppose—'

Alerted by the sound of rockfall, he glanced up and spied the unmistakable form of an ibex making its way precariously along a narrow path. Liese did not know quite how to respond to Michael, at first. As a pathologist, she had seen plenty of mortuary specimens taken from deceased coal miners.

'Well, at least the air up here is fresh and clear, Michael.'

'That it is. It's like breathing champagne. And do you know what?'

'What?'

'I'll never go down a mine shaft again, no matter what. When I see these mountains, so natural and beautiful – otherworldly, eternal, God-given – the thought of those shafts render me claustrophobic. I wouldn't wish to be anywhere else. Especially underground in the dark with just a lamp to see the way ahead.'

Liese broke off a chunk of her baguette and held it out for Michael. He took it and handed her a large piece of goat's cheese wrapped in brown paper.

'Thank you, Liese. You're not so bad for a German, really.'

She smiled graciously.

'And you're surprisingly generous for a Yorkshireman,' she said.

'Touché. You see, I don't really care,' he continued through a mouthful of food. 'If I die fighting, I shan't mind terribly. Hopefully, the Republic will triumph, rout the fascist bastards so we can all go home happy. But if it doesn't happen, so be it. I'm not going back. Not to where I was. I can never do that.'

Michael looked up again at the jagged profile of the highest two points of the Pyrenean amphitheatre. As the sun finally dropped behind them, a silver flash from the snowline between them made him squint. The deep hum of an aircraft engine somewhere high above the clouds echoed through the valley.

Florentino also heard the sound and took it as a cue to get to his feet and sling his rucksack over his shoulder. '*Vamos,*' he said in a loud whisper as he helped up the stiffest and most tired. He added something else, which only Kitty and Thiago had understood. *Time to go,* he had said, and *time to hide.*

Two thousand feet above the group trudging through the mountain pass, Jürgen Altmann sat upright against the hard metal bulkhead in the body of the heavily laden HISMA transport plane. Despite the bitter cold and the roar of the engines, he felt rather pleased about the successful roll-out of his mission so far. The battle-hardened Moroccan men of the Army of Africa sharing his space were the latest batch of fighters due to be joining those already stationed near Seville's Tablada airport. Thanks to his own well-practised subterfuge, the flight from Aéroport Tétouan via San Remo in Italy had gone completely unnoticed. Aware of a slight increase in turbulence now, Altmann estimated that the plane would be somewhere above the highest peaks of the Pyrenees where, according to reports, a small and disparate rabble were attempting to cross the closed frontier to join the rag-tag army of Republicans. No matter, he thought gleefully, fascist patrols were even now intercepting and eradicating most of them.

The huge fuselage of the Junkers JU 52 vibrated as the

aircraft struggled to maintain altitude. Soon, the plane would be dropping back down on the other side of the mountains and landing in Andalucia.

Altmann's dreams were coming true. Hitler and Mussolini had readily agreed to support Franco's Nationalists. Operation Magic Fire, or *Feuerzauber*, would soon see tens of thousands of troops on the ground together with weaponry, munitions and tanks. It's high time Germany bared her teeth, he thought, something he had longed for since the end of the last great war in Europe. The idea of the spread of communism on the Iberian peninsula was unthinkable, and at a recent Berlin rally, Hermann Goering himself had declared he would never recognise 'a Red Spain'. Yet Hitler seemed reluctant to plunge Germany into the conflict too overtly. The Nazis were cautious about escalating their involvement into another world war too soon, and had encouraged the Italian dictator to do their dirty work for them. Altmann was impatient and ready to die for the cause right now. He would have liked nothing more than to get stuck in immediately, and was convinced the end result would be the same anyway. For the time being, however, he would dance to their tune.

Altmann toyed with the Iron Cross hanging from the top pocket of his uniform. He liked others to notice it, although he still felt slightly aggrieved that the Abwehr had declined the offer of his services and felt they'd missed a trick. He had been attracted to the idea of intelligence work; the thought of being given carte blanche to carry out whatever brutal deeds he deemed necessary had a strong appeal. Despite his reputation as an uncompromising police chief and a feared member of the SS – and revered commander of the Hitler Youth – Altmann was a loose cannon and unpredictable.

Kurt von Schleicher, the man who had interviewed him, had soon realised that his interviewee was totally unsuited to the role for which he had applied. To start with, his research had cast doubt on the validity of Altmann's Iron Cross. The only one left alive from his entire regiment fighting on the Somme, and no other survivors to corroborate his story of heroism? It seemed unlikely. And he was a thug, too, by all accounts. Moreover, with his facial scars, he could never hope to become the inconspicuous type of undercover operative that could merge into the shadows. No, Altmann was much better suited to ordinary soldiering and, at heart, he knew it. He could achieve much more for the Fatherland by doing what he did best.

Germany's covert presence in Spain was a handy distraction from the growing re-militarisation at home. It would suit his country very well to ally themselves to a state friendly with his own, keeping France and Britain sandwiched in between. There was an economic imperative, too. The ore and minerals to be plundered from the industrial centres like Vizcaya and Catalonia would provide rich pickings. An existential threat from the Soviet Union, too, had to be stopped at all costs.

Altmann closed his eyes and smiled. He felt a contentment he had not experienced for years: a growing excitement at the thought of something grand and historic taking shape. The drone of the giant engines finally lulled him to sleep.

5

Mill Lane

Grace woke the next morning to shafts of bright sunlight streaming through a gap in the curtains, which danced in the breeze coming through the open window. It was still rather chilly for March, but Will liked it that way, insisting it was good for his immune system. Outside, the sound of friendly robins and goldfinches made up a familiar dawn chorus in the garden. Grace had always loved nature. She had relished precious days with her father as they had planted row upon row of crab-apple trees on the family estate at Bishop's Cleeve in Gloucestershire. She could identify hundreds of species of trees as well as the animals they fed and nurtured, and had come to recognise the individual tweets and warbles of the birds in the garden; the variable crescendo of the blackbirds, the high-pitched tones of the robins, and the variety of different notes from the song thrushes. All of them were now in full song, marking out their territory from where they perched in the elms, oaks and hornbeams down by the river. Grace had come to regard them as part of the family and topped up the birdfeeder regularly with suet, leftover bread and anything else remotely edible. The beautiful great spotted woodpecker with its black, white and red plumage seemed happy enough to chip away at anything.

It was still early, and she turned languidly on to her side. Will started playing with a lock of her long auburn hair and held her gaze. She raised her eyebrows inquisitively.

'Good morning, my love,' he whispered thickly, a smile on his face.

'Mmm,' she responded simply, placing an arm on his muscular shoulder. She was not quite awake enough to speak and was enjoying the gentle transition to consciousness.

Will, however, was fully awake. As he patiently stroked the perfect curves of her body, she let the sensations flood through her, still enjoying the beautiful, erotic twilight zone between sleep and arousal. She slid over on top of him, took his hands in hers, and placed her lips on his.

Later, flushed with contentment, Grace walked along the towpath by the side of the river, contemplating the seismic change in her career since coming to this university town. She had already challenged a male-dominated field by qualifying as a doctor and building on her impressive reputation first earned in the Great War. An accomplished surgical scrub nurse, she was now also a qualified pathologist, specialising in asepsis and disease prevention.

As Will had already secured his surgical post at Radcliffe Infirmary, they had made the move from London to Oxford. Grace had been quite willing to continue her work at St Mary's Hospital in Paddington, commuting by train. By staying with Clara in Chiswick two nights each week, she could break up the travelling and enjoy the added benefit of spending more time with Daniel, who had chosen to stay in London with his great-aunt.

A chance meeting in the Eagle and Child a few months earlier had already brought about a momentous change in Grace's life. Popping out one winter night just before

Christmas, she and Will had grabbed the last two seats in the crowded lounge bar. Sitting next to them was an unassuming Australian and his younger sidekick, neither of whom Grace immediately recognised. But the subject she had overheard them discussing was very familiar, and she had not been able to stop herself butting in as antibacterials was the subject to which she wanted to devote her life. Howard Florey had introduced himself and his junior colleague, James Kent.

Florey! Of course, Grace thought. The Director of Pathology at the Dunn Institute: a familiar name in the world of medicine. In stark contrast to the standoffishness and pomposity of most of the celebrated medical men she knew, here was a man who was refreshingly down-to-earth, with not even the slightest hint of arrogance about him.

It had been a shock to be offered a job on the great man's teaching and research team. Grace thought back to the events of that evening. Ernst Chain, the German biochemist working with Florey, had been playing the piano in the corner of the pub, and had come over to sit with them, joining in the conversation. He had been a little hesitant about Florey offering somebody a job on the spot, particularly in a department he was so proud of, and made no bones about voicing his opinion. Florey, however, was his boss, and had made up his mind. 'I don't really go in for the rigid formalities of university interviews,' he had said. 'I've been on the receiving end of far too many of those bloody things.'

Chain had glared at him but kept his thoughts to himself.

Florey had continued, 'I reckon I can assess a person's talents better over a beer than a baize table. What did Shakespeare say? "There's no art to find the mind's construction in the face"? Well, I reckon I can. And with this ambitious lady's qualifications and experience, I'm willing to take a gamble.'

Grace remembered laughing at this.

'Seriously, Dr Chain, a feisty young woman with more than half a brain and a bit of Aussie attitude is just what we need.'

'Shakespeare said that?' asked Chain, much more a pianist and chemist than a reader of literature.

'He did,' Will cut in, mentally thanking his aunt Clara for supplementing his lack of formal education with her home tutoring. 'King Duncan says it in *Macbeth*, when he learns that the Thane of Cawdor has been executed for treason.'

Florey nodded. 'I'm impressed!'

'It means what, though?' asked Chain. 'You cannot judge a book by its cover?'

'Or a sausage by its skin,' added Grace, still smiling.

Chain was privately thinking about another innocuous-looking man. Short, thin-lipped, with a perfectly square moustache and a flipped-over fringe of mousy, greasy-looking hair. At first glance, someone who might seem eminently forgettable. Yet, who could now ignore the man hellbent on dragging his own country and the whole of Europe into another inevitable conflagration.

'With Grace, I'm willing to take the risk,' Florey said flatly. 'Since we can't afford to pay her much, I don't suppose it'll matter a great deal if I'm wrong. But we'll give the girl a chance anyway. And we'll see.'

Grace laughed inwardly at the recollection of that first meeting. It had been so unexpected and surreal in many ways. So un-English, with a rather unsophisticated Aussie and a rhapsodic German refugee in charge of such a traditional and conventional British establishment. Yet Florey was not just some rough colonial genius. He might have lacked decorum, but he was nothing if not inspirational.

So far, Grace and her employer had got along famously, although he was hardly vocal in his approval, seldom offering overt praise to any of his staff. As she approached the institute for another hard day's work, she wondered if today she would prove herself the exception and earn his admiration.

6

Dunn Institute, Oxford

Howard Florey stubbed out his cigarette, took off his glasses, and looked up from the research paper he was reading. The unmistakable German voice down the hall had become a familiar and rather regular occurrence in recent weeks, and seemed to increase in volume with every passing day. Ernst Chain was a brilliant biochemist, of that there was no doubt, but if he thought his work was being hindered by inadequate equipment or the incompetence of his technicians, he would fly off the handle in an instant. That was Ernst. Voluble, demanding and temperamental. The same artistic qualities that made him such an accomplished pianist also made him a flamboyant and dramatic character around the laboratory. Sighing, Florey stood and stepped into the corridor to find Ernst pacing up and down, waving his hands about in a dramatic demonstration of impatience and dissatisfaction. 'Dr Chain!' called Florey. 'Come and share it with me.'

The German cursed quietly and entered Florey's office, where he plonked himself down heavily in a chair. 'They make such elementary mistakes, Professor. They have set back my experiments by two weeks because of this. It is intolerable. We must have more equipment and more people who know what they are doing. These people in my laboratory, you must dismiss them without delay.'

Florey had no intention of sacking anybody. He was taking over a department that in recent years had been somewhat stagnant and unproductive, and it was expected that he would cull many of the academic staff. But he had not done so. Firstly, there was no money in the pot to take on new staff, and he saw no point in rocking the boat, especially when several of the underperformers were well-connected with people he might need to rely on for funding in the future. Most had the talent and the skill, even the appetite for originality and sheer hard work, but their leadership in the past had been poor. 'No one is going to be dismissed, Ernst. We are short-staffed as it is, and most of the fellows are reliable. They just need direction. It will take time.'

Chain seemed unconvinced. 'But there is so little time and so much to do. We have just two Soxhlet extractors in the whole of the building. In Berlin, we had six in my laboratory alone.'

'We have been promised more by the MRC, but they seem remarkably unwilling to part with their funds.' The Medical Research Council had been sitting on the request for some time.

'So we have to make up for this lack of resources with our brains and our wits alone?'

'Exactly.'

'I would not be here, if working with you did not hold the promise of great scientific discovery in the future.'

'We always live in the hope that science doesn't go backwards,' said Florey, making one of his typical understatements.

'It must advance without delay, at a march, not a stroll. I am impatient to proceed.'

'You? Impatient?'

Finally, Chain laughed. '*Mein Gott!* Every day I have to bite my tongue. Suppress my anger. Explain things all over again.'

'Your results are encouraging, Ernst. Maybe you need to take a wider view.'

Before he could answer, Florey swiftly introduced a different subject. It was one he had been thinking about a lot lately. 'I want to organise a meeting,' he said, 'with the entire department. And the teaching staff. People like Leslie Epstein, Margaret Campbell-Renton, and Grace Burnett. *Six-zero-six* has been something of a novelty. A chemical dye that Ehrlich showed could alter the chemical structure of the microbes that cause syphilis. Yet he had to explore six hundred and five other avenues before he achieved success. We need to find other candidates, thousands if necessary, that might treat other infections. But we need to bypass the laborious nature of that work.'

'And Domagk has now produced Prontosil, proving very effective in the treatment of puerperal fever and other strep infections,' said Chain.

'So, let's suppose we turn our attention to exploring other antibacterial substances that can potentially treat the kind of infections that have dogged the human race for centuries.'

'This is exactly what I have been advocating for months, Professor. I want us to continue our work as before. But I want to focus on antibacterials, especially.'

'There's a paper I'd like you to read, Ernst. It was published in 1928 by a man called Fleming, when I was an editor of the *British Journal of Experimental Pathology*. Take it away and look at it. Tell me if you think it has any clinical implications of note.'

'And you?'

'I'll set up this meeting. Not just for us, but for every researcher and every scientist: the pathologists, the biochemists and the entire teaching staff. Everyone. Let's have all of them singing to our tune. We'll have the whole choir, Ernst, don't worry. And you shall be the conductor.'

'*Fabelhaft!* Just as it should be. This way, we shall create a beautiful symphony.'

7

French–Spanish Border, March 1937

The sleet blowing up the side of the ridge from the west numbed their faces and left their feet and fingers frozen. They were tired, hungry and beginning to wonder if they would ever reach the other side of the mountains. Their guide, Florentino, had promised them they would reach the warmer foothills the day after next, but warned that the dangers of the climb and the descent would increasingly be eclipsed by the even worse threat of rebel patrols. These men, he had told them, were not as familiar with the terrain as he was, but they were armed to the teeth. They were ruthless, and under orders to kill on sight anyone attempting to enter Spain illegally and swell the Republican ranks. His warning soon proved prophetic.

Descending an open area of loose scree in an irregular line, a cry rang out from the back as Leonard fell sideways, holding his foot. The rocks were wet, and he had badly twisted his ankle. Up ahead, Florentino stopped and turned. He was wiping the sleet from his eyes when he felt the bullet hit him in the back. He pitched forward with the impact, all the air knocked out of him. The others crouched down instinctively and ran for cover behind the nearest boulder. Florentino sat up and un-slung the rifle from his shoulder, sliding down the stony surface as he went. He reached a rocky outcrop and coughed. Blood spilled from his mouth, coating the front of his sheepskin jerkin.

'*No te muevas,*' he rasped. Another shot rang out nearby, ricocheting off rock and spraying Florentino with specks of granite. Then another and another, the last one from the opposite side. There was more than one shooter and they were well-hidden. Leonard was still clutching his ankle, while Frank and Neil were leaning over, trying to protect him. Michael had picked up a stone, ready to throw it at the invisible enemy. Only Fraser the war veteran had a pistol and he drew it out, looking ready for a fight. Florentino dropped out of sight, correctly anticipating an onslaught of further gunfire.

Liese, Kitty and Thiago had their backs against the cliff face. They considered their options but no solutions came to mind. There was nowhere to run, not without exposing themselves to greater danger. Yet with Florentino isolated and badly wounded, staying put was not an option either. A fusillade of shots rang out, followed by sporadic volleys, the exchange lasting several minutes. It was impossible to know what was happening.

Then there was silence; the mountain was eerily quiet once more. The only sounds came from the breeze in the pines and the drip of melting sleet from their needles. Michael, who had told Kitty he had nothing to lose, stood and cautiously made his way down to where they had last seen Florentino. He peered over the outcrop and then around the side of it. He hesitated, looked back, and held up his hand as if to say, 'Stay there.' Then he was gone.

Several minutes passed and the sleet finally stopped falling. A pale sun popped out from behind the clouds above and illuminated a small window of clear blue sky. Then they all flinched, alarmed by the sound of footsteps on the scree below them. Had the patrol come to finish them off? Just as they had finished off their guide, and possibly Michael, too? But there was Michael now, pointing up at them, showing someone with him the way. He seemed unharmed, as was the athletically built man behind him, striding confidently up the hill. The others watched as the two men approached, apparently unconcerned about any threats to their safety. Michael gestured to the figure behind him. 'This man is our knight in shining armour,' he said. 'He came out of nowhere and levelled the score.'

'Except I left the armour behind,' said the other man, smiling. 'Too impractical for mountaineering in the wet. I'm Ned. Ned Harding. I'm on my way to join the Lincoln Battalion, and, like you, trying to overcome obstacles on the way.'

Kitty stood still, mesmerised. Seconds earlier, she'd been sure she and her companions were going to be killed by a fascist patrol. Now the sun was on her face, and standing before her was an all-conquering Adonis. He was one of the most handsome men she had ever laid eyes on, his wide cheekbones and full lips framed by long black locks. Her current ordeal suddenly seemed a lot less arduous.

Shaking herself, she said, 'Michael, what about Florentino? Is he—'

'I'm sorry. He was shot through the chest but still managed to take out two of the bastards. Ned dealt with the other two.' The little group looked at each other in silence. Neil, the journalist, was scribbling notes.

'We must get going, though,' added Ned urgently. 'You can hear gunfire several miles away and there may well be other patrols nearby.'

'We must bury Florentino first,' said Kitty. 'It is the least we can do.'

'Yes. We have done that, Michael and I.' Kitty gave him a questioning look, as if to ask how they could possibly have done it in so little time.

Ned smiled again, apparently reading her mind.

'The ground is solid,' he said. 'Like cement. Not even an ex-miner like Michael could dig that. We covered him with a tombstone of rocks. He won't be seen or disturbed. And he lies in the mountains he clearly loved. It's a small mercy.'

Kitty looked into his sympathetic eyes.

'Come,' he said. 'We really must move.'

8

Dunn Institute, Oxford

Grace had just delivered another batch of pathology samples from the Radcliffe Hospital to Professor Florey's laboratories, including human matter taken from almost every different organ. She and her team were currently investigating which particular bacteria were responsible for a number of infections, and scrutinising samples under a microscope would reveal whether a patient's excised lump was benign or cancerous. Florey had invited her into his office for a cup of tea and a professional catch-up.

'I don't think I've ever seen this number of samples all at once,' said Florey.

'It's winter. And bitter. I suppose it's inevitable we'll witness a surge of bronchopneumonia at this time of year.'

'Ah, yes. The old man's friend. That reliable companion, which carries most of them off into the welcoming arms of the grim reaper. Some of them will have pulmonary tuberculosis – or at least a reactivation of a previous infection with it.'

'Of course. There is still so much poverty and malnutrition, as well as poor housing. There's only so much that rest and fresh air in a sanatorium can achieve. It's still the case that most of them will be dead within five years.'

Florey sipped his tea and gestured to a picture on the wall behind him. 'I don't know if you're familiar with this,' he said. 'It's a print of a painting by the Venezuelan artist Christobel Rojas, called *La Miseria*.'

'It's well-named, then. Showing the squalor and misery of dying slowly from consumption in some damp back-bedroom somewhere.'

'Phthisis, the White Plague . . . call it what we will. It's been around for thousands of years and has killed more human beings than any other infection. Examination of the remains of the Egyptian pharaohs testifies to that.'

'It certainly has no regard for social standing,' said Grace. 'I have it on good authority that two members of our own Royal Family are currently on the French Riviera, convalescing from it.'

'It seems incredible, Grace, that only fifty years ago, it was killing one quarter of the entire adult population of Europe.'

'But thousands are still dying,' she said. 'And despite the fact that it preys on the weak and the frail, we currently have a liberal politician and a well-known writer on our wards.'

'Well, they're in good company. Think of your English literary legends and how many have succumbed. Emily Brontë died of it, you know, at the tender age of thirty. John Keats at twenty-five. I believe Lord Byron once wrote that given the choice, he would rather die of consumption than anything else, a sentiment which has helped to popularise the disease as a condition of impoverished artists.'

'We can only hope that we will find a cure in our lifetimes, Professor.'

'At least we now know what the causative agent is, thanks to microbiologist Robert Koch. But the mycobacterium is an elusive and hardy little bugger, as you well know.'

Grace looked back up at the picture on the wall behind the director as she finished her tea.

'And him? The artist, Rojas?'

'He painted this whilst suffering from the disease himself. Dead at thirty-two, poor sod.'

9

Lleida, North-East Spain

The train from Lleida to Zaragoza was packed with people fleeing the conflict, beaten and bedraggled, most of whom had deserted their fincas and farms, bringing with them only their immediate family, their livestock and whatever possessions they could carry. Many had witnessed atrocities being carried out on their neighbours or loved ones, perpetrated by people they had known for years. The mood was sombre as the long train rattled and lurched through the flat plains of Aragon and the Ebro River Basin. Kitty gazed through the window of the carriage at the sorry-looking olive groves and the barren fields which would otherwise have been ready for planting with wheat, barley and sugar beet. Ned was asleep opposite her, his head lolling on his folded coat. He deserves a rest, she thought. Their first experience of this war had been a harrowing one, yet he had protected them as if it were the most natural thing in the world. Without him, they would have been rudderless. Within hours he had won their trust. Their journey had not been easy, yet all of them had reached Lleida safely, where the group had split up and gone their separate ways. Only Kitty, Ned, Liese and Thiago had boarded the train. Now Kitty examined Ned more closely. He had undoubtedly been their saviour, and she had every reason to be grateful. He was also unlike any other man she had ever met. He was tall and strong, softly spoken, yet commanding with it. He was classically good-looking with his chiselled jaw and broad forehead. Whenever he looked at her, she felt weakened – and safe. She kept telling herself she was being foolish. No man had ever made her feel like this. She was a fiercely independent woman who could very easily look after herself, so why was she doubting that she still wanted to? She closed her eyes and found herself daydreaming about him taking her in his arms, and pressing those perfectly formed lips against hers.

The train suddenly lurched and swayed violently. Liese had to put a hand on Kitty's knees to prevent herself tumbling to the floor. The train was slowing down. Ned woke and peered out of the window. He could see the front of the train rounding the bend up ahead, as it approached a viaduct over a gorge. The men and women clinging to the sides and the roof of the train were pointing and gesticulating wildly.

'Wait here,' he said, jumping up, 'I'll be back.' He made his way down the aisle. As the train slowed further, the occupants of the crowded carriage pressed their faces against the windows, jabbering loudly to one another. Some gathered their meagre possessions, whilst others grabbed their children and pinned them to their laps. Then there was a huge explosion and the train was hurled backwards, throwing one small child against a vertical metal upright. Liese and Thiago got up to tend to the boy, as other passengers screamed in fear, whilst Kitty set off in search of Ned. How far along the train could he have gone before the explosion? She jumped out of her carriage and raced along the shingle track looking frantically into each carriage as she passed. There was luggage everywhere, and people were blocking the aisles. If Ned was still inside, there was no way he could be making progress in either direction.

When Kitty reached the front of the train, she saw the carnage. Bodies lay everywhere. The detonation on the track in the middle of the viaduct had sent the engine over the edge and left the first two carriages teetering precariously on their sides over the precipice. Smoke was rising from the wreckage of the engine three hundred feet below, and the tortured metal of the carriages creaked and squealed under the strain.

'Ned!' she yelled. 'Ned!' There was no way he would hear her over the noise of others shouting. Where was he? What should she do? Boarding either of the carriages could be disastrous. They were already on the brink of pitching over the edge of the viaduct, so any extra weight or movement would prove hazardous. Two or three passengers were climbing out through the rear doors, but there was no sign of Ned. She glanced down at the pulverised engine in the gorge. *Ned would not have got as far as the engine itself, would he?*

The screaming of the metal couplings between the two carriages was getting louder. Only the chain linkage between them was holding the leading one in place, and the front of it was beginning to yaw over the chasm below. Then she saw him: trapped in a twisted compartment, unable to reach the aisle, and trying to kick the glass out of the window without success. He was frantic, but she felt powerless. Looking around her, she saw debris from the train everywhere. Lumps of coal, mangled metal panelling, the driving wheels of the locomotive still attached to their side rods and the twisted remains of the tender. Partly hidden under the dented steam dome, she spotted something bright red. It was the wooden handle of some kind of hand-tool. Pulling it out, she saw it was attached to a metal claw at the end. It was a railroad-spike hammer, used for maintenance of the track.

She ran back to Ned's window and waved at him to move out of the way. But the carriage was already beginning to slip. She lifted the hammer over her head and brought it down against the window with all the force she could muster. The glass shattered and bowed in the middle but still held. Ned put his boot against it and the whole thing blew apart. He dived out of the opening with Kitty clinging desperately to his shoulders, just as the carriage tipped over and plunged into the abyss.

10

Berkshire and Buckinghamshire Joint Sanatorium

Will made his way along the long line of hospital beds, stopping to speak with each patient in turn. It was still a little chilly, but fresh air and rest was the best natural therapy the tuberculosis patients could hope for, and all of them were well wrapped up in pyjamas and gowns beneath their heavy blankets. Being wheeled out from the wards on to the veranda overlooking the low-lying hills was a routine daily occurrence, provided it was not raining.

The nurses scurried this way and that, carrying sputum pots and kidney dishes, with clinical records and medicine charts tucked under their arms. Many of the bedridden chatted idly to one another while some, despite their failing health, even managed a wry joke and a laugh. As a result, one man, who had become a little too excited, experienced a spasm of coughing, bringing up copious amounts of blood-tinged phlegm from the cavities deep within his scarred lungs. Others, pale and haunted, were too exhausted to engage with anyone else, hanging on to life by a thread.

Will visited every Friday, making the short journey from Oxford in his second-hand Riley Nine with its two-tone blue-and-black steel Merlin chassis, manufactured just up the road in Coventry. It had been in a sorry state when he had bought it, the bodywork battered and its 1087cc engine backfiring and spluttering, but it had been relatively cheap for that very reason. Grace, who had always loved tinkering with cars, had jumped at the chance of repairing and maintaining it, and with Emily's help had soon ironed out its numerous mechanical defects and got it running smoothly.

'Dr Burnett?' Will heard someone behind him and he broke away from the patient he'd been tending. Sister Drewett stood nearby, with her sleeves rolled up.

'We will be ready for you in theatre in ten minutes, Doctor. Mrs Castellano is fully prepped and consented.'

'Very well, Sister; I'll be right there.'

Annestas Castellano had not responded as well as expected to bed rest and clean air. She had continued to lose weight and was becoming increasingly breathless. She regularly suffered night sweats, a debilitating, undulating fever and severe episodes of coughing. Sputum samples had confirmed the teeming presence of mycobacterium and X-rays had shown several large cavities in her lung. All clinical signs indicated that her consumption was galloping along apace. If she continued on this trajectory, she might be dead within a few short days. She lay, pale and apprehensive, on her healthier left side, with a wedge-shaped bolster under her bony thorax and her right arm raised above her head, her hand acting as a cushion.

'How does this treatment work, Doctor?' she asked. Will was taken by surprise; not many patients enquired about the procedure. Either they did not consider it their place to question the doctor, or they would rather not know. Mrs Castellano was obviously one of the more curious. Perhaps she had been wondering about it for a while.

'It's designed to give your infected lung a rest,' replied

Will. 'By allowing air into the space inside your chest, the lung will contract under its own elasticity and close off the thousands of little air sacs. That enables the circulation to bring along all the cells that will promote healing.'

'I understand.'

Will was not sure she did. He was only grateful she had not asked about risks, or potential complications. He decided to give her a little background, which he hoped she would find interesting and diverting. 'Like many surgical discoveries,' he said, 'the value of this treatment came about by way of a chance observation. An Italian physician noticed that soldiers with chest wounds experienced an improvement in their tuberculosis symptoms upon recovery. The outside air sucked into the chest through the wound led to exactly the same results we are hoping for today. So it was on the battlefield that the procedure was born.'

'Santa Maria de Dios,' said Mrs Castellano. 'So now I'm a casualty of war!'

Will smiled. He bent down and crouched in front of her. 'You understand what I am going to do, Mrs Castellano?' he whispered. 'You will feel a pressure in your side but the local anaesthetic will stop most of the pain. If it is too much, you must tell me, all right?'

'*Esta Bien. Confio en ti.*'

Somehow, her trust in him made his task seem even more onerous than it already was. Will made his way to the other side of the table, and, with his gloved finger, felt the indentation between her fifth and sixth ribs, below her armpit. There was precious little fatty tissue, so he easily infiltrated the area with the liquid cocaine and waited a few minutes for it to do its work, chatting quietly to take her mind off what was about to happen. He asked about her family, her previous job and her favourite pastimes. He asked her about Spain, where she was born, and asked what it was that had brought her to England.

Will tested the injection site by prodding it with a sharp needle, but there was no reaction. The anaesthetic had kicked in. 'I'm going to start now,' he said, 'so we won't be able to speak for a little while.' Mrs Castellano nodded.

No sooner had Will begun than his patient let out a low moan. Sister Drewett held her hand and silently mouthed her reassurance. Will waited a few moments before resuming, but when he did, Mrs Castellano let out a sharp cry. Her back arched and she immediately passed out, limp and unconscious. Will's eyes met Sister Drewett's. Sadly, they both knew from experience what had just happened. Vasovagal syncope. A devastating drop in heart rate and blood pressure due to intense pain.

11

Zaragoza

The overladen bus lurched along the dusty track towards Bilbao, over two hundred miles to the north. Liese was asleep, resting her head on Thiago's shoulder. Thiago himself was still in a murderous mood, silent now and gazing through the window of the bus. The sabotage of the train had hit him harder than it had the others. A gentle and rather timid soul by nature, he had come to Spain more to ensure the safety of his grandparents than to fight. Now he seemed hellbent on revenge. He could not comprehend how anyone could deliberately take the lives of so many innocents, and struggled to understand how the country of his ancestry could be so riven by division and hatred. He had never before seen bloodied and broken bodies, let alone torn, mangled corpses of women and children. Thiago had uttered hardly a word since they had left the site of the wreckage. Kitty and Ned were still too exhausted and angry to sleep.

'Could we have done more?' he asked quietly, turning to Kitty.

'We did all we could,' she replied. 'You know that.'

The four of them had toiled for hours at the site of the train wreck, manufacturing makeshift splints from branches to stabilise broken bones, and applying tourniquets made from strips of ragged clothing. When help had begun to arrive from local villages, they had realised it was time to move on. Despite their efforts to lend assistance, some of the passengers were beginning to cast suspicious glances their way and murmur accusations that their unfamiliar presence on the train may have been responsible for the attack.

As some of their fellow surviving passengers started to disperse in all directions, the four of them had carefully descended the ravine on foot, and after a long hike, joined the traffic on the main road between Lleida and Zaragoza. It was the first time they had had a moment to try to make sense of it all.

'Who would've planted those explosives?' Kitty mused. 'And why? There were no soldiers on that train. No armaments, nothing of military importance. Just ordinary people.'

'Collateral damage,' murmured Ned. 'It was the train they were targeting. And the main line connecting north and south.'

'But why blow up the train? Why not just destroy the bridge and the track?' Kitty pressed.

'Tracks can be repaired. Bridges rebuilt. But no train company will want to lose another locomotive. Nor any train crew their own lives. For all intents and purposes, this strategic route no longer exists.'

'Nationalists, you think?'

'Who knows for sure among all this chaos? They have more to gain, I suspect. It's a strategic conduit for reinforcements from the south.'

'But the train was full of women and children. Farmers, livestock.'

'And us, Kitty. The four of us. And for all we know, others joining the Republican cause. They don't know how many we are.'

'Or how few!' Suddenly, she felt like a liability. She turned to look outside for anything suspicious and scanned the passing countryside for signs of armed militia or patrols. Their destination was hours away, across unknown territory. Who knew how dangerous and eventful the journey would prove to be? She closed her eyes and let her head fall back on to the rucksack she was using as a pillow.

Ned studied her face. She was physically and mentally spent and had worked tirelessly looking after the sick and injured before hiking at least thirty miles across rugged terrain to reach the road. And she still looked radiant and beautiful. Her auburn hair framed her delicate features – her full lips and her sweet button nose – and her long eyelashes fluttered as she fell into a deep and well-earned slumber. He had never before been so enchanted. Or grateful. A few hours ago, this lovely girl had hurled a railway spike at the train window that had been blocking his escape from a doomed carriage, and had saved his life.

12

Maudsley Hospital, South London

Daniel sat in the great, echoing hall just inside the entrance of Maudsley Hospital, waiting to be ushered through to see his grandfather. He knew as much as anybody about Robbie's life and the tragedies that had befallen him, and could barely even imagine the pain of losing a beloved wife in childbirth, let alone the trauma of witnessing the carnage of trench warfare. His chronic grief and deep clinical depression were understandable, and it was not surprising that the psychiatrists who attended him had concluded that Robbie was incurably insane.

'We won't keep you long, Mr Burnett,' said the young girl behind the desk. 'We just have to track him down and give him notice that you're here.'

Daniel knew he might be anywhere. Wandering the grounds, slumped on a bench under the cloisters somewhere, or curled up in bed facing the wall, lonely and withdrawn. He did not react well to surprises, so although this was Daniel's regular visiting time, Robbie would still need a reminder of that, and would need a few minutes to gather himself.

Unlike his great aunt or his parents, loving and compassionate as they were, Daniel never found his time with Robbie distressing or awkward. He was intrigued by the few sentiments he was able to coax out of him, and had a knack for painstakingly piecing together the disjointed fragments of his grandfather's thoughts, as if he were solving a complex jigsaw. It was a puzzle of tiny interlocking images, which somewhere in his head had been exploded into a thousand jagged pieces, just like the German shells that had detonated and shattered above the trenches. Over time, the full picture was beginning to take shape. Robbie had become more forthcoming, even animated at times, but whilst occasionally these outbursts of energy would trigger a fit of tears or uncontrollable shaking, it seemed to Daniel that his outlook on life was becoming a little more positive.

Sigmund Freud was well known by now for expounding his theories about the workings of the human mind, although Daniel found fault with a lot of his work. Besides, Freud worked mostly with the milder neuroses rather than full-blown psychoses. Disappointingly, there were still no dramatically effective treatments for the latter. Were some people just hardwired for greater resilience than others, and born into coping better with adversity? Or was it related to parental nurturing, childhood environment and learned behaviour?

Daniel had set himself a challenge: to help his grandfather get better gradually, removing the heavy cloak of depression and chipping away at those stratified layers of sadness.

Robbie's doctors here had effectively written him off as a lost cause. They were more interested in seeing more acute cases on a voluntary outpatient basis, and had recent ties to eugenic research. Daniel knew there were revolutionary new treatments on the horizon that sounded exciting, which even offered the promise of mental reawakening; remission brought about by induced convulsions or malaria. Insanity cured by insulin shock therapy or injections of Metrazol. These treatments sounded barbaric. Would they be suitable for Robbie?

At that moment, his thoughts were interrupted by a dishevelled old man stumbling along the corridor in his nightgown, wide-eyed. He was quickly caught up by two white-coated orderlies and bundled away. At the same time, desperate cries and moans echoed from farther along the corridor. This was not a place in which Daniel wanted Robbie to spend any more time.

But for now, he would carry on doing what he was doing. He would find Robbie, sit down calmly next to him, and after a few minutes of silence and only when his grandfather was ready, he would gently open up a conversation.

13

Mill Lane

Will stood beside the bath and poured a kettle of warmed water into it as Grace lay back against the copper tub and relaxed. Will sat on a chair at the other end of the bath and gazed at her.

'You know, my love, you are just as beautiful as the day I met you.' Grace looked back at him and smiled.

'But you didn't see me naked, then.'

'More's the pity. But you are just as lovely as ever – if not more so.'

'I couldn't agree with you more. And, Dr Burnett, you are not so bad yourself. Those heavenly, deep-set blue eyes are still to die for. I think I might keep you.'

'That's good to hear. Quite reassuring.'

'How was your day?'

'Didn't start too well. A lady fainted on me when I stuck a trocar through her chest. No one likes seeing a metal cannula, I suppose. Luckily, she recovered soon after, and we're still friends. Other than that, fairly routine, really. An appendix. A ruptured spleen. And a woman whose ear had been bitten off by a horse.'

'That's routine?'

'You know what I mean. What about you?'

'Four patients discharged from the septic ward, two admissions with polio, three with measles, and one with God knows what.'

'Is that a technical term?'

'It is until I find out more. We lost Arthur Scammel, though.'

'I feared you might.' Will paused in remembrance of the man he had seen too late to be able to save him with surgery. 'And you are having a bath to wash the smell of the mortuary from your hair?'

'I am.'

'And here I was just about to join you.'

Grace smiled and held out a bar of soap. 'I can always wash my hair later.'

14

Bilbao, Northern Spain

It had taken over a week by road and on foot, but they had finally arrived at their destination without further incident. In Bilbao, Pedro Ibanez had welcomed his nephew Thiago with undisguised delight. He had never met him before, as his parents had emigrated to England before the boy was born, but they had frequently corresponded by letter, and he had followed his fortunes as if he were his own son. Kitty and Liese had looked on as the man had hugged the lad to his chest and shed tears of joy. If only it hadn't taken a civil war to achieve their reunion. Pedro was explaining that Juliana and Raphael, the grandparents Thiago had come to protect, had already fled to the apparent sanctuary of Lalin in Galicia. They were safe. At least for the moment.

The modest house on the Calle Sendeja between the river and the Parque Etxebarria was small, cluttered and dusty, but arrangements had been made so Thiago and Ned had their own room, and Kitty and Liese would share one at Pedro's sister's house, until it was time to leave for the Jose Fina Hospital in Guernica. They were due to start work the following week.

Pedro had lost his wife to pneumonia some years before

and had brought up his son, Leandro, on his own. The boy was now seven, intelligent and engaging. His name meant 'lion-man' and he seemed determined to live up to it.

He was full of questions. 'How long can you stay,' he had asked, and 'Have you come to kill the rebels?'

Thiago, who was determined to suppress his festering reaction to the train sabotage, had been patient and kind, telling him all about life in England, and the little house he lived in, which he said Leandro could visit as soon as the troubles in Spain were over.

Liese had noticed the little boy limping and asked what was wrong.

'It was the bombing two months ago. Opposite his school,' Pedro replied. 'A bit of flying debris hit his leg and it's been sore ever since.'

Liese offered to look at it and noted, with some concern, a reddened area of sore, shiny skin.

*

It was a fine morning and the sun had risen over the hills, dispelling an early mist and warming the still, November air. The markets were full of people bustling about purchasing fresh produce of all sorts: fish from the rivers and the sea, vegetables from the fields, and whatever wildlife and game the hunters had been lucky enough to catch. With unreliable supply chains, there was plenty of competition for the spoils. Liese had gone to meet her cousin, a teacher at the Universidad Erandio on the other side of town, leaving the others to walk along the riverbank to a family-run restaurant just off the busy market square. They perused the menus, smelling the mouth-watering aromas coming from the kitchen, while Leandro became transfixed by a game of pelota taking place nearby.

Liese had arranged to bring her cousin and meet them all at the restaurant at two o'clock, while the sun was still high enough in the sky to allow them to sit outside and watch the world go by.

'This is Matthias,' said Liese, as they joined the others and made the customary introductions.

'You are a teacher at the university?' Pedro asked Matthias.

'Yes. I teach science and German. I'm afraid to say my own command of Spanish leaves a lot to be desired.'

'No. You speak it very well, with hardly a trace of your own accent, either. Our students are lucky to have you.'

'My teacher went to fight the fascists,' piped up Leandro, leaving an awkward pause in the conversation.

Liese jumped in. 'Matthias is from Germany and, like me, he got out of the country as soon as he realised he was no longer safe there.'

'Just because you are both Jewish?' asked Pedro.

'Although I was raised as a Catholic, my grandmother was Jewish, which in the eyes of the National Socialist Party makes me Jewish, too,' said Liese.

Matthias glanced at Liese and she nodded her reassurance. It was all right to speak freely.

'I'm a Communist, Pedro,' Matthias explained. 'Persona very much non-grata back home. My beliefs are the main reason I chose to come and work in Republican Spain.'

'Then you are very welcome, Matthias. One of us. But I'm afraid your fellow countrymen have followed you here. Most of them want to destroy us.'

Matthias nodded and looked embarrassed. Leandro took his father's hand.

'They won't destroy us, though,' said Thiago defiantly. 'There are people from all over the world joining the fight to defend our freedoms, and I'll be one of them!'

Ned frowned. He had heard that the Nationalists were fast approaching from the east and the future was anything but certain.

'Liese and Kitty are hoping to help, too,' Thiago added. 'They are going to be working for the Red Cross in a big hospital in Guernica.'

'Can I go and fight, too, Thiago? With you?' asked Leandro.

'You are a bit too young for that just yet,' he said, putting a hand on Leandro's shoulder and drawing him closer. 'And thankfully, by the time you are old enough, the war will long be over and we'll all be living peacefully again.'

'Oh,' said Leandro, sounding rather disappointed. 'Well, hurry up and win the war, then, because I want you to play pelota with me.'

15

Jose Fina Hospital, Guernica

Kitty was now utterly exhausted. The sheer volume of casualties she was dealing with had taxed her reserves of stamina and resilience, and for days she had hardly slept. She had not realised how much she was going to miss Ned. She missed his reassuring presence and his easy smile. She missed his gentle humour and physical warmth. She missed the smell of him. Now she found herself wondering if she would ever see him again. He had always seemed rather reluctant to talk about himself or his family, being reserved and almost secretive about it. But before she had left Bilbao and they had said their goodbyes, he had finally managed to share a little of his past with her, knowing he could trust her – but perhaps also knowing he may never see her again.

'I'm Canadian, but I'm also from a much older world,' he'd said. 'Against the wishes of his family, my father married what the locals disparagingly called a "redskin", and raised a family. As a result, they were ostracised. My older brother, a warrior in form and spirit but kind and generous in his heart, was attacked by a gang one night in the town and killed. They scalped him. No one was ever held responsible.'

Ned had taken a deep breath and Kitty had taken his hand.

'My parents were the most loving people you could ever

hope to meet, Kitty. Welcoming, forgiving, wise, hard-working. My brother and I wanted for nothing. We were brought up with the best of both cultures. My mother was an inspiration and truly wonderful.'

'*Were*, you said?' asked Kitty. 'Are they . . .?'

'They're still alive – as far as I know – but they were forced out of the farm they loved, their livestock was stolen, and their crops burned. They have encountered prejudice and discrimination at every turn. I tried to do everything I could to protect them but there was only so much they could take. One day they packed up and left without warning, leaving a note to say I'd be better off without them, and encouraging me to make my way in the world alone. They thought it was the most loving thing they could do, I guess.'

'Where are they now, Ned?'

'I have no idea. I tried to find them. Knowing them, they'll have gone back to the prairie. They'll survive somehow. They still know the old ways.'

'I'm sorry, Ned. That's awful.'

'It's why I volunteered to come to Spain. I'm not so much of a patriot in my own country. But here, I have a lot in common with the Republicans, the dispossessed, and the downtrodden. I can fight for what I feel is right, Kitty.' He'd laid his head on her shoulder then, and she'd hugged him. She had relived the moment often.

But that was a distant memory now, and her emotions had been diverted by those resulting from the trauma and carnage around her in the hospital.

Every patient she treated, every wounded soldier or civilian, had a human face and individual story. She tried to remain professional and objective, and hide most of her emotions and feelings, but it was never easy.

Only a couple of weeks after she arrived in Guernica, Kitty had been devastated when they had brought Thiago to the triage area. Kitty mopped his brow and helped him with a cup of water. 'Here, take a sip of this. That's it.'

She discovered that he had been wounded a fortnight earlier, fighting for the Republic, but in the chaos of battle he had been cut off from his lines, trapped, and only just rescued and brought in for treatment. Had it not been for Ned, who had recognised him and brought him to the hospital, he would still have been lying there now. At least he had been given a chance, and she was temporarily reunited with Ned.

The Jose Fina Hospital was a reputable establishment, usually well-staffed and equipped with antiseptics, bandages and dressings. But the number of casualties had severely depleted their stocks. Thiago's injuries, although superficial, had become impacted with dirt and soil and were now infected and weeping. He was sweating profusely, had a raging fever, a rapid pulse, and was delirious. At regular intervals, his body became wracked with painful spasms. Today, his back had contracted so powerfully his whole body had become arched unnaturally backwards and his breathing had stopped for several minutes.

Kitty knew he was suffering from tetanus. She also knew he was dying. At that moment, she felt helpless. As she looked up and saw the other Red Cross nurses tending to the other patients, she was temporarily buoyed by the good work they were doing and knew that many of the injured men and civilian casualties would survive as a result.

But then one young man collapsed in one of the nurse's arms, convulsed, and died. For him and Thiago it was already too late.

Kitty felt faint and shaky and was overcome with grief.

Liese took over while Ned took her in his arms and held her close. He stroked her hair and whispered to her as she broke down and sobbed. Now, for a moment at least, she was in a safe and peaceful place.

16

Villafria Burgos Airport, 26 April 1937

Fifty miles to the west of where Kitty was working, Jürgen Altmann took his place behind the podium at the front of the stage. He studied the sea of expectant faces in front of him: some two hundred or so air crew and pilots, though he could not be sure exactly how many. Yet each of them, whether German or Italian, hung on his every word.

'Guernica must be destroyed,' he began. 'Our troops have made significant advances in Biscay and throughout the north-east, and are now on the outskirts of this very town.' A loud cheer went up at the back of the room, swiftly followed by a round of whistling and clapping.

'It is thanks to your bravery and your skills that this has been achieved. At Durango, you took them by surprise. At Tolosa, you crushed their resistance. In Vergara, you smashed their infrastructure. Now, thanks to you, all that territory is in the Nationalists' hands.'

The men got to their feet, embracing and laughing, slapping each other on the back.

'And also thanks to you, our army is just thirty kilometres from the frontline.' As the cheering and the stamping of feet escalated, Altmann raised his arm and bade everyone be silent and take their seats. He had the men in the palm of his hand, and he savoured the moment.

'But Guernica still stands in our way. The enemy has retreated and dug in to the town. The Spanish Nationalist command has ordered Oberstleutnant Wolfram Freiherr von Richthofen to conduct a raid on Guernica and take out its bridges and roads. We must restrict any Republican movement of equipment and impede any further Republican retreat.'

Altmann was not a naturally gifted orator, but he had studied the style and delivery of the leader he so worshipped, and had rehearsed his speech relentlessly. A ripple of excited conversation coursed around the room; Altmann raised his arm again for quiet.

'Our generals require a decisive and rapid victory in the Basque region; we must destroy the Basque Army and their lines of communication completely. We will use our success as a stepping stone to overwhelm Bilbao and secure total victory in the north.' Altmann paused for dramatic effect. 'The town's population has been swelled by the retreating enemy, and by refugees. General Emilio Mola seeks a rapid surrender in return for sparing their lives by confining our bombing to bridges and roads outside the town. Precision bombing will be the order of the day. So be it.' He looked around the room and saw only enthusiasm and approval. 'Dismissed!'

As the men filed from the room, he called over Günther Lützow, the commander of Jagdgruppe 88's 2nd Squadron. 'Herr Altmann?' Lützow was wary in tone. He seemed to instinctively distrust and despise Altmann.

'Lützow. You will lead the subsequent raids.'

'The subsequent raids?'

'You will lead raids three, four and five, and any others that become necessary. Your orders will be conveyed on a need-to-know basis. Guernica must be destroyed in its entirety. The bridges and roads, certainly, but the infrastructure, the arms factories, and the iconic Assembly House in particular.'

Lützow eyed Altmann suspiciously and wondered what was coming next.

'We must also destroy the morale of the people and show them that resistance is useless. We will sacrifice Guernica so that we can take Bilbao unopposed. We do our army's fighting for them, Lützow.' Altmann smiled, in the hope of receiving the commander's agreement. It was not forthcoming.

'You know as well as I do, Altmann, that there is double the number of people in Guernica now. Seven or eight thousand certainly, and mostly civilians, many of them innocent women and children. A blanket-bombing raid on a civilian target is out of the question. It is a repugnant idea and would be widely condemned throughout the world.'

'It will be a historical first, Lützow,' Altmann retorted.

'I will have nothing to do with it,' he spat.

'No, Lützow, you won't,' Altmann said, having anticipated the officer's reaction. 'But your squadron will. You will be absent, on leave. Your well-earned trip home has been arranged, by me personally.'

17

Guernica

Kitty and Liese had just finished their shift, but satisfied they had done a good day's work, they headed towards the farmers' market arm in arm. Still mourning the passing of Thiago and having said her final goodbyes at his hastily arranged burial, Kitty was grateful for the distraction.

It was five o'clock on a fine April day. Ahead, they could see the street stalls laden with produce from the local fields. Young women, dressed in traditional Basque costume, were offering samples of wine for tasting. Men, clothed in bright shirts and berets, cut small pieces of cheese, meat and fish to accompany them. The aroma of paella, octopus stew and chicken wafted on the gentle breeze towards them, and Kitty gratefully accepted two small green Padrón peppers from a little girl. 'My mother's,' she said proudly. 'The best in Spain.'

'Good God!' spluttered Liese, taking the pepper quickly from her mouth. 'Certainly the hottest in Spain. My mouth is on fire!'

'I need some cold vino blanco!' Kitty said, as Liese nodded furiously.

The market was bustling and noisy. Cheerful greetings passed between acquaintances, people embraced openly, and bargains were snapped up. Kitty and Liese became one with the crowd, mingling with the same locals they had been doing so much to support and care for during the fighting. The Republican Army was struggling. Their forces, despite resisting fiercely, had gradually been beaten back by the greater Nationalist Army. Many of the casualties lay wounded, dead, or dying from infection, back at the hospital where the two women worked. But the joyful scene around them reminded them briefly of a more tranquil time where families could go about their usual business, enjoying the simple pleasures of life.

A massive explosion erupted at the farthest end of the market. A huge fireball of red and yellow leapt into the sky, swiftly followed by a thunderous roar, which left their ears sore and ringing. The crowd froze, rooted to the spot. Then there was a second blast, just a few metres from the first, which flung trestle tables, produce, livestock and bodies high into the air in a pall of smoke. The sound of aeroplanes reverberated from overhead, just as people on the ground started screaming. Terrified shoppers began to flee in all directions as more bombs dropped, blowing walls out of buildings and burying people under their weight.

Kitty grabbed Liese and hauled her into one of the doorways. As random projectiles whistled horizontally past them, the acrid smell of cordite and burnt flesh was overpowering.

Through the thick, cloying smoke, they could make out the shapes of mangled bodies on the ground. The first cluster of bombs had fallen, while another cluster dropped from a second wave of aircraft coming from the west, peppering the ground in a criss-cross pattern. The two women held on to each other for support as one ear-splitting explosion after another threatened to blow them off their feet. They instinctively crouched forward, their backs to the door jambs and their knees flexed at right angles. The roar of detonations was incessant and the heat from the incendiaries intense. As the ground shook violently and rocked her body, Kitty looked frantically around for a means of escape but there was nowhere to run, and no effective cover from the destruction that continued to fall from the sky.

A huge hole had appeared in the building behind them, leaving a massive crater deep in the ground where apartments and offices had stood only moments earlier. The front facade of the warehouse opposite had collapsed into the courtyard behind it, and flames licked hungrily through the windows of residential properties either side. Kitty looked up and saw that the decorative stone lintel above her lay slightly askew, powdery concrete falling like snow from one end. It was intact and still holding up the remaining brickwork above. As everything around them was pummelled and smashed, the two women huddled under their protective arch, increasingly convinced they were about to be blown to pieces. Liese was shaking uncontrollably.

Directly above them, the Dornier Do17 approaching from the south released the last of its massive bombs, which toppled downwards towards a decorative concrete portico.

To the south-west of the city, Jürgen Altmann listened to live radio communications at the airfield. The element of surprise had achieved almost every objective. His own objectives, at least. 'Guernica is extinguished.'

Altmann's eyes turned skyward. Perfect, he thought. The ruins of Guernica were lit up like a Christmas tree. Two dozen bombers had delivered twenty-two tons of explosive. Few of the Republicans, holed up in their boltholes, would have survived, and besides, any survivors now had nowhere to hide. He turned back to the radio and flicked a switch.

He said loudly, in German: 'Attention, all pilots. Squadrons one, two and three will continue the bombing attack on any enemy group seen fleeing. We will strafe any surviving stragglers on the roads leading out of town. Anyone moving is a legitimate target. Understood?'

Other than the crackles of static and a distant rumbling, the radio was silent.

'Understood?' he yelled.

'Understood, Herr Altmann,' came a disembodied voice. It was an acknowledgement of the order, but only just.

'We will be like the invisible hand of God, flattening the symbolic oak trees, the Gernikako Arbola, like a scythe reducing a cornfield to stubble.'

*

With a badly broken leg, Liese crawled towards Kitty's limp and bloodied body. Her eyes were closed, her face deathly pale, and her head was at an awkward angle. 'No! Kitty!' she implored, shaking her.

'Kitty, Kitty, wake up!' She shook her again. Slowly, Kitty's eyelids fluttered and she moaned softly.

'Liese?'

'Oh, thank God!'

Kitty opened her eyes fully and tried to move. Too soon. She winced as she straightened her neck. 'Ouch,' she said, rubbing her sore muscles. 'That last one was too close for comfort. Who turned all the lights out?'

'It's dusk, Kitty. Night is falling. The planes have gone. At least, they have for the time being, but they bombed the hell out of the city, and it's been burning for hours. They must have known that the casualty count would be enormous. We must move whilst we have the chance.' Liese grabbed an arm and helped Kitty up, despite her own injuries.

Kitty staggered briefly and fell back against her friend, who let out a little cry with the impact. That's when she saw that Liese's right leg was bleeding. She was holding it off the ground and putting all the weight on the good leg.

'Liese!'

'It's all right. It's just my leg, Kitty. It'll mend. But that last bomb threw your head against the stone door frame and knocked you out cold.'

'I feel so dizzy. How long was I out?'

'Several hours, I think. I was dazed myself by the blast. The Church of San Juan and the Republican headquarters took most of the damage. God knows if the hospital is still standing. We must go and see if we can help. Come on, we'll hold on to each other.' Blocking out the pain of her fracture and limping on her left leg, she leaned on Kitty as a crutch. They navigated carefully through the rubble, avoiding the fallen masonry and burning rafters still cascading around them. As they turned right into the next street at the Plaza De La Paz, they both gasped. Every building in the street had been obliterated.

'Oh!' cried Kitty, putting her hand to her mouth. 'Oh no!' She crouched and gathered up the body of a little girl. Her head fell back as Kitty cradled it. The eyes were unseeing, and the blonde hair matted with congealed blood. Kitty looked up hopelessly at her friend.

'It's the little girl who gave us the Padrón peppers.'

Liese's eyes filled with tears and she looked away. Kitty closed the girl's eyes. She took off her shawl and covered her up. It was all she could do as any thoughts she had about finding her a more suitable resting place were interrupted by the sound of machine-gun fire. Half a dozen enemy biplanes were flying along the rubble-strewn street, shooting at anything that moved.

18

Jose Fina Hospital

By picking their way through the narrow side streets and avoiding the main thoroughfares, Kitty and Liese managed to make slow but steady progress without further injury. Liese leaned heavily on Kitty as a crutch to keep her broken leg off the ground and when they finally hobbled around the last corner, they saw the smouldering ruins of the Jose Fina Hospital in front of them. Only a small part of it was still standing, and since the main entrance had been completely destroyed, nurses and orderlies were busy passing patients out on stretchers from a shattered window at the side. Some were still alive, but only some.

In their injured state, the two women were unable to do much in the way of assisting with the evacuation, but at least they could help with the wounded once they were set down on the ground in relative safety. Kitty tended to Liese first, stopping the bleeding from her leg with a tight bandage and creating a makeshift splint to keep it stable, then they toiled for what seemed like hours, and it was long into the night before the hospital had been completely emptied. Some were still buried inside, but there were no signs of life and the ruins of the building were threatening to collapse.

Liese was exhausted now and the pain in her leg

excruciating. She propped herself up against a stone bollard in the street, her face drained of blood and her shattered, bandaged leg turned outwards at an unnatural angle. Kitty sat by her side, equally drained.

A quietly spoken fellow, dressed in a bloodied doctor's coat, came over and knelt beside them. He removed the bandage and splint and examined Liese's injury. 'They tell me you are a nurse here. With the Red Cross, yes?'

Liese managed a little nod.

'So you know you have compound fractures of the tibia and fibula, with the risk of infection?'

Another nod.

'. . . And that we must treat it immediately?'

Liese studied him. She had been working at the Jose Fina for several weeks and had never seen this doctor before. 'My name is Josep,' he said, 'Josep Trueta. I'm a surgeon. Usually, I am head of trauma services at the main hospital in Barcelona. It is only by chance that I am here this week.'

'Your timing is terrible, then,' said Liese, attempting a smile.

'I think maybe it is good for you, though,' he said, returning the smile. 'With your permission, I am going to reduce the fracture and correct the displacement. Then I'm going to dress the wound with the closed method used by Alphonso Guerin in the days before Lister.'

This doctor seems to know what he's talking about, thought Kitty. It wasn't the usual method of fracture treatment, not one she was familiar with, at any rate, but he sounded very sure of himself. 'I can change the dressings regularly for her,' she said.

'No! You must not. The dressings must remain totally undisturbed for at least twenty to twenty-five days.'

This surprised Kitty even more, and she knew Liese would have her own views about his proposals.

'Your patient is not just a nurse, Josep. She happens to be a pathologist specialising in infection control. I'm not sure she will consent.'

Liese and Josep exchanged glances. Liese seemed too tired to argue.

'You are a pathologist?'

She nodded.

'I'm achieving remarkable results using this technique in Barcelona. Come. Time is passing. Do you wish me to proceed?'

Liese took his hand and squeezed it. 'Whatever you say, Doctor. I'm in your hands.'

*

Kitty and Ned had stood at the quayside at the port of Bilbao and waved goodbye to the SS *Habana* as the ship eased away from her berth, taking Liese, Leandro and four thousand other Basque refugees to Southampton. Kitty had just been able to make out Liese on her crutches standing by the rail at the bow of the ship, surrounded by a gaggle of small children all waving scarves and handkerchiefs at the crowd below. Liese was waving frantically at Kitty, too. She had not wanted to leave her, but her leg, although healing nicely, could still not bear her weight. Leandro had only been persuaded to leave for the safety of England because he had a bad leg, too, and felt they were comrades. Besides, Matthias, who had already been tasked with evacuating the youngest children at his school, would be on hand to look after them. That was three weeks ago. It seemed like a lifetime.

19

Radcliffe Infirmary

The mortuary was Grace's least favourite part of the hospital. Buried deep within its vaults, two floors underground, it was cold and bare. Despite the meticulous cleaning and sterilisation procedures, there was always the lingering smell of death. She could do nothing more for the people down here, but as a pathologist, she could still pay her respects and, more importantly, learn from them.

Arthur Scammell's body lay on a bowed metal table, the rib cage sawn down the middle and each side hinged outwards, not unlike the twin flaps of Grace's medical bag. The infection that had taken hold of his kidneys had invaded his bloodstream and affected nearly every organ of his body. Grace had only to look at his skin to know what she would discover inside him. And sure enough, the purple-red bruising that peppered his face, torso and limbs was matched by identical signs of haemorrhage in his internal organs and there was evidence of uncontrolled bleeding – everywhere. These were the typical signs of the end stages of septicaemia.

Grace meticulously examined every cadaver the same way. She would take each organ in turn and slice them into tiny sections, embedding tiny samples in wax-covered glass slides, to be scrutinised later under a microscope. If she persevered long enough, she might one day discover the physical mechanisms behind the bleeding. How would that advance medical treatment and save lives, though, if the underlying cause of the problem – the bacteria – could still multiply?

Dear God, she thought, for what felt like the thousandth time, please let Florey and his team come up with that magic bullet soon.

20

Croydon, South London, December 1937

On the train to Croydon, Grace thumbed through her copy of *The Daily Sketch*. The headline read 'Croydon in 1937 is a Dangerous and Frightening Place'. There were dozens of people in hospital apparently suffering with typhoid, and the outbreak had already led to several fatalities. Grace had been summoned by a Mr Rimington, who worked for the Bank of England. His son had been admitted on to a local isolation ward and was seriously ill. Rimington felt that local doctors and public health officials were proving less than competent and, as Grace's reputation had preceded her, he had insisted on securing her services, asking her to name her price. She had agreed, but refused the offer of money.

When she arrived, Rimington was able to tell her that a neighbour had recently developed typhoid, as had a little girl nearby. He had already ascertained that their milk had come from different sources, that no shellfish or watercress had been consumed, and that the only common denominator appeared to be their water supply.

It did not take Grace long to carry out her own investigations. The origin of the infection was a polluted well at Addington, which supplied almost one fifth of the Croydon area. The well collected water from the surrounding ground, some of which came from cesspools and a pig farm. Normally, that water was filtered and chlorinated, but recent repairs at the pumping station had meant that these measures had been overlooked. Everyone had assumed that the ground itself was contaminated, but it soon became apparent that one of the repairmen, who was now known as 'The Index Case', had become unwell with typhoid during the First World War and had unwittingly become a carrier. Grace identified him as the original source of the outbreak and her contribution to the inquest proved invaluable. Rimington thanked her profusely, not least because his son had survived. She had probably saved the lives of many other people, too. Despite her protestations, he pressed a cheque for one hundred pounds into her palm as a donation to Will's charity for the sick and impoverished. Grace felt a little embarrassed to be given so much credit, but at least she would be returning to Oxford with a good idea about the subject of her next tutorial at the Dunn Institute.

*

Grace's lectures were frequently well attended as she always made the subject interesting and encouraged audience participation. Today was no exception. The tiered lecture hall was packed to the rafters.

'So, what are the fundamental principles of the medical consultation?' she asked, searching the sea of faces.

'Careful listening, and observation of the patient,' came the reply from an earnest young man in the second row.

'Because?'

'Because if we listen hard enough, the patient will tell us

the diagnosis. According to Hippocrates, if we look hard enough, we will see it, too.'

'Yes,' said Grace, 'usually, that is true. But what if the patient has nothing to report and we spot nothing untoward about them, either?'

'Then clearly there is nothing wrong with them at all,' said a self-assured young man, with a dismissive shrug of his shoulders. 'And they can be confident they are free of disease and suffering from no more than hysteria.' No one else in the room seemed willing to contradict him.

Grace paused for a moment, as if taking in the response. 'Look at these pictures,' she said, showing an array of different skin infections likely familiar to most of the undergraduates. 'Cellulitis: the bright red, inflamed, burning skin of bacterial infection. Folliculitis: germs flourishing in the hair follicles. Furuncles, or boils, if you like: those enlarging volcanoes of pus that develop into carbuncles when there are clusters of them. Impetigo: the characteristic crusting rash usually around the mouth or nose in children who are poor and malnourished.'

Grace described one slide after another. The nonblanching rash of meningococcal septicaemia, the diffuse pustular eruption of smallpox, the scaly and flaking stigmata of fungal infection, the disfiguring lesions of leprosy.

'What do all these have in common? I'll tell you. They are all characteristic visible features, and together with what the patient tells us, we can make an accurate diagnosis.'

'Yes. But what if the patient tells us nothing, and nothing is visibly wrong, either?' a student asked.

Once again, it was the cocky young man who responded. 'They clearly aren't unwell at all, as I said. They are malingering.'

'Let me introduce you to this stern-looking lady, then,' said Grace, sharing a picture of a tall, heavy-set woman in her forties. 'This is Mary Mallon, who was born in County Tyrone, Ireland, and emigrated to America at the age of fifteen. At the turn of the twentieth century, she started work as a cook for an affluent family in Mamaroneck, New York, where within two weeks, several residents developed typhoid fever. They had high temperatures, abdominal pain, headaches, muscle weakness, exhaustion, sweating and a dry cough. Some had a skin rash with rose-coloured spots. A year later, in Manhattan, several members of a family Mary was working for became ill, and the laundress died. In the years that followed, she left a trail of typhoid fever victims in her wake. Yet she remained completely well throughout. This pattern continued, and she is thought to have infected up to one hundred and twenty-two people in all, with as many as fifty of them dying. So, how did we find out? Well, eventually, the sheer number of victims and the fact that the disease did not normally occur in sporadic cases within affluent families led to investigations, all of which pointed to one common denominator: Mary Mallon. Did she know she was the source? Of course she did. How could she not have noticed that everywhere she went, people were falling sick with the same illness? Why else would she move on to new employment so swiftly?'

Grace looked around the room at the students. 'When she was eventually tracked down and confronted with the evidence, what did she do? I don't know what any of you might have done, but our Mary picked up a carving fork and threatened to kill the investigator. She also refused to give samples and protested that she was being made a scapegoat. Was she as innocent as she claimed?'

Grace pointed to two students and invited them to come up to the front of the lecture theatre.

'You,' she said to the first, 'will role-play the part of Mary, and you' – pointing to the arrogant young man – 'will represent George Soper, whose article in *The Journal of the American Medical Association* led the woman to be nicknamed 'Typhoid Mary' by the popular press. She was finally arrested under the Greater New York Charter as a public nuisance, and forced into an ambulance by five police officers and a public health doctor who had to restrain her.' Grace waited for the students to settle down.

'The case still raises important medical and ethical questions about personal responsibility and public protection. We'll have some fun with the debate presently, with a vote at the end to see whether you think she was treated appropriately or harshly. But the point I really want to make is that her illness was asymptomatic and invisible. She herself was perfectly well, yet she was transmitting a potentially lethal infection to hundreds of others. In bacteriology, we cannot always rely on what patients tell us or what we see. We must delve further. In this case, Typhoid Mary's stool samples showed millions of salmonella typhi bacteria, emanating from the reservoir in her gallbladder, an infection she had presumably acquired from her mother in childbirth. She had been an unwitting carrier of the disease all her life.'

'Why didn't they just take out her gallbladder?' somebody asked.

'Because back then, it was an invasive procedure, and dangerous. It could have killed her. She never consented to it.'

'So why didn't they ask her to work in a different capacity other than as a cook?'

'They did, but she found out that working as a laundress

paid less than half the salary of a cook. So she continued in the kitchen. They tried to quarantine her, but on her release, she reneged on a number of the promises she'd made to never again work in a kitchen, to wash her hands meticulously, and to regularly report her whereabouts.'

'So she spread the typhoid fever a second time?'

'Yes,' Grace said. 'Several times, actually, until eventually, she had to endure a second quarantine, which effectively triggered a nervous breakdown that lasted until her death twenty years later. Was she badly treated? Pilloried unfairly and compared to some kind of leper? Even if she didn't initially fully understand that she was the source of the outbreaks, was she, in all but name, a murderer? You have to remember that at the time, the germ theory of disease was still relatively new. To many, the concept of a healthy person transmitting disease to others was ridiculous. Typhoid Mary was the first ever case of an asymptomatic carrier being identified and officially described in a medical journal. As pathologists, this is incredibly important, with major implications for public health and medical ethics now and in the future. So, over to our actors here at the front. Who wants to start?'

'I have been cruelly and unnecessarily incarcerated, and I deserve to be compensated accordingly,' said the feisty young girl taking the role of Mary.

Professor Florey, eavesdropping in the corridor outside, smiled approvingly and chuckled. He had been wanting to spice up the teaching at his school of pathology for some time, but until recently, had struggled to recruit anyone with sufficiently fresh ideas. He had had a feeling about Grace from the start. And she was proving him right.

21

Teruel, Spain, February 1938

It was only through their lovemaking that Kitty could forget the tragedy of the turmoil raging around them. Ned Harding was a generous and considerate lover, his gentleness and skill a complete contrast to his physicality and recklessness in battle.

Kitty watched him as he slept; it was difficult to reconcile his baby face with the soldier he had become. Peaceful now, she had seen the rage and hatred rise within him as he had fired at the enemy at close range. He was equal parts philosopher and warrior. She looked over as a heavy clump of snow slid off a branch high above them and landed with a soft thump, waking him.

In her letters home, Kitty maintained she was working as an International Red Cross volunteer. With her nursing training, her teaching experience, the friends she had made in Barcelona and her excellent command of five languages – including her growing fluency in Catalan – nobody could deny that her services would be very valuable. But that was a year ago, before she had trekked over the Pyrenees to join the Spanish Red Cross in Zamora, and before she had waved Liese off on the SS *Habana*, along with thousands of desperate refugee children. It was before she had witnessed the terrible atrocities meted out by both sides, the indiscriminate bombings, and the public executions – often carried out by those they had previously called neighbours. Gradually, her compassionate nature had started to evolve. Her heart had hardened, inured to the brutality and heartlessness.

'What are you thinking about, Kitty?' Ned whispered. 'You've got your sad face on.'

'That seems to be my go-to expression these days. Except maybe when I'm with you.'

Teruel was known to have the lowest annual temperatures in the whole of Spain; this winter had been the coldest for twenty years. Kitty shivered and looked up at the clear night sky. The moon was full and bright but hidden behind the high fronds and needles of the trees. Stars sparkled in the cosmic blue-black tapestry above. Gone were the storm clouds that had dumped so much snow over La Muela, Teruel's Tooth, a high ridge to the west of the town and a key strategic position for the battle. Gone as well, at least for the time being, were the German planes that had dropped hundreds of bombs on Republican parts of the town and maimed thousands of fighters holed up in the surrounding mountains. Kitty had been there for two months when the siege had first begun.

The Communist commanders had begun the attack in December, while snow was falling heavily. La Muela was conquered, the city encircled. Within a week, the Nationalists were cornered, the buildings they occupied bombarded with artillery and then infiltrated by Republican soldiers. Kitty kept her primary roles as nurse and translator, but she also carried a revolver and had become hardened enough to use it if necessary.

It had been impossible to remain impartial. Kitty was a

libertarian, a freedom fighter. Back in London, she had marched with the suffragettes, and her niece Emily was even named after one of them. When she had taught in Spain, she had been angered to find that half the country was illiterate – and had deliberately been kept that way.

Madrid was still in Republican control when Kitty was there, but the incessant bombing and frontal assaults had killed thousands.

She had spoken in her best Polish to the Brigadista of the Dabrowski Battalion, whose spine had been broken by falling masonry. She had written a letter in German to the parents of a Jewish boy from Dortmund, dying from an open skull fracture. She had translated battle commands to a group of French Communists joining a Spanish division. But what she witnessed in Zamora had trumped it all.

Kitty was a feminist. She knew that it was the women of this world who were usually the negotiators, peacemakers and healers, and so it was the violence against women meted out by the partisans of Franco's military coup that had cemented her allegiance to the Republican cause. She recalled her Red Cross jeep entering the town of Zaragoza. It passed women tied to stakes in the street, often naked, their heads shaved. Others were languishing in overcrowded and unhygienic prisons, raped, tortured, or killed as punishment for withholding the whereabouts of their menfolk. She had heard rebel leaders actively encouraging such depravity.

On 11 October, the day Kitty learned that Pedro Ibanez had been captured, Amparo Barayón, a mother whose only 'crime' was to have married and borne children with Ramon Sender, an anarchist sympathiser, was executed.

So now Kitty was no longer officially with the Red Cross,

but carrying out the same work as a nurse behind the lines for the Republicans. Among her family, only Fitz, her brother Will's brother-in-law, knew what she was really doing and her letter to him held the truth about her actions.

He was also trying his best to persuade the ruling Liberal party members to change their minds about the non-intervention pact agreed several months earlier, which had banned the supply of weapons or manpower to either side.

A bursting artillery shell and gunshots nearby woke Kitty from her reverie. 'We need to move,' she said urgently to Ned. 'While we still have some cover of darkness. We're not safe here.'

Ned yawned. 'What? No breakfast in bed? No hot shower and shave before our luxury Buick sedan arrives? What's the world coming to?'

'The only things coming our way are the fascists. And by the sound of it, they're not far off.'

The Battle of Teruel was over. National reinforcements had retaken the town and now the remaining Republicans were the ones besieged. In January, the reserves of the International Brigades had been ordered to join the struggle, but any minor territorial gains had been temporary. Ned had thrown himself into the fray of course. Kitty had seen him running forwards, hooting wildly, while singing *L'Internationale* in broken Spanish, unbothered about taking cover. It was lucky he had not been killed already.

Finally, in February, a massive rebel cavalry charge to the north of the town had broken the Republican forces and scattered them. Many lay dead while thousands of others were surrounded and trapped in the town. The rest, like Ned and Kitty, were on the retreat. The higher they climbed, the colder and more rarefied the air became.

Teruel itself stood at 3,050 feet above sea level; it was a natural fortress ringed by mountains and perched on a high knoll above the junction of the Turia and Alfambra rivers. The Republican Army were now just a motley group intent on saving their own skins. They would cross the river Ebro and regroup.

*

Kitty held Ned's hand as they descended the steep, rocky slope, stopping only briefly when they heard voices below or the unmistakable scrape of heavy boots crunching on loose gravel.

They continued making their way down for several hours as stealthily as they could, searching in vain for an escape route, jumping from boulder to boulder and inching around stony protrusions jutting from the cliff walls. When they reached a fast-flowing river at the bottom of the gorge, they had nowhere else to go. Kitty felt resigned to her fate. She calculated they had three choices, each bleaker than the last. They could swim for it, but they would surely either drown or freeze to death. She could be captured, and risk being raped and tortured before being executed. Or she could give Ned a final loving embrace, put a gun to both their heads, and blow their brains out. A romantic suicide pact. Her legs felt weak and shaky, but her head was strangely controlled and calm.

'Kitty,' said Ned, standing in front of her with his strong hands on her shoulders. She looked up into his eyes, glowing silvery-black from the reflection of the light on the water. She imagined he had come to the same conclusion. 'Take your clothes off.'

She jerked her head back and frowned. Despite their imminent danger, she let out a quiet, ironic laugh.

'But—'

'Don't ask questions. Just trust me.'

Taking her cue from Ned, she unbuttoned his shirt and trousers and took off her jacket. Voices somewhere close by were becoming louder now.

When the six-strong Italian fascist group they'd heard talking arrived at the bottom of the gorge, the first thing they saw was a pile of discarded clothing. A woman's tunic, a long skirt, a blouse and shoes, and her male companion's greatcoat, trousers, waistcoat, shirt, boots and pistol. Glancing at the river, their leader spotted someone swimming frantically away about thirty yards ahead, struggling to cope with the turbulent water around them. They raised their rifles and opened fire. A bloodied hand was raised, and then sank as the figure disappeared beneath the surface. The men watched in silence for a moment before one of them spoke.

'He's gone,' he said.

'Yes,' agreed a comrade, 'and the bullets should only take him to the bottom faster.'

The others laughed. The leader kicked the woman's clothing with his steel toe caps. 'Shame. She could have provided us with some entertainment.'

'Drowning in cold water is what she deserved.'

Monsters, thought Kitty, in her tiny hiding place beneath a huge pair of boulders not three metres away from them. Even after the men left, she dare not move. She was frozen to the marrow, shivering uncontrollably. It was as cold as the mortuary compartments at the university campus in Madrid. At some point she would have to risk wriggling free, but did she still have the strength? She could hardly feel her legs and feet as it was. She had heard a fusillade of rifle shots, but had not been able to see what had happened. Had they killed Ned after he had sacrificed himself for her? And even if they had not, what terrible fate would he have met in those swirling, freezing waters? Surely nobody could survive that. She felt desolate. They had been through so much in such a short time together.

The tears came easily and she let them tumble. But then, all she felt was rage, and all she could think about was survival. Survival and revenge against these depraved murderers and rapists. Her family had warned her about the risks, but she had not listened. She had been determined to fight, to make a difference. Maybe they had been right all along.

She wriggled free from the rocky tomb and quietly recovered the clothes she had abandoned, pulling them on. The Italians had taken Ned's greatcoat and pistol, but his waistcoat and shirt would at least offer her an additional layer of protection against the cold.

*

She walked for two long days. Kitty knew in her heart that Ned's chances of survival were negligible. He had told her several times that he loved her and would gladly lay down his life for her. Now, he had proved it. His quick-thinking and selflessness had saved her life. She could keep warm by continuing to move, but every step was an effort, and she desperately needed to rest. The cold was punishing, her muscles ached from cramp and fatigue, and she was starving. It was midwinter in the mountains and the only bushes and shrubs that were not covered in snow were bare of fruit or foliage. There was plenty of water, but the only thing she had eaten were the charred remnants of a rabbit left by the retreating Italian soldiers. She had become a scavenger. She thought again of Ned, of her aunt Clara, and her two brothers. It was as if she could hear them talking to her. *Come on, Kitty. Keep going. Never give up. You have the strength to find a way through.*

She had believed it at the start, but increasingly, with the crest of every hill she reached, her hopes would be dashed when she would find an even higher one further on. Her spirit was beginning to break. She knew she had to cross the river to travel south, and had followed its course whenever she could. Finally, on the evening of the third day, she spied a primitive rope bridge with many of its wooden slats missing or broken. It seemed entirely unsubstantial, hanging across the gorge. But it was a bridge, albeit over a drop of some one hundred and fifty feet. There was no going back. Kitty closed her eyes and took a deep breath. The longer she put it off, the greater the fear that would grip her. She glanced around and saw a long, dry branch that had fallen from a tree. She snapped a few straggly twigs from either end and held it out in front of her, as though she were a tightrope walker. Looking straight ahead, she edged forward on to the bridge, leading with her right foot. Originally, there would have been four sturdy ropes spanning the ravine, with vertical connecting ropes between them, and wooden planks fixed across the floor of the bridge. Now only half the wood remained, with only two shredded ropes on either side. The bridge was a death trap. Yet the enemy would not be far behind her; Kitty had little choice.

But which rope to hold? The higher one to hang from, and pass one hand over the other until she reached the planks, or the lower of the two, where she could then try to lever herself up from below? She removed her heavy shoes, tied the laces together, and slung them around her neck. She wheeled her arms in a circle to get the circulation going; her life would depend on a firm grip. Closing her eyes, she thought of her gymnastics training as a teenager, the rope climbs and the vault, the monkey bars, traversing between two uprights, the floor exercises, the parallel bars. How she wished she had a tub of resin now to dip her hands into. She took a deep breath and jumped, clinging to the higher rope. The rope creaked a little and sagged, but it held. Then, slowly but surely, she passed one hand over the other, gripping the ice-cold cable with her flexed fingers. After three overhead hand exchanges she found herself floating free, a diminutive figure suspended in space. She glanced down and felt dizzy. She heard her family's voices, shouting louder. *Come on, Kitty, come on!* Finally, with a supreme effort, she clambered up the last rocky step and dropped to her knees with exhaustion. She had done it. She had crossed the river.

When she looked up to check her surroundings, she was shocked to see two men standing six feet in front of her. She tried hard not to let her panic show.

'That was quite a spectacle,' said one of the men in German. 'We didn't think you'd make it.'

Kitty stood stock-still. Had she risked her life only for it to be finished now?

'The last three people to attempt this crossing fell to their deaths,' said the second man, 'but we didn't care. Ammunition is scarce. It saved us wasting bullets.'

'So why didn't you shoot me, then?' asked Kitty, bitterly.

'Because you're one of us, right?' said the first man, softly this time. 'You're running away, not conducting an all-out assault on your own, I think?'

'You're German, yes?'

'I am with the Edgar Andre Battalion. My name is Johann, I'm a German Jew. This is Izsak, a Hungarian Communist with the Dimitrov Brigade. We each have different reasons to fight Franco's animals in Spain.'

Kitty saw that their uniforms supported what they claimed. 'I was in Teruel,' she said. 'I was with my friend, Ned, a Canadian fighter. He jumped into the water in the ravine down there as a diversion when we were being followed. I don't know what has happened to him.'

The two men looked down into the gorge. They knew nobody could survive such a torrent. Johann thought of the bloated corpses they had been pulling out of the water downstream, almost every day. Looking at Kitty's stricken face, he simply said, 'I'm sorry.'

Kitty was close to collapse. He took off his greatcoat and slipped it gently over her shoulders. She nodded gratefully. 'You are safe with us now, Comrade,' he said. But Kitty was understandably wary.

'I'm hungry and I'm cold. And I need to sleep,' she said.

'Then come with us. The relief sentries will be here soon enough. We only have rough peasant wine, but plenty of it, and the best hot goulash anywhere in the whole of Aragon.'

They each took an arm and lifted her up. She reached for the laces of the shoes she had slung around her neck, but they had gone. She would have to walk barefoot. Later, as the three of them walked into the camp, several soldiers sitting around a fire got to their feet in astonishment. 'Where did you find such a treasure?' asked one, with a huge grin on his face, exposing missing and blackened teeth.

'We found a lamp in the heather and rubbed it. Out popped a genie who gave us one wish. And here she is.' The other men laughed.

'Well, it must be true, because the only other explanation is that she managed to get over the bridge by herself. And that's impossible.'

'There you go, then,' said Johann. 'Next time you're on sentry duty up there, you should look around to see if there are any other lamps lying about. You never know your luck.'

He looked around to see Kitty's reaction. She was curled up close to the open fire, covered with a rough blanket, and already fast asleep.

22

Southwark, London, March 1938

Fitz re-read the letter, then placed it gently on the coffee table in front of him. He took the silk handkerchief from the outside pocket of his neatly tailored suit, wiped the tears from his eyes, and sniffed defiantly. It was the third bit of bad news he had received that day, and something unfamiliar within him was stirring. It was a feeling to which he was generally unaccustomed. Usually a gentle and thoughtful man, he was not given to outbursts of anger or impatience. The weak heart he had been born with also meant that any physical expressions of irritability had to be controlled. Nevertheless, it did not prevent him picking up the porcelain vase beside him and hurling it at the wall. It smashed into smithereens and the water and flowers within it slid to the floor. This was a Fitz he would never otherwise have recognised in himself. But today, he supposed it was understandable.

Before he had left for Westminster that morning, his wife had announced she was setting off on a jaunt to the French Riviera with a couple she had recently befriended. Shauna would initially be travelling down by train with the gentleman alone. There had been no discussion on the matter, and nor had she any notion of inviting Fitz. It was another low blow in a series of similar events. He knew by now that there would never be any romance in the relationship, not that there had ever been, not in the physical sense at least. But formerly, there had certainly been mutual respect, trust, and companionship. He was not possessive or jealous. Not at all. He was disappointed. Were it not for the kindness and devotion of Stephen, his young parliamentary assistant, he would have felt even more lonely and rejected.

That afternoon, he had attended his routine medical check-up at Wimpole Street, and, after a cursory examination, had been told rather curtly by Professor Brewin, the cardiologist, that his long-standing heart failure was getting worse.

'It's a nebulous term,' he had said. 'There are various degrees of severity, of course, but in essence it means you could drown in your own secretions when your heart is too weak to pump anymore. The swelling of your feet and ankles is evidence of venous congestion. Cardiac oedema. Your heart can no longer circulate the blood efficiently enough. So fluid builds up in the extracellular spaces.'

'I see,' said Fitz, not really seeing at all.

'The likelihood is that once your lungs become waterlogged, you will be increasingly overcome by a feeling of suffocation.' Fitz could hardly believe what he was hearing. 'But do try to look on the bright side,' the professor continued, attempting a reassuring smile and scribbling notes, 'medicine may yet come up with a solution.'

'But when?'

Brewin, as it happened, had recently read an article by a chap called Robert Edward Gross, who had performed the first successful ligation of a patent ductus arteriosus on a seven-year-old girl in Boston. The same condition that Fitz had been suffering from since birth. But given that the long-term effects had not yet been studied, he didn't think the news was worth sharing with the patient in front of him, so he did not take the trouble to voice it.

Instead, he simply muttered, 'When indeed?'

While Fitz could accept the thoughtlessness of his wife and the rudeness of the physician, whose fees were crippling him, it was the letter from Kitty that had so upset him. Posted from somewhere near Albacete and scribbled on poor quality, water-stained paper, it seemed to have been written in a hurry. She had told him everything about her dreadful experiences, about Ned, the shooting, the bridge, and still, she was fighting for a cause. Still, she was trying to help.

I know that you are in a position to raise questions in the House, she'd written. *Please do what you can.*

Fitz stared at the damp patch on the wall for several minutes. He knew Kitty was holding back in her letter and sugar-coating her news. He feared for her safety and her health. She was still young, idealistic and independent. As always, she was rebellious, and all too ready to take risks. Just like her sister-in-law.

23

Mill Lane

Will's right eye was stickier than ever, and now the left one was red too, a sure sign the infection had found a new home. It would not affect his vision, and it would not stop him operating, but it would not be comfortable, and he was worried the germs might contaminate his patients' incision sites.

The front door swung open, and in came Grace with a laden shopping basket on her arm. Will went to meet her, gave her a hug, and grabbed the basket from her.

'You come with gifts,' he said, suddenly hungry.

'Bread, cheese, beer, and a big surprise!'

'A surprise? Let me guess. Coffee? Bananas? Eggs?'

'Come off it. Not that much of a surprise. There's a war on, you know. It's this.' Grace withdrew a small pot of creamy-looking froth wrapped in a tea towel.

'It looks revolting. Certainly not edible. If I didn't know better, I'd say it looked like something you'd taken from the laboratory. What is it?'

'It's mould juice.'

Will frowned. 'Mould juice? Professor Florey's mould you've been trying to grow?'

'The very same. And you're privileged to be offered it. The stuff inside it can inhibit bacterial growth. We just can't extract whatever it is yet, and this raw product loses its potency within half an hour.'

'I suppose I should be honoured, then. What am I supposed to do with it?'

'Pour that beer for us and I'll tell you.'

The ale was welcome, and despite being rather too warm, it was still refreshing and tasty.

'So,' said Will, looking at the pot of goo on the kitchen table, 'why are you bringing your work home?'

'The professor and I wanted to try something out.'

Will hesitated. 'What?'

'You know you've had that sticky eye for a few days . . .'

'Ah. No chance!' Will laughed. 'You're not using me as a guinea pig, and you can stick your mould juice somewhere else!' Grace smiled but would not be dissuaded.

'Look. Think about it. This stuff can inhibit bugs in a culture medium like nothing else. For superficial infections in people, it might well eradicate symptoms. We won't know until we try.'

Will jumped up from his chair. 'You must be joking! You might blind me!'

'No, I won't. We tried it out on our rabbits and their vision is fine.'

'I'm not a rabbit.'

'You are . . . *in bed*.'

'Not funny, Grace. Does it sting?'

'The rabbits didn't flinch. The pH is six point five. So not alkaline, and not acidic.'

'You really are serious?'

'Deadly.'

'Poor word choice.'

'Shut up, sit down, and open your eyes.'

Will, realising she was not going to relent, sat back down. Despite his reservations and protestations, he did trust his wife.

'You might as well shove it in both eyes. The other one's red now, as well, so why not catch the infection early? But be gentle with me. It's my first time.'

'One eye at a time, Doctor. The right eye is the treatment eye, and the left the control. That means we'll have a better idea whether it works or not.'

'And this was Professor Florey's suggestion, was it?'

'Oh, no, absolutely not. This was entirely my idea.'

Before he could react, Grace had pulled down his lower eyelid with her index finger and spooned a thimbleful of gloop inside it. Will screwed up his eyes in discomfort. 'God, Grace!' he cried, blinking furiously. 'It's like looking through porridge!'

'Don't be such a baby,' she replied. 'I've always known doctors make the worst patients, and you must be the worst of the lot.'

Will *harrumph*ed.

'And besides,' added Grace, 'if this stuff works on you, it might be worth trying on little Leandro, too. My mother brought him to the Radcliffe and the X-ray confirms he has osteomyelitis. His tibia is slowly being eaten away. And I don't imagine he wants his leg amputated.'

24

Daniel

Will was secretly delighted with his son's chosen career path. As well as being a surgeon, Will had an innate understanding of the human psyche. He would often put himself in his patients' shoes and consider what he would feel like if he were suffering from their condition or faced with their options. His wartime experiences had made him even more considerate and gentle in his approach, and his bedside manner was impeccable. It was one of the main reasons he was so popular with his patients, and why he was the doctor they trusted. It was also the reason why the few wealthy private patients he saw on Saturday afternoons, who paid their fees directly into his charitable fund for the poor and sick, flocked to him.

Daniel had his father's natural gift for being able to establish a close rapport with his patients, but he specialised in torments and disorders of the mind. His initial interest in his grandfather, and his continued support for him, had paid substantial dividends. Robbie could now talk objectively about his previous traumas and was beginning to express the feelings he had bottled up for so long. It was as if the mental torture within his head had been released. The electroconvulsive therapy that had been touted no longer seemed necessary. Robbie remained unable to talk about the devastating loss of his wife in childbirth, a wound far too painful to be reopened. However, the visceral and terrible experiences he had witnessed in the slaughterhouses of Flanders, and the hell of no man's land, had dissipated. Daniel had somehow succeeded there, where no one else could.

Will was impressed by his son's unique approach, and knew that thousands of men suffering comparable symptoms could benefit from similar tactics, if only they had the means to be able to afford such treatment.

Daniel had helped his father personally, as well. At unexpected moments, Will would find himself becoming enraged whenever he thought about the Great War, and especially when reminiscing about his friend and mentor, Captain Jacob Daniels. The man had been put to death by firing squad, by his own army. He had been charged with desertion, when in truth, he had simply been out of his mind with shellshock. Will talked about him a lot. Jacob Daniels had been a decorated soldier of extraordinary courage, who commanded the loyalty and respect of his men. The fact that the man who had passed the unjust sentence against Captain Daniels was now serving fifteen years himself, for other crimes, was no consolation.

Daniel had often talked to his father about what had happened, gently and patiently probing for any details. As a result, the intrusive thoughts that would sometimes distract Will from his work and family seemed to be diminishing. Yes, Daniel was very good at what he did, and Will was proud of him. He was affable, engaging, and seemed confident about his purpose and direction in life. Will had no reason to worry about him.

The interests and exploits of Daniel's twin sister, Emily, however, concerned him.

25

Emily

As Will drove Daniel in the old Riley Nine towards the aerodrome with his vision surprisingly restored and his eye pain relieved – thanks to the application of the muck Grace had brought home from the institute – they resurrected their conversation from the previous evening. 'Emily's always been headstrong, Dad. You can't stop her doing what she loves.'

'I know, but she's chosen to enter a male-dominated field, with patriarchal concepts and prejudices. She couldn't have made it harder for herself if she'd tried.'

'Come on, Dad. She's always liked a challenge, and if she wasn't good at it, they would never have taken her on as a trainee ground engineer in the first place.'

Will grudgingly conceded the point. 'She's still my little girl.'

'She always will be. But she's quite capable of looking after herself.'

Will went quiet, his worries growing. There was no denying that war was on the horizon once again.

They parked outside the main hangar, where they found an oil-smeared Emily brandishing a spanner inside the cowling of a bright yellow de Havilland Tiger Moth.

'Daniel! Dad!' she cried as they approached. 'What a lovely surprise! What brings you here?'

'Just came to say hello,' said Will. 'I got a few hours off work.'

'Excellent. How about you, brother?'

'I'm down visiting the parents for a day or two, and thought I'd tag along. How's it going here?'

'I'm really enjoying it.' Emily pointed the spanner at the Tiger Moth's engine. 'Just got to tighten up a few nuts and bolts and she'll be as good as new.'

Will eyed the fragile-looking aircraft dubiously. 'You're not going to fly it yourself, though, are you?'

'Of course I'm going to fly it. What on earth's the point of fixing it up otherwise?'

'It just doesn't look very . . . reliable.'

'Are you kidding? The Tiger Moth's a simple trainer. Built for being thrown about and tested. You can come up with me if you'd like.'

'Another time, maybe.'

Emily regarded them both a little warily. She realised something else was coming. This wasn't just a social visit to exchange pleasantries.

'Look, Emily, Dad isn't just worried about you flying. He is worried about *you*. There are so few women in this line of work, and we know the pay is lousy and your accommodation hardly luxurious.'

'Who cares about accommodation? It's just a bed for the night, that's what it is.'

Emily turned to her father and took a deep breath. 'You don't have to worry about me. I'm in my element here. It's partly *because* women are so underrepresented that I want to do this. I want to change all that.'

'But you have to understand, it's a dangerous occupation. I've had patients brought to me after crashes that I've had to put back together, some of whom—'

'That's rare. I'll bet you've had a lot more patients injured in motorcar accidents.'

'True, but far more people drive. As your father—'

'As my father? As my father you should remember the risks my mother took! Going to war at fifteen. Driving a field ambulance and being bombed off the road. What about the risks you took, Dad? Volunteering to join up when under age, and working as a stretcher-bearer on the Western Front.'

Will looked to his son for support.

'That was wartime, though, sis. War means people take risks out of necessity. I think what Dad's saying – and remember, it's his job to keep people healthy – is that unnecessary dangers should be avoided.'

'Life without challenges and risks is dull as ditch water, as you well know. It's not worth living,' replied Emily emphatically.

She came over and gave Will a tight hug, before looking up again, meeting his eyes. 'Dad, I love you, you know that. I love that you care for me and want to protect me. This is what I'm born to do though. You've always been a supporter of equal rights for women, so has Mum. You even named me after Emmeline Pankhurst. There's no reason on earth why we women cannot do what men do. Amelia Earhart flew solo across the Atlantic six whole years ago now.'

'But Amelia Earhart is dead, love.'

'I'm not intending to fly across the Pacific. I've never told you this, but I've begged and scrounged my way into flying fourteen different aircraft now. No one actually says it around here, but they know I'm as good as any other pilot.

Trust me, flying will soon become accessible to women who don't come from wealthy backgrounds. The ninety-nines will see to that.'

'The ninety-nines?' said Daniel. 'What's that?'

'It's an international organisation of women pilots based in Oklahoma. Amelia Earhart was its first president. It provides flight scholarship opportunities for anyone who shows the right aptitude.'

'Or altitude,' whispered her brother.

Emily pulled a face. 'So there you are. For the women of the future, the sky's the limit!'

'At least promise me one thing.'

Emily was smiling broadly now. 'What's that, Daddio?'

'You won't join the RAF. Not with another conflict looming.'

'There's no chance of that. We women aren't even considered; more's the pity. There are plenty of girls like me who'd jump at the chance to take a pot shot at the Nazis.'

'I'm sure. But I'm glad to hear the RAF is a no-go.'

'I can still take an interest.' She gazed at her father, knowing she had won him over, and rather fancied teasing him a little. 'I was up at Duxford Aerodrome a fortnight ago and Sir Sydney Camm unveiled his latest prototype of the Hawker Hurricane. What a machine! Imagine a superbly aerodynamic monoplane with retractable landing gear and equipped with a powerful Rolls-Royce Merlin engine. It's a thing of absolute beauty and that is a plane I'd *die* to fly in one day.'

'So tactfully put,' said Daniel, dryly. 'That's really going to smooth things over.'

'I'll probably never fly it, don't worry. But here's the thing: it's been put together using purely conventional construction methods. Methods we are very familiar with.'

'Meaning?'

'Meaning, even if I can't climb inside it and pilot the thing, I can certainly help to maintain and repair it on the ground, even without any support from Hawker themselves.'

Will was secretly impressed by Emily's knowledge and enthusiasm. He had seldom seen her so happy and animated. He would have to compromise. Nodding in reluctant acquiescence, he was thinking that he would much rather his daughter was busy as an engineer with her feet safely on solid ground than mixing it up in the skies with the Flyboys in their dangerous fighter planes.

26

James

Will had asked Emily to come over for dinner the following evening, so Grace had gone to pick their daughter up from the airfield. When they returned home, a letter from America was waiting for her. Grace was always excited to read her brother James's news, not least because he kept in touch with their sister, Amy, who was also living over there. She tore open the envelope and read the letter to Emily.

Dear Grace,

Thank you for your recent letter, and apologies as always for the infrequency of mine. I could make excuses and claim that work has been hectic, but I cannot be anywhere near as busy as you must be! I have been tasked with publicising and selling the new Ford Saloon to the public, especially to the female market, as it has been dubbed 'The Woman's Car' (as it's easier to park and to handle in congested traffic). No, that's not a joke . . . and I know that as something of a mechanic yourself, those words will infuriate you. I promise that with you in mind I'll try to downplay that strategy!

On a more serious note, I am of course aware of the impending war. I do hope you are all safe. Could you come to the US? Amy would love that, too. She is flourishing in her new job, I must say . . . You would be entirely safe; over here, we are all for staying out of the conflict and leaving Western Europe to fend for itself. Personally, having lived through what we did before, and particularly after the loss of our beloved Charles, I am distraught by the apathy of the American people. What would Charles's sacrifice mean if we were prepared to surrender to the same aggressor? I fear Britain might find herself alone in any potential conflict. Even at Ford there is no appetite for fighting. Henry Ford himself has said he does not wish to participate in any Allied military effort. I've spoken up, of course, but I've been warned that if I persist, I'll be shown the door. It's difficult to fathom, but Henry Ford is openly antisemitic and even received the Grand Cross of the German Eagle. I find it galling to be associated with such a company, so I have been minded to try to change things from within. That's the kind of path I think our dear brother Fitzy would take, don't you agree? How is the funny little brainbox, anyway?

On a happier note, Amy, as I say, seems to have fallen on her feet. She is ensconced with a lovely man who works for the American government – in defence, I think. I suspect wedding bells may be imminent. She has also secured work with a major French fashion house (Lanvin – do you know them?) which suits her down to the ground. Talk about falling into the you-know-what and coming up smelling of roses . . . but that was always our Amy, wasn't it?

I'm sorry to have gone on so long. Guilt, I think. Must do better. Please send love to Mother, God knows how anxious she must be feeling. Love to Fitzy, Henry and Ru, and best wishes to Will and the children. Please seriously consider evacuating to the States whilst you can. Time may be running out.

Write soon. Your loving brother, James.

Grace tucked the letter back into the envelope and placed it on the mantelpiece for Will to read later. Emily took her mother by the hand and made her sit down. 'I don't think the picture is quite as bleak as he makes out, do you? And good news about Amy, I know you still worry about her.'

'It is good news about Amy, yes. Though I wouldn't entertain the idea of moving to the States, I do believe we are going to need their help in some form or another before long.'

At that moment, they heard the front door open and Will threw his keys on to the little hallway table.

'Until then, Mother, we must keep our spirits up, whichever way we can.'

'Talking of spirits,' said Will, coming into the room and brandishing a bottle in his right hand, 'how about a little drop of Macallan malt whisky before tea?'

Grace's expression read: *How the devil could you afford that?*

Will smiled. 'Present from a grateful patient.'

27

Aragon, Spain, June 1938

Kitty's summer had been miserable. She'd been adopted by her rescuers in Aragon and had ingratiated herself into their affections through her sheer dedication and professionalism. She had attended to many of the soldiers' wounds, and some swore they owed their lives to her. 'Angel Funambulista' they called her, after her tightrope performance over the ravine. The Republican Army was in disarray after the Battle of Teruel, demoralised, disorganised and outnumbered. The Nationalists' Aragon offensive had pushed them farther south, and by April, had reached the Mediterranean at Vinaros, cutting the remaining Republican territories in two. They had overwhelmed the towns of Lleida and Gandesa, and taken control of Barcelona's hydroelectric dams in the Pyrenees, which provided much of the Catalan industrial area with electricity. Without power, the supply of arms for the defenders had come to a halt, and at the same time aid from the Soviet Union had begun to dry up.

As Kitty had retreated, along with the bedraggled band of fighters, across the flat plains back towards Zaragoza, the enemy air force had been able to land just behind their frontlines to equip and relieve their troops. Unlike the mountainous regions to the east and west, the low, barren landscape provided little protection, and the Republican air force had all been wiped out. Kitty's group had been the last to leave the demolished town of Belchite, leaving the surrounding area firmly in Nationalist control. In the battles that followed, thousands of men had been killed or captured.

She was now holed up with Colonel Duran's Mounting Group in the Maestrazgo, the rugged mountainous region of southern Aragon, but it was clear this was the beginning of the end. The Republicans were licking their wounds and talking of regrouping, but Kitty saw resistance falling apart. Communist officers refused to share munitions with their anarchist brothers and Kitty witnessed more than one officer being arbitrarily executed in front of his own men. Even the unity of the International Brigades had been severely tested. Like the remaining few men she had come to know, Kitty realised the campaign seemed all but lost. Yet her spirit was still not broken. The sub-zero temperatures she had endured at Teruel had given way to the blistering heat of Segovia and Aragon. Kitty could have accepted defeat and headed home. She had been in the thick of it for eighteen months now, and had done her best. Her search for Ned kept her going. Not a day had passed without her wondering about his fate. The man she had loved and who had saved her life. Suppose he had somehow survived being shot? How long could he have lived with all those whirlpools and eddies of the river threatening to pull him under? However hard she tried, she had not been able to shake those thoughts from her mind. Johann and lszak, the men who had welcomed her at the top of the gorge, had been fatalistic. Farther downstream, they had pulled dislocated bodies out of the water regularly and had seen corpses everywhere over the past month – in war, this was commonplace. Yet Kitty had not yet found Ned's dead body, and so could not admit he was really gone. The search for an answer continued.

28

Lower Ebro Basin, Spain, August 1938

The Ebro River Basin covers over one fifth of Spain's landmass. It rises in the Cantabria mountains in Northern Spain and flows east-south-east between the Pyrenees in the north and the Iberian mountains in the south, before entering a broad delta and discharging into the Mediterranean Sea. The Popular Republican Army had chosen this spot to launch a major offensive against Franco's armies.

Kitty had never been so busy. She had been brought to the river's edge one night with several other nurses and doctors, ready for the first assault. There was no moon, and the river flowed silently past like dark treacle. She watched as the commandos paddled across it and were then joined by other troops in little boats, each carrying about ten men. As she sat in the stern of one of the vessels, she looked back to see that several pontoon bridges were being hastily assembled, ready to ferry over the remainder of the 50th Division of the Republican Army. Following just behind the advancing frontline, the initial progress was swift and took the enemy by total surprise. In the first two days, many prisoners had been taken and hundreds more enemy soldiers had deserted. The medical teams were overwhelmed; no matter how hard they worked, increasing numbers of injured men were being brought in. Outside Gandesa, the limestone rocks and sparse forest cover of the mountain ranges provided no significant shelter, and despite their valour, the Republicans proved no match for the Nationalists' air and artillery superiority. At Hill 481, the 15th International Brigades were all but annihilated.

Kitty worked herself to the point of exhaustion. There were times she had to be physically removed from the medical tents to sleep, eat and recover. Like the campaign itself, her work was proving a losing battle. The high temperatures accelerated the decomposition of the dead, who lay fallen, reeking of decay.

Half a dozen Nationalist counter-offensives had succeeded in forcing the Republican Army back over the river. Ultimately, the Republicans were losing ground and men continuously. Back in Fayon now, only the presence of Dr Josep Trueta, the man who had treated Liese's leg fracture, and who had travelled up from Barcelona to lend his assistance, had been able to lift her spirits. He was a good, kind man, who had discovered the best and most efficient way of treating open wounds and avoiding amputation or death. She was rather in awe of him. Sometimes, if it was quiet, they would sit and talk about their families and the holidays they had enjoyed. Kitty told him about her brothers and her sister-in-law and the work Will and Grace were both involved in at Oxford. Trueta listened attentively and then told her about the Trauma Department he headed up in Barcelona. Inevitably, they shared their views about the progress of the war and reluctantly agreed it was all but over.

'As the Republicans face defeat,' Trueta said, 'my family and I will need to leave our home. Not just the house, but the country, too. We must leave it all behind.'

'I'm so sorry. That must be terribly hard.'

Trueta nodded slowly and placed a hand gently on Kitty's shoulder as a tear ran down her cheek. 'And just as bitterly hard for you too, I would imagine.'

Kitty sniffed and wiped her face with the ragged sleeve of her tunic. 'When I leave Spain, I will be leaving behind any remaining hope of seeing Ned. I shan't even discover whether I leave him alive or dead.'

29

Dunn Institute, Oxford

In the bare, oak-panelled library on the second floor of the Dunn Institute, the informal weekly staff meeting was taking place. Ernst Chain and Howard Florey sat smoking behind a grand mahogany desk, while Grace mingled with the technicians and students of Magdalen and Lincoln Colleges. The weekly meeting was a chance to share news and ideas, and discuss the latest funding decisions by the Medical Research Council.

'Right, listen, everybody,' Florey began. 'We have no equipment, no chemicals, no stationery, and no money for recruiting more personnel. As a result, I have removed half the light bulbs in the building to save on juice.'

A low murmur of disappointment swept around the room.

'Other sources of income are drying up. The Dunn School has no endowment to maintain it, the university is freezing funds in favour of other departments, and the Rockefeller Foundation has not been persuaded to cough up either.'

'You all know what is happening in Germany,' said Chain. 'Not only to scientists, but to academics and artists among others. This is why the MRC's priority is for funds to go to our German colleagues who are struggling to survive.'

This was news to the group. 'But because they are struggling to survive and continue their work, so are we,' said Grace.

'Their scientists have achieved great things,' added Florey. 'It was only fifty years ago that Koch described germ theory.'

'Less than thirty since Erhlich developed Salvarsan to treat syphilis,' said Chain. 'But we cannot afford to wait thirty more years for another such medical advance.'

'I agree. I'm convinced we can find better ways to control and manipulate bacteria to our advantage.'

'Even now, we use viruses, fungi and moulds to clean our culture mediums of unwanted contaminants.'

The Florey–Chain double-act held the audience captive.

'Where are we now with all this?' said Florey. 'Well, Dr Chain has been investigating lysozymes. They are interesting compounds and are present in many areas including tears and nasal mucus. Also in pike eggs, dog saliva and human breast milk. In addition, they dissolve certain bacteria. We have spent four years looking into them.'

'And my conclusion?' Chain waited for a reaction before continuing, 'They are not acids, as some researchers first thought. Nor are they viruses that invade bacteria, things we call bacteriophages. No. They are nothing but enzymes that lyse and dissolve susceptible bacteria.'

'Disappointingly . . .' Florey left the sentence hanging as a cue for Chain to continue.

'They only have an effect on harmless bacteria, not the ones that cause serious disease.'

'So,' said Florey, 'Dr Chain's magnum opus has proved once and for all that further research into lysozymes is a dead duck.'

Chain, a sensitive and at times rather suspicious character, was uncertain of the professor's meaning. Was it a slur on his hard work, or just one of his attempts at humour?

'So we must start again. Together, we have uncovered all sorts of information on the physiology and pathology of mucus, on tetanus, on lymphatic systems and gastro-intestinal secretions. Dr Chain has explored the carbohydrate metabolism of cancer cells and described scientifically just how snake venom paralyses the human nervous system.'

Chain smiled, once again feeling appreciated.

'But now I want us to go all-out in another direction, on a renewed and relentless search for effective antibacterial substances. I want you all to scour the medical literature for anything that might kickstart our odyssey. From Germany and France to the USA and Russia, to my home country, Australia and beyond. Go back as far as you wish, right back to Leviticus and the Bible's advice on the treatment of lepers. Come back to me with ideas. Devise your experiments and let's get cracking.'

As the staff filed from the room, Florey called Grace and Dr Chain over.

'Grace, I like what you're doing with your tutorials. The students are fizzing with energy and I've never seen the auditorium so full. Keep it up. Dr Chain, I want you to read these publications. Start with this one from Gratia and Dath at the Institut Pasteur. The second one is a 1928 paper by Papacostas and Gate. Then read Alexander Fleming's paper published that same year, which I oversaw at the time as editor of the *British Journal of Experimental Pathology*.'

Chain examined the pages handed to him, titled: 'On the antibacterial action of a culture of penicillin with special reference to the isolation of B. influenza.'

'And finally, this one. Harold Raistrick's 1932 paper

detailing how he tried to purify Fleming's penicillin but found it impossible.'

'Impossible?' queried Chain, his ears pricking up at the sound of a challenge.

'To quote him verbatim, "The production of penicillin for therapeutic purposes is almost impossible".'

'*Almost* impossible,' said Chain under his breath. 'I wonder.'

'You're the best biochemist I know, Dr Chain,' said Florey, before adding in his typically derogatory fashion, 'although I don't know many. If anyone can have a good crack at it, you can.'

Chain snatched the paper from the professor, turned on his heels and left. Grace frowned.

'Do you enjoy baiting the poor man?'

'He's big enough and ugly enough to take it. If it spurs him on to prove me wrong, so much the better.'

'If I may . . .?'

'Speak freely. I know you will anyway.'

'Just be a little careful, Professor. You know his family history, and antisemitism is barely concealed, even here in Oxford. He was hospitalised with anxiety and depression not so long ago, remember, and he is never far from his rages and rants.'

'You'd better look after him then. The best way I know to keep the troops happy is to secure this establishment some decent funding and pay their meagre salaries.'

Florey exited the room. The mere mention of the word 'troops' had flipped Grace's train of thought. She might have been working flat-out for poor financial reward, but at least she was safe. Where was her sister-in-law Kitty? And was she in any danger?

30

Kindertransport, London Docks, December 1938

Not so very long before the arrival of the merchant steamship *Warszawa* at London docks, Liese had welcomed Kitty back from Spain with open arms and free-flowing tears. Will, Grace, Emily, Daniel and Clara had all been there, too, relieved to find Kitty physically intact, if somewhat battered and bruised. They had spent the last fortnight catching up with her, ensuring she also got the rest and recuperation she needed.

Now Liese and Kitty stood together at the quayside watching hundreds of Jewish refugee children making their way down the gangplank on to terra firma. Some of the teenagers looked apprehensive. Several of them held the hands of much younger children, some as young as four or five.

In the last few days, Kitty and Liese had reminisced about their original journey to Spain and their dreadful experiences in Guernica. Kitty had described the last few weeks of the Civil War and how in September the Republican prime minister, Juan Negrín López, had announced the unconditional withdrawal of the International Brigades. She told of her lightning visit to Barcelona to make Josep Trueta promise he would get out and travel to Oxford to meet Professor Florey and his team. She also talked of Ned and how impossible it had been to forget him, never knowing his fate. Liese had listened sympathetically and had told Kitty all about her journey from Bilbao with the thousands of Basque children. It had turned out to be a hellish crossing because of the terrible weather in the Bay of Biscay.

'And here we are,' she said, 'with another boatload of refugee children. When will it stop?'

'No time soon,' Kitty replied, 'and I fear these poor lambs will face all sorts of trauma.'

'Will you help me?' asked Liese. 'Help them to learn English and get settled with foster parents?'

'Of course I will. I'll have them fluent in English in no time. Leandro has settled in so well with Clara and Daniel. He is nine now, thriving under my aunt's guardianship. He's given her and my father a new lease of life, too, and Daniel is like a brother to him. Of course, he mourns his father, Pedro; we didn't tell him the whole truth, and we know Franco is still wreaking his revenge on his opponents. My sister-in-law's mother, Dorothy, has a big home and time on her hands and says she is willing to take in one of the refugees as well.'

As the bedraggled little children were filing past to be processed by a row of government officers, one of them stopped and tugged at Liese's coat tails.

'Will I see my mummy and daddy again soon?' he asked in Yiddish.

She crouched down to his level. 'I hope so, little one. I hope so.'

31

Houses of Parliament, London, 3 September 1939

Fitz sat with Stephen in their parliamentary office waiting to hear Neville Chamberlain's BBC radio broadcast. It seemed that Winston Churchill's dire warnings had been prescient. It had been a year full of foreboding: in March, Hitler had invaded Czechoslovakia and annexed Austria; early in April, Mussolini had ordered the Italian Army to invade Albania; in May, those two countries had signed the pact of steel. Then, in August, while the Soviet Union signed a non-aggression pact with the Nazis, Britain and Poland had signed a mutual assistance treaty. Now everyone was preparing for conflict, digging air raid shelters, hoarding supplies, putting up blackout curtains and evacuating women and children from the cities. Fitz's nephew, Daniel, now aged twenty, was liable for a four-year call-up under the military training act, and Rupert, Fitz's brother, a commodore first class with the Royal Navy, had already proceeded to war stations in readiness for what might lie ahead.

Neville Chamberlain had abandoned the offer of a negotiated peace between Germany and Poland, and had finally delivered his ultimatum to Hitler. Now, all around the country, families gathered around their wireless sets to hear what the prime minister had to say. In Oxford, Grace sat with

Florey, Chain, and another colleague, Norman Heatley, all having temporarily abandoned their posts at the institute. Daniel was tuning in with his fellow psychiatrists at the Maudsley. At Kidlington, Emily was at the aircraft hangar, listening in with the engineers. Liese and Kitty were listening from the Bureau for Jewish Refugees in London. Will was operating on a teenage boy with acute appendicitis, but the theatre nurses had installed a wireless in the corner. Just after eleven o'clock, the radios crackled into life and Neville Chamberlain dropped a bombshell.

'I am speaking to you from the Cabinet room at 10 Downing Street. This morning, the British Ambassador in Berlin handed the German government a final note stating that unless we heard from them by eleven o'clock that they were prepared at once to withdraw their troops from Poland, a state of war would exist between us. I have to tell you now that no such undertaking has been received, and that consequently this country is at war with Germany.'

32

Dunn Institute, May 1940

Ernst Chain would never get used to the English way of doing things. Trained in Berlin and fully accustomed to state-of-the-art laboratories, he despaired of the apathetic attitude of some of the technicians and their lack of investment in biochemistry. Neither could he understand why Norman Heatley did not seem to mind. Quiet and unassuming, stick-thin and industrious, Heatley went about his business with enthusiasm and, even when the equipment let him down – which it frequently did – he was more inclined to see failure as a challenge and already had a considerable reputation as an inventor and innovator. He had just come down from the roof of the institute with his latest batch of crude penicillin broth; it was five degrees up there, and he had discovered that lower temperatures were better for growing the medium to produce penicillin. Chain had to admit the man was certainly ingenious.

'You look every bit the mad scientist, Dr Heatley. But if you can furnish me with more material to test, I would be grateful.'

'Oh, I'm quite happy to play the crazy boffin,' Heatley replied. 'And I do believe we're getting somewhere with increased extract and fewer impurities.'

'Good. I am pleased to hear this. However, there are still too many contaminants mixed with the penicillin. The compound makes up a tiny percentage of the solutions but without a pure active compound, there are too many confounding factors.'

'Ah, yes. "Eye of newt and toe of frog, wool of bat and tongue of dog" . . . and all that other *Macbeth* stuff.'

'We can't rely on witchcraft, Heatley,' said Chain. 'If I'm ever to discover the true chemical nature of penicillin, I need enough of it to analyse. So I, too, have made some progress.'

Heatley looked up from the vertical column of glass pipes and tubing in front of him as Chain continued. 'The professor was not particularly interested initially, but I did the experiment anyway. As I think you know, I have no Home Office licence to perform animal toxicity tests, but with the help of Dr John Barnes, we injected two mice with forty milligrams of the compound. I thought it was about time we tested it on something other than germs on a Petri dish.'

'You did? What happened?'

'Nothing happened, Heatley,' Chain said, grinning. 'Nothing at all.'

'But that means . . .'

'Yes. The compound is non-toxic, even in this most impure form full of contaminants.'

'That's a big step forward, Dr Chain. This has huge implications.'

'But that is not all. We collected the urine from the mice, which was tinged with a brown pigment. We spread it on an agar plate, growing colonies of streptococcus, and incubated it.'

'And?'

'Whatever the active ingredient within the pigment, it still retained its own antibacterial power.'

Heatley beamed and slapped Chain on the shoulders.

'My God, Chain, that means it is not only non-toxic, to mice at least, but that it is not inactivated by the body, and is almost certain to fight bacteria inside the living body.'

'Precisely!' Chain laughed gleefully.

'So what are you going to do next?'

'I'm going to go and tell Professor Florey. I think he will be more interested now that we have embarked on biological testing.'

'He can't fail to be. Penicillin is no longer just a chemical, my friend. You've proved it has become a drug.'

*

As soon as Grace heard about the results of Dr Chain's penicillin toxicity test, she realised the substance had the potential to save human lives across the country. Historically, the life's work of many a scientist was founded on mere potential, but realising that potential was quite another thing. Encouraged by Florey, and much to the disappointment of the students, Grace wound down her commitment to undergraduate teaching and ramped up her animal experiments at the institute.

Between April and May she carried out countless tests on cats, rabbits, rats and mice, carefully analysing the effects of penicillin, on the way it was excreted and absorbed, the changes to the animals' blood providing a reliable marker of the presence of infection. She observed the way penicillin caused different bacteria to swell and elongate under the microscope. Peering through the eyepiece, she looked on in amazement at how, in the presence of penicillin, the germs puffed up and exploded before her eyes. While it clearly had an antibiotic effect on germs spread out on a microscope slide, would it work on living animals that were sick? And would it have any horrible side effects? More to the point, would it work on humans?

In the last few days she had prepared a standardised batch of streptococcus bacteria, capable of killing a mouse within thirty-six hours. They had carefully calibrated the dose: enough to prove fatal to the mouse, but still dilute enough to give penicillin the chance to alter the outcome. Today they were going to find out if it was enough to protect the mice.

33

Eight Mice, 25 May 1940

It was eleven o'clock in the morning, and an air of anticipation filled the room. Will had wanted Grace to accompany him and Emily to an Oxford United match, but she was not going to miss this experiment for the world. She was even more excited to be introduced to the well-respected Dr Josep Trueta, who had recently joined Florey's team, after being introduced some months earlier by Kitty. The Dunn Institute was more than happy to give him a home.

In separate cages, eight white mice of similar size and weight scuttled about in the sawdust-and-biscuit powder under their feet. The bacteria they had been injected with had not yet taken effect. Florey and Kent picked up the first two mice and injected five milligrams of the experimental penicillin solution into their tail veins. This would be repeated frequently, ably assisted by Trueta. Mice three and four were similarly treated, but with double the dose, and only once. The remaining four were not treated at all, to act as controls. All the researchers had to do now was wait. What happened in the next few hours would tell everyone exactly what they wanted to know.

By six in the evening, mice one and two looked chipper and alert. Mice three and four, however, were less active. By comparison, the other four mice, the untreated ones, all looked withdrawn, curled up and sickly. Four hours later, Florey administered the last injection and went home, leaving Norman Heatley to finish and lock up. Heatley was too excited to leave now. At 3.45 a.m. he placed a fourth red cross in his notebook to denote that half the mice had died. Then he put on his coat, snapped on his bicycle clips, switched off the lights and headed downstairs. He was dog-tired and longing for his bed, but he was almost certainly not going to be able to sleep.

Just as the first glimmers of daylight were appearing on the horizon, Heatley freed his trusty Raleigh bicycle from the air-raid shelter where he kept it, and headed off towards home. He had only reached the corner when he was unceremoniously challenged by an aged and rather officious member of the Home Guard. Without giving away any secrets, he explained as best he could where he had been working and why, but the man seemed to need more convincing.

'It's a strange time of night to be out and about, isn't it?'

'It is indeed,' replied Heatley, 'but like you, we've got a job to do – and we're never really off duty, are we?'

'That's true enough,' said the man philosophically, 'although I doubt anyone appreciates it. On the other hand, I don't suppose either of us is likely to change the course of history for that matter, either.'

We'll see, thought Heatley, as he cycled off across the park. You might just be wrong about that.

34

Result!

Grace had been tossing and turning all night, yet despite her rolling from one side to the other, adjusting the blankets and plumping her pillows, Will remained deep in blissful slumber. It was four-thirty, and it would be another half hour before the Oxford sunrise illuminated the trees in the garden. She eased herself out of bed quietly, dressed, and went downstairs. A pot of tea and some marmalade-toast failed to calm her busy mind, so she left a note for Will and set off for Radcliffe Infirmary. There were plenty of patients to attend to before she joined the rest of Florey's team over at the Dunn Institute.

Six hours later, she climbed the steps flanked by stacks of sandbags, showed her pass to the three military policemen guarding the front door, and ran up the stairs two at a time, to the second floor. Ernst Chain was pacing up and down the corridor, chuntering impatiently and complaining.

'Grace!' he cried. 'We are locked out of the laboratory, and Heatley has the key. I want to see the results.'

Just as she was about to remind him that the meeting had been arranged for eleven o'clock on the dot, Heatley and Florey appeared at the other end of the corridor, Heatley brandishing a set of keys.

'This is a first,' said Florey, dryly. 'Four members of my elite team all present and correct at the allotted time.'

'I have been here an hour already, locked out of my own laboratory!' protested Chain.

'My laboratory, actually,' corrected Heatley. 'But no matter. Let's take a look.' They entered the room and inspected the cages in silence. Grace felt the hairs on the back of her neck stand up and her heart was thumping rapidly against her ribs.

The four control mice were all dead. The two mice that had received a single shot of penicillin looked sluggish and worse for wear. But the pair who had been given five shots looked just fine and dandy. They were moving about freely, as if nothing had happened.

Chain clapped his hands on Florey's shoulders and shook him. 'Do you realise what this means?' It was a rhetorical question as Florey knew instantly what it meant. 'Heatley, it's unequivocal. Grace, do you see?'

Heatley certainly did. So did Grace. She turned to the professor to gauge his reaction. He was looking intently from one cage to the next, his forehead furrowed. For a moment or two he said nothing, then, with the hint of a smile, he turned to them each in turn and shook their hands.

'This, my friends,' he said slowly, 'looks like something of a miracle.'

They all knew Florey was not a man given to hyperbole. If anything, he would tend to downplay things. Florey immediately started planning to extend the trials to include greater numbers of mice and other animals, using different dosages of penicillin and for different durations. He would also try it against a whole battery of different bacteria. He looked once more at the exhausted figure of Heatley.

'The next experiments are vital, Heatley. We may be on the cusp of something truly special. But to do more trials, we need more penicillin.'

Chain jumped in. 'And if I am to discover the exact chemical composition, I need more, too.'

Heatley had already worked for months to produce the small quantities that had made this first trial possible. 'I'm currently producing a hundred litres of mould juice every week,' he replied defensively.

'Double it,' ordered Florey. He knew Heatley was a brilliant scientist and a man he could rely on to solve biological problems with micro-chemical methods. It was what he did.

'You ramp up production as fast as you can. Dr Chain, I want you to carry on investigating the chemical structure of penicillin. Grace, galvanise the whole team into performing more animal tests. I'll get out the begging bowl and prostitute myself before the powers that be for funding.'

By now, other members of the department had made their way into the laboratory and were listening to the animated conversation.

'You all know what the next big step must be.'

Grace had known for some time.

Florey continued, 'The next step is to see how penicillin works in humans. But, Dr Chain, we may require the exact chemical structure before being allowed to do that. Grace, we will need consent from the patients and from the hospital authorities. We must perform all the interim stages first, so Heatley, whichever way you look at it, we need more of the stuff to test. We've already learned that the dose is critical. Currently, we're taking a week or more to produce enough of the juice just for a mouse. The average human would need almost three thousand times as much.' He looked around the room for dramatic effect. 'Gentlemen, ladies, it is within our reach to change the world. But we face a number of major challenges: production, purification, payola and proof. Let's get to it.'

35

Dunkirk, 27 May 1940

There were around four hundred thousand men currently trapped on the beach at Dunkirk.

Bessie was a sturdy Thames sailing barge made for transporting heavy cargo. Although built for the river, she was nevertheless seaworthy, and would often make cross-channel trips to industrial ports in Holland and France. She was flat-bottomed, weighed over a hundred tons, and rode very low in the water. Only the high gunwales prevented her from taking on too much water in choppy seas, and now, she was wallowing badly in the heavy swell.

Jack was looking rather green; he would have preferred the challenge of an unexploded bomb, any day of the week. Usually, *Bessie* was crewed by at least two men, but her captain, Spike, had lost the services of his usual deckhand. Jack had done a bit of recreational sailing over the years, so had agreed to join him.

The *Bessie* had left Ramsgate two days after the evacuation had started, Churchill having appealed to those with anything that would float, to help rescue the stranded soldiers. The boat's shallow draft had allowed them to bring her close to the beach, where the waves were breaking and a stream of desperate, weary men were wading out towards them. They were shivering and shaking as Jack and Spike hauled each of them aboard, wet through and exhausted. Most were English, although some were French, and all but one of them could do no more than collapse silently in the relative shelter of the hold. One chap, who spoke with an unmistakably French accent, immediately discarded his rifle and got to work pulling yet more men out of the sea and wrapping them in warm, dry blankets. One or two still in the water obviously recognised him and were calling his name. 'Sam Grefria!' they shouted to him. 'Sam Grefria!' He quickly hauled them aboard. Jack reckoned the name sounded more Spanish than French, but either way, the fellow seemed to be bilingual as he understood Spike perfectly and carried out his instructions to the letter. He cut quite a figure, tall and powerfully built, with long black hair, a broad, slightly protruding forehead, and slanted jet-black eyes just above wide, noble cheekbones. He was a handsome fellow, for sure. Jack watched him working tirelessly whilst at the same time calmly reassuring the rescued men in his native tongue.

When the barge was fully laden, they turned the boat around and made for home. Jack looked out to sea. It was bedlam. Hundreds of little craft bobbed about in the swell. He could just make out the paddle steamer *Victoria*, a familiar Thames fire boat, and he recognised the elegant motor yacht, *Dora*. Through the smoke and the spray, he could also see the MV *Royal Daffodil* over to starboard as it was being attacked by six oncoming aircraft. He watched helplessly as one bomb penetrated both her decks and blew a massive hole just below the waterline. Miraculously, it seemed she could still make headway and was now setting off for home.

Jack looked back at the forlorn column of men still queueing on the beach. Black smoke obscured much of the view, yet could not hide the corpses lying on the sand and floating at the water's edge. The dive-bombing Ju 87 Stukas were relentless. With their inverted gullwings and fixed, spatted undercarriages, the scream of their ramair sirens struck fear into everyone on land or sea as they swooped to launch another ground attack. Hopefully, the Spitfires would turn up and see them off, but where were they? Jack surveyed the sorry group of men huddled together below *Bessie*'s decks. The Spitfires could not come a moment too soon.

36

Dunn Institute, 18 June 1940

Grace had called the team into Professor Florey's office. Downing tools and leaving their experiments in the hands of their assistants, they ambled into the cramped little room and gathered around the battered Bakelite radio perched on the desk. Florey sat behind it, his face half obscured by the wisps rising from a partially smoked Chesterfield cigarette in the ashtray. Dr Chain sat beside him, his expression a mixture of anger and despair. The others stood around the desk two or three deep in places, glued to the words of Winston Churchill.

'. . . The whole fury and might of the enemy must very soon be turned on us. Hitler knows that he will have to break us in this island or lose the war . . . if we fail, then the whole world . . . will sink into the abyss of a new Dark Age made more sinister, and perhaps more protracted, by the lights of perverted science. Let us therefore brace ourselves to our duty, and so bear ourselves that, if the British Empire and its Commonwealth last for a thousand years, men will still say: This was their finest hour.'

Grace switched off the radio and looked at Florey for his reaction.

'Ladies and gentlemen,' Florey started, picking up his

cigarette, 'Churchill talks of perverted science, but science should be a cause for good, a catalyst for progress, for the advancement of mankind. I've been telling anyone here who will listen – and others in higher echelons of power and authority – just how important our work might prove for the war effort. The Battle of Britain is about to begin, and a German invasion on these shores is a possibility. Dr Chain knows from personal experience how the bastards could behave, and I for one am determined to ensure that whatever happens, we continue our work. We must prevent the invaders from getting their hands on everything we have strived so hard to achieve. Penicillin must not fall into Nazi hands.' A murmur of approval washed across the room.

'We already have bomb shelters outside and soldiers guarding the entrance to the building. We must be ready to destroy everything here if we have to, rather than let it be stolen and used against us.'

'It would not be enough,' said Chain. 'The Nazis are well-informed and totally ruthless. I don't believe aerial bombing is the main threat, not to Oxford at least. The enemy may be merciless, but so far they have respected the sanctity of the top university cities – after all, they will be of both architectural and scientific value to them should they ever be captured.' The men and women huddled around him pressed forward.

'So what are you saying?' asked Arthur Gardner, who headed the MRC's Standards Laboratory. 'We turn the institute into a fortress and ask the Army to defend it at all costs?'

The idea seemed too ridiculous to even consider. They were doctors and scientists, not an elite band of desperados.

'I have a suggestion,' said Norman Heatley from the back. 'If we need to evacuate the building, rather than destroy everything we have worked for, we should take our work with us.'

'And how will we do that?' someone asked.

'*Penicillium notatum* is a mould, is it not? In its resting state, it forms spores. Hardy, microscopic particles that allow fungi to reproduce, just like plant seeds. And just like those seeds, the spores can survive without water or sustenance indefinitely, often lying dormant for many years.'

'So we take the spores with us, if nothing else?' asked Chain.

'Precisely,' said Florey. 'That's logical.'

'What if we get caught with them?' asked Chain. 'The very fact that we are selecting only the spores will merely highlight their importance, and would hand our precious treasure to them on a plate.'

'But we won't get caught with them,' said Heatley, looking smug.

'How can you be so sure?'

'Because we will hide them in a place no one would think of looking.' Heatley beamed as he looked around the room, clasping both lapels of his lab coat.

'Ah, I think I know what you mean,' said Grace, 'and I like it.'

'Look,' said Florey, stubbing out his cigarette, 'wherever you hide agar plates, microscope slides or even brown paper parcels, you're never going to be able to guarantee they won't be found.'

'I beg to differ, Professor. Listen. We can rub the spores into the very fabric of our coats.' Heatley pulled at his lapels and stroked them with his thumb and forefinger for effect.

'The little brown specks will be lost among all the other marks and stains and we can revive the dormant spores at any time in the future.'

'It's brilliant, Heatley,' Florey said. 'Ingenious as always.'

37

White Waltham Airfield, Berkshire

At the request of Dickie Burns, the chief aviation engineer at Kidlington, Emily had flown down to White Waltham airfield in the de Havilland Tiger Moth to meet someone called Pauline Gower. He had not told her any more than that. The meeting turned out to be a wonderful surprise and a most unexpected opportunity.

In 1940, Pauline Gower had been tasked with organising the women's section of the air transport auxiliary, and had already recruited a number of women pilots operating designated RAF ferry pools to transport military aircraft from factories to maintenance depots or operational airfields. Since women were banned from combat duty, skilled women pilots were required to take the burden of transportation and aircraft delivery from the RAF. Gower had heard about Emily's engineering skills and flying experience on the grapevine.

'There are risks, of course,' she had warned. 'We fly not just newly built planes but also repaired and damaged ones. We often just have basic instruction manuals to fly them, too. We have lost over a dozen pilots so far to any combination of factors – bad weather, bad judgement, bad luck – but we are making a good fist of it.'

'So, is it an engineer you're looking for?'

'That expertise certainly comes in handy, Emily. I'm hoping you'd also be willing to train as one of our pilots. Dickie Burns is obviously an admirer of yours. But with us, you'd be flying a great many more planes: Hurricanes, Mosquitoes, North American Mustangs, and Lancasters, to name a few.'

Emily was so overcome, she did not know quite what to say. It was what she had always wanted to do.

'We have our own training programme and you'll progress from single-engined aircraft to more powerful and complex types, one stage at a time. Once qualified to fly a plane of a certain class, you could well be asked to fly a different aircraft in that class, even if you've never clapped eyes on it before. You'll just have the standard ATA pilot notes: a ring-book of small cards with the critical statistics and notations needed to ferry the aircraft about.'

Still Emily said nothing. She was trying to process it all. Gower continued, 'They don't pay us as much as the men for doing exactly the same job yet, but I believe that will change.'

'I'd do it for free, Miss Gower, if the truth be known.' Emily grinned from ear to ear. 'When can I start?'

38

The Blitz

If Florey had hoped his *Lancet* paper would light up the pharmaceutical world overnight and stimulate a frenzied rush to produce penicillin in bulk, his dreams lay in tatters. The only thing ignited was London. By the first day of the Blitz, which had begun the day after his publication on 7 September, three hundred and fifty German bombers flew along the Thames estuary, dropping tons of high-explosive bombs and parachute mines over the docks, railway lines and other strategic targets.

As London burned and night fell, the flames lit up the darkness like monstrous fingers beckoning the next wave of bombers, shining a spotlight on the Thames and the buildings and streets either side of it.

Jack, dressed all in black and wearing his customary cloth cap, looked up as he stood beneath the crane at St Albert Docks, his face reflecting the flickering yellow-and-crimson glow of the fires all about. He was used to bombs and detonations. He was accustomed to the flash and thunder of explosions. It was his job.

He knew instinctively how many bombs would have been needed for this mission and how much preparation must have been involved. It was clear to him what this new onslaught meant. A new phase had begun. Germany had failed to destroy the airfields and the resistance of the RAF. The Battle of Britain had been won, but Germany was still intent on winning the war. As things stood, nobody would bet against them. Not even Jack – an inveterate gambler and a master at tipping outsiders – could guess the outcome.

Just then he heard the screech of metal on metal and the crump of an entire warehouse wall falling on to a crane nearby. There was a group of men sheltering under it, but they did not stand a chance. The entire construction bent and collapsed under an avalanche of bricks and dust. The arm of the crane fell towards the water, impaling the deck of a fire barge with its tip, snapping it in two and forcing it under the choppy water. Jack felt the bile rising in his throat. He probably knew some of those men. How many times would he have to endure the aggression of the German military machine? They had already taken his childhood best friend, and countless others. They had turned his father into a shambling wreck. And Jack, like so many others, had endured the ghastly fighting in the trenches and had seen the civilian consequences of the war. Yet here they were again, intent on mayhem and destruction.

Jack could not stand back and watch. He walked the streets of London in a blind rage. People of all descriptions wandered about helplessly, dazed, some clutching precious possessions, some weeping, some battered and bloodied.

Still strong in mind and spirit, but deemed too old and medically unfit for conscription, Jack still had skills and expertise with explosives. Civilian work in demolition was now non-existent, but there would be bombs aplenty that failed to detonate, and parachute mines whose fuses were faulty. There would be ordnance everywhere that was a significant danger to the public. Jack could not prevent the bombs from falling but he could make safe many of those that had failed to explode. He would offer his services to the bomb disposal teams of the Royal Engineers.

39

The Fox and Hounds, Oxford

'He's a strange fellow, that Alexander Fleming,' said Grace at the bar of The Fox and Hounds. 'Everyone was rather perplexed by him.'

'In what way?' Will downed the last of his pint and ordered another.

'First of all,' she said, 'he arrives almost unannounced. And he didn't bother to tell us he was bringing company.' Fleming had brought along E. J. King, a biochemist from the Postgraduate Medical School at the University of London, and Douglas Maclean, from the Lister Institute.

'Then he mooched around in all the laboratories, inspecting our processes, and even the storage facilities.'

'And?'

'And nothing. He hardly said a word. He took it all in, mumbled a half-hearted thank you to the professor, and just pushed off, without so much as a backward glance.'

'How bizarre.'

'It is, given that he discovered the source of penicillin all those years ago. You'd think he'd be at least a little excited about witnessing its production and development for the first time.'

Will took another gulp from his ale. He had performed six

operations that day and had worked up a thirst. 'Maybe he's envious. It is over ten years since he came across his precious mould. But what did he do with it? Nothing. Did he realise the importance of what he'd discovered and what significance it might have for the human race? Possibly not. Now he sees other scientists reaping the benefits and he probably feels under-appreciated.'

'No,' said Grace firmly. 'That's definitely not the case. Florey has always kept him in the loop, and if anything, Fleming has repeatedly asserted that penicillin is too unstable to keep, impossible to purify, and unlikely to have any therapeutic application. You'd think he'd want to collaborate with Florey, but he gave up on the work years ago. He is clearly not a man with whom it is easy to communicate.'

'Maybe he's finally realised the greater purpose of his discovery and feels it is being usurped by others?'

'Listen, Will, the man did nothing with it. His original paper merely indicated an antibacterial action of penicillin cultures on an agar plate. He didn't carry out a single test to see if it might have any clinical application.'

'That's what I'm saying. I think he simply didn't know its significance.'

'Florey, Chain and Heatley put two and two together, put in the hard graft, and got us to where we are now.'

Confronted with the facts, Will found it hard to disagree.

'Penicillin is just too difficult to process. The yield is too small against the huge production costs. And they are not convinced that it's commercially viable or that the clinical trial results are conclusive.' Grace picked up her tumbler of whisky sour and swallowed it in one.

'They think that the exact chemical structure of the drug

will soon be elucidated, and once that happens, it would be produced synthetically at a fraction of the cost.'

'Making current expensive fermentation methods obsolete.'

'Indeed.'

'How did the boss take Fleming's visit?' Will asked.

'He was as puzzled as the rest of us. I'm not sure what he expected, but he certainly went out of his way to make Fleming feel welcome. They say credit where credit's due, but the prof deserves a lot of it, and got none whatsoever for all his efforts. Not from Fleming, anyway.'

'It's a competitive world, Grace, and the scientific community is full of ego. I suppose it's hard to let go of something you consider your own baby.'

'But progress can only be made by collaboration. If penicillin is to become a game-changer, it'll take a whole group of individuals – maybe even an international effort – to bring it to fruition.'

'Is that likely?'

'If Florey has his way, it is. He's in talks with the MRC now about travelling to the States to garner their support.'

'Is he, indeed? Well, if anyone can put fire in their belly, it's him, I suppose.'

40

SOE: Special Operations Executive, St Ermin's Hotel, London

From the outside, the Queen Anne-style red-brick building in Westminster resembled an old, neglected gentleman's club more than anything else. Kitty had not even hinted at what the interview might entail, nor what her role might be if she was appointed, asking Liese not to push her on the subject. 'It'll become clear soon enough!' she'd said. Their heels clacked noisily on the marble tiles as they reached the second-floor landing, and within minutes of their arrival they were promptly ushered into an austere room with blacked-out windows, furnished with comfortable armchairs and Persian rugs. The walls were lined with bookcases, and an impressive collection of oil paintings bedecked the walls.

Sir Andrew Morrison sat behind a walnut desk and looked up from the paperwork in front of him. 'Ladies,' he said, getting to his feet, 'please make yourselves comfortable.'

Kitty and Liese moved over to the cushioned burgundy Chesterfield. Sir Andrew took a seat near to them in a high-backed armchair. The two women eased themselves forward to the front of their seats and sat upright; a more rigid and correct posture instinctively seemed fitting.

'Thank you for coming,' he started, looking directly at Liese. 'Miss Burnett would have been aware of the reasons we have invited you, Ms Fischl, but at our request, she will not have shared them with you.'

Liese was more intrigued than ever.

'You are an eminently qualified bacteriologist with a wealth of experience in the field of pathology, I understand.'

'Yes, I qualified at the Charité Hospital in Berlin, where my father held the position of Chair. I came to Britain in 1936 and was appointed as director of pathology at the Royal Infirmary in Edinburgh a short while later.'

'Quite so.' Sir Andrew paused to study his interviewee more closely. 'Then you left that position voluntarily, just a few weeks later, without explanation.'

Liese blinked rapidly. It seemed like an accusation.

'The Dean, Douglas Monro, was quite upset about it, was he not? He'd pulled quite a few strings to secure your appointment there.'

Liese had always felt rather guilty about letting the poor man down. So now she found herself blushing. 'Am I in some sort of trouble?' she ventured, looking at Kitty for support.

'Not at all, my dear. Quite the opposite. It's we who are in trouble, and we need your help. Your work in the medical field is well known and your expertise is enviable. However, your contribution to the Republicans' cause during the Spanish Civil War is perhaps rather less appreciated, as is your German origin, your Jewish ancestry, and your tireless assistance in finding work for the refugees.'

Liese was curious. How does he know all this?

'We know about your parents and their internment by the German authorities, Miss Fischl. We know you have been brought up as a Catholic although your grandmother was Jewish. We are fully aware of what that means in Nazi Germany. We also know that you had a lucky escape with the help of Miss Burnett's sister-in-law.'

'It seems there is very little you don't know about me!' Liese sounded affronted. She wanted to protest at this personal intrusion, and felt rather uncomfortable about the inquisitorial tone of the conversation.

'Let's start again. My name is Sir Andrew Morrison, and I work for an organisation called the Special Operations Executive. Miss Burnett has been involved with us since her return from Spain, and suggested we approach you for help.' He let the implication linger before continuing. 'Many of our operatives are university graduates, intelligence officers, policemen, civil servants, or ex-soldiers, and most of them are men. But a smaller proportion of women – who come from all walks of life and backgrounds – have become invaluable.'

Liese wondered where this was leading.

'None of them works in the field of microbiology, though. Many of our recruits are recommended by existing personnel. Provided they work independently of each other and cannot be compromised by friendship and loyalty, it is not usually a problem.'

Liese looked at Kitty in a new light, now understanding her recent disappearances and her secrecy about this meeting. 'I am a bacteriologist,' she said, still perplexed. 'How can I possibly be of value to you?'

'That is your specialist field, yes. That is what defines you first and foremost. But you also speak fluent German and Dutch. You have experienced the ruthlessness of the Nazis first hand, and joined the struggle against the fascists in

Spain. You will be fully aware that your parents' liberty has been taken.'

Kitty looked aghast. She knew Liese prayed every day for her parents' safety, and had never given up hope, despite knowing nothing of their fate.

'Ms Fischl, we will do what we can to help you, if you would consider helping us.' He let the statement sink in.

'Helping you how?' Liese asked. It was time to get to the point.

'As you've highlighted, you are a bacteriologist. Your profession is comprised of an esoteric band of friends and colleagues. Thanks to them, you are acquainted with the work being carried out at the Dunn Institute in Oxford and the extraordinary potential of a revolutionary compound they are attempting to produce. The Chair of Pathology there is convinced this compound, once he can produce enough of it, could change the course of medical history. If that is the case – and we have no reason to think otherwise – it could very well change the course of military history, as well.'

The two friends had spoken at length with Grace about this, but Liese had no idea the research had piqued the interest of anyone else outside the medical fraternity.

'So,' Sir Andrew continued, 'Florey is a brilliant scientist, as is his right-hand man, Chain. A compatriot of yours, Ms Fischl, I believe? But unlike so many other academics, these two do not work in isolation. They know the outcome of the war hangs in the balance. They are currently working behind barricades and sandbags. In between experiments, they are under military police protection and retreating to their air raid shelters and cellars. They run the emergency blood transfusion service at the Radcliffe Infirmary on a shoestring, and, somewhat reluctantly, house refugees and medical student evacuees from London in their building. We all have to do our bit. But they also know that whichever side in this war is first to produce penicillin in significant quantities will be afforded a hugely significant military advantage and could save millions of servicemen's lives.'

Realisation struck Liese. 'Not to mention the lives of countless innocent civilians,' she said. 'We should be sure to include them.'

'Quite so.'

'All right. So where do I come in?'

Sir Andrew turned to Kitty. 'Miss Burnett,' he said, 'would you be so kind as to fetch us some coffee?' She took her cue and left the room. Liese felt very alone.

'The Germans are not unaware of the potential of penicillin. So much more promising than their own sulpha drugs, I'm told.'

She knew this to be true. Penicillin was many times more powerful than sulphonamide and could treat a wider range of infections. 'In short,' he said, 'they are desperate to get hold of it.'

'But as far as I know,' countered Liese, 'Florey's team are the only ones working on penicillin.'

'I will risk being accused of teaching my grandmother to suck eggs, but I imagine that by now, you will be familiar with a chance discovery by Alexander Fleming in 1928. He gave that mould to the world. He was sending samples to anyone who requested them.'

'That's what scientists do, isn't it? They collaborate internationally in the spirit of medical advancement and the well-being of mankind.'

'Some more than others, apparently. I believe your German colleagues at Bayer, for example, were deliberately slow to reveal the active ingredient of their antimicrobial dyes at Farbenindustrie. They sat on their discovery for years.'

Liese was silent for a moment.

'But Florey and his team must be streets ahead of anyone else attempting to extract and produce penicillin. It's an almost impossible job. How would anyone else know what to do with Fleming's mould?'

Sir Andrew laughed out loud. 'That's what Edward Mellanby thinks. Oh – he's someone I know at the Medical Research Council. Unfortunately, the clues are already in the medical literature. Fleming's publication may not have stirred up much excitement at the time, but Oxford's more recent publications have not gone unnoticed overseas. And, as I say, others – the Swiss in Berne, the French at the Institut Pasteur in Paris, Dr Schmidt in Berlin, for example – have plenty of samples of the mould to work on.'

Liese was stunned. She knew very well that the German chemical and research industry was the envy of the world. Their pharmaceutical powerhouses were highly efficient, generously resourced, and their pioneers had been at the forefront of the majority of medical discoveries for decades. By contrast, the British equivalent was a poor relation, starved of money, short on equipment, and living off scraps. It was quite possible that the work of the Oxford group could be mimicked by anyone in Germany smart enough to have been alerted to their activities.

'We need to know how much progress they've made,' he said. 'While Florey can redouble our efforts to produce penicillin in bulk with the help of our American allies, we have a pressing imperative to delay progress elsewhere.'

'You mean sabotage progress elsewhere?'

'If you like.'

Liese was momentarily speechless.

'Well,' she said eventually. 'I don't like the idea of deliberately holding back a treatment that could save the lives of millions. It's against every doctor's principles. I'm sure you're familiar with the Hippocrates quotation: "Above all, do no harm." You're effectively asking me to refute my whole life's work. Not to actively fight infection, but to allow it to flourish. The whole idea is repugnant to me.'

'All right, I understand. But you must appreciate that your German counterparts in concentration camps across Eastern Europe do not seem to share your qualms about medical ethics. It seems they are prepared to stop at nothing.'

Liese didn't know what he was referring to.

'The more penicillin we can produce, the more Allied soldiers we can save, and the better our chances of survival as a nation. As you say, the same goes for our civilian population, too. As a doctor, you might save hundreds of patients during your career. But working for us, you could save tens of thousands. Isn't all fair in love and war?'

Liese took a deep breath. 'I need to think about this,' she said. 'Even if I were to agree to help, how could I possibly make any difference?'

Sir Andrew lowered his voice. 'We already have agents on the ground. In France, Italy, even Germany itself. But, as I've said, they are not bacteriologists and lack medical knowledge, with no access to the research laboratories. You, however . . .'

'I—'

'You're wondering where we might start? I'll tell you. We want to secure you a post at the Centraalbureau voor Schimmelcultures in Utrecht in the Netherlands. It has the largest collection of fungi and moulds in the world, as you likely know, and their collection includes samples of Fleming's *penicillium notatum*. Dr Johanna Westerdijk will offer the position, and we want you to be her chosen appointee.'

'But the Netherlands is under German occupation,' she protested. 'All medical and research establishments are closely guarded. I would be recognised and arrested immediately.'

'As Lieselotte Fischl, you would, yes. Arrested, and worse besides. So, we will give you false papers, a new identity, and glowing references from academics who never existed and therefore cannot be traced.'

'Being a spy isn't on my curriculum vitae.'

'It's a tall order and you don't have to decide now. All I ask is that you think about it. As I say, it is we who are in trouble, not you.'

'I have no experience in espionage, Sir Andrew.'

'Few of us do so that's par for the course. But consider the greater good.'

'What if I fail and get caught? By going to these lengths, wouldn't they be even more convinced of the need to accelerate their own research?'

'Miss Burnett is convinced we can afford to put our trust in you. The Germans have other priorities to distract them, and we believe it is a risk worth taking.'

The spymaster was encouraged that his potential recruit had not rejected his proposal outright, and pressed his advantage. 'I won't pretend there are not inherent dangers, but we would offer you full training. Liese, if I may call you that, I will make a solemn promise: my department and I will do whatever we can not only to track down your parents, but also to protect them.'

Liese had lived in hope for so long that she desperately wanted to believe it was possible she might be reunited with her family. She had worked all her professional life with people she trusted. They were dedicated, reliable and decent. Why should this dignified and respectable man be any different?

41

SS-Sonderlager Hinzert, Germany

Jürgen Altmann was finding it difficult to understand the true nature of what he was being asked to do. But if SS Standartenführer Hermann Pister himself was requesting his undivided attention, then Jürgen Altmann would provide it without question. He would carry out his orders as if his own life depended on it. It was a pity, he thought, to be diverted from his current activities at Hinzert, as he rather enjoyed his exalted role there. After all, how many of his SS colleagues had the privilege of being the arbiter of who would be deemed fit to be put to work for the Nazis and who could be discarded? Who else had the power to welcome the innumerable hordes from the railway carriages and herd them into disparate groups to decide who would live and who would die? For him, as absolute power went, it did not get much better than that.

He would miss the look of fear in the eyes of his captives, and the satisfaction he drew from knowing their fate. He would miss the delight on the faces of the medical staff when he brought them another set of identical twins on whom to experiment. He would miss being a supernumerary witness to the results of those fascinating clinical interventions, especially where slow extermination was involved. But most of all, he would miss the extraordinary pleasure he derived from sexual gratification. After all, he was able to select women without restraint or censorship.

No matter, he thought. War was a great provider in that respect. There would surely be other occasions where he could have his pick of women ripe for exploitation. Of that he was certain.

His orders were to go and meet with a Dr Schmidt in Berlin to glean more about a new substance the doctor was working on. He did not understand much more than it was highly secret, and was frustrated by the scant briefing he had been given. *But look on the bright side.* For all he knew, he might get the opportunity to really make his mark. He might even get the chance to impress the Führer.

42

Radcliffe Infirmary, 27 January 1941

Will hated to admit defeat, but he had to accept there was nothing he could do for his patient, other than to make her comfortable. She was going to die of an inoperable cancer and had no more than a couple of months to live. He knew his colleague Dr Charles Fletcher was looking for a suitable candidate to act as a guinea pig to try out a new chemotherapeutic agent, and the fifty-year-old Mrs Akers had struck him as a possibility. He had established a good rapport with her, and she had taken the news of her approaching mortality with resigned acceptance and composure.

'Good morning, Mrs Akers.' As was their custom, Will grabbed her hand and took a seat on the side of her bed. 'And how are you today?'

'All the better for seeing you, Doctor!'

'Oh, you charmer, you! I'll bet you say that to all the doctors!'

She winked. 'Only the good-looking ones. And please, call me Elva. You've already made me feel part of the family here.'

Will patted the back of her hand. 'I wonder if I might ask a favour of you, Elva?'

'Of course, but I have no idea how I can possibly repay you for everything you have done for me.'

If she agreed to Will's request, Mrs Akers would be the first ever patient in Britain to be given a dose of the new compound, which had not yet been tested on anything other than small animals. If it proved toxic, it could kill her almost instantly. In her already weakened state, it was a distinct possibility. Furthermore, the drug would offer her no relief in terms of her own condition, because she was not suffering from any infection. Logically, he should have been asking a patient who was struggling to overcome a disease caused by germs, but if that patient died, the researchers would be none the wiser. They would not know which had killed her, the drug or the original infection. Effectively, this was a toxicity test on a patient who was dying anyway, from a non-infective cause. If it proved safe in this case, the medical team could then go on to use it on a patient with a severe infection.

Will explained the implications of the favour he was asking, including everything they might learn, and any possible side effects. 'Dr Burnett,' she said confidently, 'if it helps somebody else, then I'm happy to do it. I might as well make myself useful in these last few weeks of my life.'

'It's a lot to ask, I know.'

'No, I really don't think so. I've enjoyed a good life. A happy life. More than most, I imagine. But my days are numbered, and you have a ward full of patients. There is also a war on, which I know from my own experience during the last one, will make the need for newer and better treatments all the more pressing.'

Will was moved by her altruism.

'If I can make even the tiniest contribution, Doctor,' she continued, 'I'm more than happy to do it. In fact, I insist.'

'There is nothing tiny about it,' said Will. 'For us, it would be a truly significant step, and we are very grateful. *I* am very, very grateful.'

'Go on, then. Go and get your instruments of torture. And if you bring me a cup of sweetened tea and a biscuit, you can do with me what you will.'

'Thank you,' he said, shaking her hand before heading down the corridor to break the good news to Dr Fletcher.

*

Later that morning, with Will standing beside him, Dr Charles Fletcher administered 100mg of penicillin intravenously to Mrs Akers, the plunger forcing the cloudy liquid out of the glass syringe into her vein at the elbow. Initially, there was no reaction. Two hours later, though, the patient began to feel feverish; she was shivering and suffered a rigor. Will was dismayed. Was the experiment already doomed to failure?

The boffins from the Dunn Institute were already on hand. Grace stood behind them with Charles Fletcher. 'So it seems our new wonder drug is toxic to humans after all,' said Fletcher, rather regretting that he was the person who had administered it.

'Not necessarily,' said Florey. 'I'm not a clinical physician, but I've certainly seen reactions like this to incompatible blood transfusions, or to bacterial breakdown components in contaminated medicines or saline diluents.'

'You think this could be an inadvertent pyrogen?' asked Chain, referring to a fever-inducing substance. It would be awful if the drug turned out to be a cause of sickness, rather than a treatment.

'It could. Can you help us here, Grace?'

'I can run the next proposed dose through a more stringent course of chromatography,' came the reply. 'That should remove any remaining impurities.'

The six scientists gathered around Mrs Akers' bed. Will was the first to speak up.

'It's entirely up to you,' he said softly to his patient.

'There's only one way to find out,' she said rather weakly. 'So take out the tonic from your cocktail, and just give me the gin.'

43

Radcliffe Infirmary, February 1941

After the impurities in Mrs Akers' first injection had been identified and removed, the second injection produced no side effects whatsoever. The purer formulation proved non-toxic. This was a triumph in itself. Now that it seemed clear that penicillin was harmless to humans, the next step was to test it in an infection scenario. Florey issued an edict to all practising clinicians at the Radcliffe: 'Please find any suitable patients with a severe and widespread infection that has proved resistant to all other treatments.' He knew the wards were full of such patients. In fact, one currently on the septic ward had been admitted to the Radcliffe quite a while ago, and was not doing very well at all.

Albert Alexander was a forty-three-year-old police constable in Oxford, whose face had been accidentally scratched by a rose thorn whilst he was tending his garden. The wound had become infected with streptococci and staphylococci bacteria, which had spread to his eyes and scalp. Sulfa drugs had been administered initially, but these had had no effect other than to bring the poor man out in an itchy red rash. Will had performed a number of expert surgical procedures to drain numerous abscesses, but he'd had no other option than to remove the patient's left eye. A week later, the infection had spread to Albert's shoulder and lungs; he was coughing up copious amounts of phlegm and every incision was weeping. He was terribly ill and in great pain.

Will looked at the semi-conscious man from the end of his bed. He was reluctant to subject him to any further surgery. It would almost certainly prove futile, and the patient was in no fit state to endure it. As things stood, Albert Alexander was a dying man but an ideal candidate on whom to try out penicillin. He had nothing to lose. With the agreement of his despairing wife, he consented to the new treatment trial.

He was given 200mg of penicillin, followed by three further doses of 100mg every three hours. Will found himself hanging about the ward over the next twenty-four hours, using any excuse not to leave. In between ward rounds, he took care to check his patient's progress and vital signs, but despite himself, he eventually fell asleep. When he woke two hours later, Albert Alexander was dramatically better. When the news rippled through the staff, the research team increased the dose.

Eight injections later, Will examined the patient again and noted that the scalp wound had stopped producing pus. The discharge from the shoulder and the one remaining eye had abated, too. The patient's fever had disappeared, and he was enjoying breakfast for the first time in weeks. His urine had been put aside to allow Dr Fletcher to cycle it over in a container to the Dunn Institute so that the penicillin in it could be extracted and reused. Every tiny milligram of the substance was precious.

Will continued to monitor his patient's progress over the next week, and was delighted by the ongoing recovery. The pathologists at the Dunn Institute could hardly contain their excitement. Grace described for Will how Chain had leapt about with happiness at the prospect of such a revolutionary breakthrough. Even Florey, always more reserved and thoughtful than everybody else, had also shown an uncharacteristic ebullience and elation.

'I've never seen him so animated!' Grace told Will.

Will and Grace's excitement was equally palpable and they decided to celebrate by splashing out on some very expensive tickets for a performance of *Swan Lake* several miles away in Stratford-upon-Avon. They drove there in Will's beloved old Riley, chatting excitedly all the way about the results. The implications for every patient in the hospital, in fact for the entire human race, were staggering.

For the duration of the performance at least, their minds were temporarily diverted. But the story of Odette, the princess turned into a swan by an evil sorcerer's curse, seemed a terrible premonition of what was happening in Oxford.

Just as their patient seemed on the verge of recovery, the supply of penicillin was exhausted. The small amount they had painstakingly managed to produce had all been used up, and another metamorphosis was taking place.

Grace had started the next day by giving Will a friendly pinch-and-punch for the first of the month. It was a fine, sunny day and she had skipped off happily to the hospital. What she found on her second ward round changed her mood completely. Albert Alexander had remained well for a full ten days since receiving his last dose, but this morning he looked totally washed out. He was sallow in colour and had a fever. She saw no outward sign of his skin lesions flaring up again, so she placed a stethoscope on his chest and listened. Air entry was poor, especially on the right side, and there were tell-tale signs of fluid in the lungs. *Pneumonia.* Grace cursed. His treatment had been such a triumph, the euphoria at the initial results still resonating throughout the laboratories and corridors of the institute. Now she would have to report that their efforts had been in vain. It would be a blow for the research, and more so for Albert Alexander. Unless more penicillin could be procured immediately, the poor man was doomed.

*

Albert Alexander died on 15 March. His widow was distraught, having seen her husband plucked from the jaws of death and restored to good health by an apparent miracle, only to lose him again a fortnight later. The nursing and medical staff, despite their training, could not help being moved by the demise of the stoical patient. The pathologists were devastated, too. Their hopes had been dashed. Florey conducted an inquest with his inner circle. The mood was sombre, but much to everybody's surprise, he soon adopted a somewhat upbeat tone.

'It's a setback, of course. But what have we learned? Firstly, we have confirmed that there is no significant toxic effect of penicillin, even when used for more than five days. We also now know that it is excreted rapidly and needs to be given intravenously, topped up with however much can be recovered from the urine and reused. But the most important lesson is that we've confirmed we need more of the stuff. The dose is either too small, or the course of treatment too short. We must find a way to produce greater quantities of it.'

'But how can we, Professor?' asked Chain. 'Heatley has done everything he can. He has grown his mould juice in everything from bedpans, kidney bowls, baking trays and children's potties. His reverse extraction process has been refined and improved countless times. Yet still we are producing minimal amounts.'

'It's true,' added Heatley. 'It's like trying to fill a sieve with water.'

'I understand the problem. Although I rarely say it, I really do appreciate the work you are all putting into this. We have six girls pulling out all the stops under difficult conditions to farm the penicillin. Some of the chemicals make them ill. Until we can secure help from the pharmaceutical giants we'll just have to do more with less.'

'How do we do that?' asked Chain.

Florey paused before providing the answer. He knew it would raise some ethical questions.

'We will do the next trials on children. Children are smaller. They only need a fraction of an adult dose.'

Will had had his doubts at first. Involving children in clinical trials of new medicines was most unusual. Their smaller bodies and immunity were less developed, less able to withstand external and unknown challenges. They also needed parental consent. Any setbacks or negative side effects on a child would almost certainly be widely reported and quite possibly kill off the research project for good. It had been a gamble, but one which Grace had persuaded Will to take.

Arthur Jones, a fifteen-year-old boy under Will's care, had badly fractured his hip and needed it orthopaedically pinned via open surgery. Will had duly performed the procedure under the most stringent sterile conditions, but even so, as so often happened, streptococcal infection ensued. Despite his operative record being exemplary compared to many other surgeons, and with the understanding and support of the boy's parents, both he and Grace were devastated, and knew the lad could die. Initially starting him on sulphonamides, no dramatic improvement had been forthcoming. But now, the result was an unequivocal triumph. Arthur Jones's fever abated, his wound healed, and the infection never returned. The teenager, who had never really understood what all the fuss was about, continued to make a full recovery and was delighted to be discharged from the children's ward two weeks later.

44

Canada House, Trafalgar Square, London

Canada House had served as the offices of the High Commission of Canada in London since 1925. The tall, recessed windows directly overlooked the Dartmoor granite of Nelson's column with the four bronze lions at its base. Kitty had visited the building since returning from Spain more times than she could remember, and each time had been disappointed. Today was no exception.

'No, miss. I'm sorry,' said the clerk in the Ontario room. 'As I've told you before, we have no one by the name of Ned Harding registered with us as living or working in London.'

In her heart, Kitty knew Ned must have died in Spain. Still, she found herself searching, always hoping, constantly dreaming that by some miracle, the love of her life would appear before her like a phoenix rising from the ashes.

Daniel had invited her to join him at the Maudsley to see her father Robbie, and she had been impressed by the way her nephew seemed to be able to coax interest and conversation out of her mentally stricken parent. It was only afterwards that the real reason he had invited her became clear.

He was concerned about her enduring grief, the lack of closure about Ned's fate and her apparent inability to move on. By all accounts, she functioned well and was doing sterling work with the Ministry of Information. She was still nursing, and he felt she was a vibrant, attractive young woman who should have been enjoying herself. He knew it might seem odd that he was psychoanalysing his own aunt, but helping people to overcome their conflicts and traumas was what he did. She was only nine years older than him anyway, so she was more like a sister to him.

'You're very sweet to worry about me, Dan, really you are. I've come to terms with it as far as I can. It's difficult to completely forget, you know – we went through so much together.'

'I don't think you need to completely forget. Even if you could, it's more a matter of just closing the lid on that emotional box and only opening it up to take a peek inside when you don't feel so vulnerable. Love can endure beyond life itself, Kitty.'

She had thought about his words, and she had tried to compartmentalise her memories of Ned. What had he told her about the stages of grief? First disbelief, then anger, then searching, and finally acceptance?

'Thank you, Dan, for being you. You're my favourite nephew, you know.'

He laughed. 'And you, Kitty, are my favourite aunt.'

She had given him a hug and hurried away.

For a while, Daniel's advice had called a halt to her searching and her visits to Canada House, but only temporarily. Then her brother Jack had casually told the family about a heroic soldier he had brought back from Dunkirk on his mate's sailing barge. He was only talking idly about the whole evacuation venture, but it was something he had said about 'a bloke as strong as Hercules' who had pulled several drowning men out of the sea single-handedly. Kitty's ears had pricked up at this and she'd pressed Jack to tell her more.

'His name was Sam Grefria, or something like that. Maybe Griffier? His unit was mostly French Canadian – Native Americans, I suppose. From Québec.'

'What was it about this one particular man, then, Jack, that caught your interest? What was so special about him?'

'Like I say, he was just a whirlwind, I guess. A modern-day Geronimo. Never seen anything like it. Anyway, we got everyone back to Blighty all right, and that was the last we saw of them all.'

Sam Grefria. Sam Griffier, repeated Kitty in her head, thinking that was more likely for a French Canadian. *Sam Griffier.* Not Ned Harding, then. She had felt foolish letting her fantasies get the better of her again, but today, unable to resist her impulses, she had returned to Canada House. As she exited the building, she skirted the large bomb crater just outside the front entrance and set off for the other side of the square to catch the omnibus that would take her to the Canadian Army HQ. As she boarded the number 14 in the Strand, she looked across at the entrance of Canada House and saw a man climbing the eight steps between the two stone pillars. From the back it could easily have been Ned. The figure was tall, with long dark hair and an athletic gait that seemed to help him glide up the stairs effortlessly. Maybe it was him? Maybe she had just missed him? As the bus pulled away, she thought once more about the hallucinations a grieving person could experience, which Daniel had told her about. The hoping against hope. The laying out of a table for two when only one person was present. Sleeping on one side of the bed to make room for the non-existent person on the other side. Ridiculous, she thought. Her mind was playing tricks on her again. Despite that, she looked back. By God, it looked like Ned. The distinctive way he walked. His posture. She could not help herself. What if this time it really was Ned?

She rushed to the front of the bus and faced the driver. 'Stop! Stop the bus! I have to get off!'

'I can't stop here, miss, it isn't an official bus stop. Besides, you've only just got on.'

'Stop the bus, please!' Kitty insisted, thinking furiously. 'I think I'm going to be sick.'

The driver pulled the vehicle to the side of the road. She pushed past the other passengers and jumped off. She took off her shoes and sprinted back across the square and up the steps.

'That man,' she said breathlessly to the doorman at the top, 'who just came in. I need to see him. The tall man with the long black hair.'

The doorman thought for a moment. 'The only person matching that description would be Mr Sam Grefria. He picked up a letter from the front desk and has just left.'

'He left? Where did he go?'

'Your guess is as good as mine, miss. He went that way towards Pall Mall and Lower Regent Street.'

'Thank you,' Kitty said, and hurried away. She ran up the west side of Trafalgar Square, past the four massive pillars on Canada House's front facade, and turned left on to Pall Mall East. There was no sign of him. She was aware of people staring at her, without shoes on her feet. Feeling defeated, she sat on a bench and chastised herself for her own stupidity.

She closed her eyes and took a deep breath. She needed to do what Daniel had told her to do. To put these foolish thoughts into a mental box, close the lid, and return to it at another time.

'Kitty?' came a familiar voice. 'Is that really you?'

45

Radcliffe Infirmary

Will and Grace had come across some unusual medical cases in their time. None so much as the life-threatening cavernous sinus thrombosis, often present following a severe facial or head wound. Since many of their patients these days were soldiers, they were now more than familiar with it. The impact of bullets, blasts and shrapnel could cause blood clots that would play havoc with a patient's circulation.

Little John Cox was only four and a half years old, and had come down with measles five weeks previously. The fever and hacking cough had left, but some of the small red blisters on his eyelids had popped and turned septic, with a secondary bacterial infection. He complained of a severe headache, and kept rubbing his eyes. The eyelids and tissue around both orbits were swollen and bulging. He could see two of everything and spent most of the day asleep. A common antiseptic had not helped, and his prospects looked bleak. His parents had agreed to try penicillin as a last resort.

Within three days the little boy had turned a corner. Within a fortnight, he was chatting away happily with his parents and playing with his favourite toys, including a small model Spitfire, which he flew about with outstretched arms, making whooshing sounds and *gdug-g-dug-g-dug* noises to mimic the sound of firing cannon. He was eating anything and everything, his vital signs were completely normal, his parents were ecstatic, and the patient himself was keen to go home. It was a little too early yet, but the signs were very good.

46

Haymarket Hotel, Lower Regent Street, London

They sat in a quiet corner of the Haymarket Hotel. Kitty and Ned could not take their eyes off each other. Every day for the last two years, she had wondered about Ned.

'I took two bullets in the back, which I later discovered had shattered my left shoulder blade,' Ned told her. 'They must've lodged there in the bone – luckily, they missed my heart. I was pumped with adrenaline and it was so icy cold I hardly felt a thing. I could still use my right arm, and I just kind of pushed myself away until I hit the rapids and kept myself afloat as long as I could. I don't know how long I was in the water or what happened later. I passed out and woke up three days after they found me.'

Kitty put her hand against his cheek. 'It's incredible you survived at all. I was told nobody could survive in that river for long. They told me they regularly dragged bodies out of it downstream.'

'What about you, Kitty? I've lived with the guilt of leaving you all this time.'

'There's nothing to feel guilty about! If I'd gone in the water, I would never have survived, and if you hadn't thrown those guys off the scent, I wouldn't be here now.'

She told him of her escape over the rope bridge and her

chance meeting with the rest of their Republican comrades. 'You said you were unconscious for three days?' she queried, her nursing instincts getting the better of her curiosity.

'When the medic pulled me from the water, they thought I was dead. Apparently I was floating face-up, blue, stone-cold, and not breathing. But when he turned me over he noticed a trickle of blood oozing from my back. It made him question whether my heart was still pumping. He found a faint, irregular pulse, so quickly got me out of there. Later, he told me my core temperature had been very low, at a level from which he'd never seen anyone recover. He had me warmed up very gradually, gave me some intravenous fluids and medicines, and three days later I woke up. Without any doubt, that doctor saved my life. I got to know him very well over the next three months as my shoulder blade healed; the repair and rehabilitation took a long time. I might've lost a few brain cells, the doctor said, but then I didn't have that many to lose in the first place!'

Kitty smiled. 'It must have been painful.'

'Worst pain I've ever known. But those nurses are wonderful. You know that. They said the pain was something I should embrace. They said it was proof I was still alive.'

'That's one way of looking at it.'

Ned nodded. 'Yeah. They couldn't believe I had actually survived. I was a bit of a talking point. The medics and nurses would all come in and tease me about my miraculous escape from my watery grave. A man risen from the dead like some kind of holy saint. That's how they came up with my Spanish nickname.'

'What nickname?'

'San Grefria.'

Kitty looked puzzled. 'What does that mean?'

'And here was I, thinking you were an expert in languages, Kitty!' Ned was smiling. 'Because I survived against all the odds, they joked that I wasn't human. That I must be cold-blooded like a freshwater fish.'

'So? Is San Grefria the patron saint of freshwater fish or something?'

'*Sangre fria*, Kitty. *Sangre fria*.'

Realisation struck and she laughed out loud.

'Cold-blooded. Now I get it. Very good!'

'It was the doctor who saved me who coined it. Then all his staff adopted it, too. I've kept it. That doctor was killed shortly afterwards by an enemy sniper, and I've held on to the name in his memory. It's also an affirmation of my Navajo roots and the tradition of naming people after some kind of significant event or rite of passage in their life. So I am San Grefria. The cold-blooded one.'

'I looked for you everywhere, Ned. I never lost hope. First in Spain, then here. I often went to the headquarters of the Canadian forces, the Canadian High Commission, too. They told me no Ned Harding had joined up since Canada had come into the war.'

'They were right! I'm officially Ned San Grefria. When I returned from Spain, I had no identification. I didn't know how the authorities would react to my having fought on the losing side in Spain, and I was unable to find out anything about my parents back home. So I applied for a Canadian passport in my new name, and got an ID card here. They needed every man they could get, I suppose. So this is me. Lieutenant Ned San Grefria of the Canadian 4th Battalion Corps.'

'So that's why I couldn't find you.' She pushed him playfully on the arm. 'Did you never think that doing what you did would make it impossible for me to track you down?'

'It never occurred to me that you might try. I thought you'd have given me up for dead long ago. I didn't know if you had survived, either. But it wasn't for lack of trying.'

'You tried to find me?'

'Of course I did. But you hardly made it easy. I only ever knew you as Kitty. You never told me where you were born, and what with the war on no registrar of births and deaths was remotely interested in searching the national archives for a Kitty with no last name. You'd left the Red Cross, so they couldn't help. You never officially served in the International Brigades, so neither could they. Why do you think I came to England rather than heading back to Canada?'

'You came to find me?'

'Yes. My parents always told me to follow my heart. That's why I went to Spain to fight. That's why I came here to find you.'

'And you did.'

Kitty took him in her arms and kissed him on the lips. Something was stirring in her head. A thought had been nagging at her. 'Ned,' she said thoughtfully, 'when did you join up?'

'As soon as Canada declared war. September last year.'

'Were you at Dunkirk?'

'Unfortunately. With thousands of others.'

'Did you get away in a Thames sailing barge, by any chance?'

Momentarily, Ned looked stunned. 'How the hell did you know that?'

'I think you may have met my brother.'

47

Radcliffe Infirmary, 3 June 1941

Will and Grace were able to distance themselves from their medical work when they chose to. After all, they had a large family and several different interests outside medicine. Devoted to their vocation as they were, and conscious of the injustice and unfairness of the inequality of access to healthcare, they could still switch off when it was needed. Usually, anyway.

But on 27 May, young John Cox's recovery took a downward turn. The boy suffered an unexpected but serious and prolonged convulsion. Thorough physical examination certainly pointed to something neurological, but it did not appear to be a recurrence of the initial condition. Despite the team's best efforts, further seizures occurred and he lapsed into a coma. He died four days later. Once again, the research team was confounded. What on earth had happened? Did penicillin have a delayed toxic effect after all? Florey had to find out, if his trial work was to continue.

Simultaneously, Percy Hawkins, a forty-two-year-old labourer, had survived after being given penicillin a few days earlier. Admitted with a four-inch carbuncle on his back, in which dirt and cement dust had mingled with bacteria, Will had lanced and drained the abscess, but the swollen glands and high fever had not responded to treatment until Percy had been given penicillin. His condition had improved immensely, and after halving the dose, he was considered completely cured three days later. He had shaken Will's hand vigorously, thanked Grace and the medical crowd who had come to see him off, and left to get on with his life.

So why had little John Cox not been saved? Florey was a pathologist. His entire ethos was to discover the nature of disease processes, their causes, their effects on the body, and their treatment. He had never performed a post-mortem himself, but if he was going to find out the answer to the riddle of John Cox's demise, he realised one was needed. He approached the bereft parents with the request but they were reluctant to give their consent. Tactfully, Florey suggested Grace have a word with them, and after an hour's patient explanation and encouragement, they agreed.

Down in the mortuary, the cause of death soon became apparent. Examination of the brain clearly demonstrated a ruptured major artery, which had been weakened by the infection. It was not the cavernous sinus thrombosis they had feared. It was not the penicillin, or any side effects resulting from its use. It was an awful tragedy, of course. But Florey and his team felt relieved. Their research could continue.

Florey sat down alone in his office and looked vacantly into space. This had been but a very small trial; just six patients, two of whom had died, albeit for reasons unrelated to penicillin itself. He knew that a 33 per cent mortality rate would not look good in published research and would need to be explained. Nobody would be remotely interested in a drug that apparently killed one third of patients taking it. His next medical paper would have to be convincing. And if a more significant, full-scale research trial was going to take place – and that was now a necessity – they would need to quickly produce the greater amounts of penicillin required to make it happen. They would need commerce and industry to achieve it.

48

St David's Church, Fulham

After three nights, Kitty and Ned were completely loved up. They had tried their best to make up for the last two years spent apart. Their bodies ached, and as they lay in Kitty's bed, they finally began to address the reality of their future. Ned would have to rejoin his unit for further training, but had no idea where that would be. Kitty confided that she would soon be flown into occupied France to make use of her linguistic talents for intelligence purposes. She revealed no more than that, knowing she had already broken protocol, but she trusted Ned completely and there was no other way to explain why she would not be able to stay in touch with any degree of certainty. They had been separated for so long and forced to live with the unknown, she felt she owed him this, at least. Ned searched her face and gave her a squeeze. He did not probe further. He understood.

'Promise me you will look after yourself. It will be risky.'

'I know. But they've trained me well.'

He knew it was futile to argue with her. He took a deep breath. 'What time do you have to be at work today?'

'Not until this afternoon. I'm on the late shift. Why do you ask?'

'I've a crazy idea.'

'Which is?'

'Let's get married.'

Kitty smiled at him and sat up. 'You're serious, aren't you?'

'Deadly.'

Half an hour later, they left the little flat. After three attempts, they found a sympathetic vicar who agreed to act as an official witness. At three o'clock that afternoon, they married at St David's Church in Fulham. They had never felt happier. They gave each other a final, lingering kiss and made their promises for their future. By five o'clock, they were more than forty miles apart, back on duty in their respective professional roles.

49

Arisaig, Inverness-Shire

Liese could just make out the rough silhouette of the shooting lodge in the distance. She was cold, wet through from the horizontal rain, covered in cuts and bruises, and utterly exhausted. The ten-mile trek up and down the Arisaig mountains had been unpleasant enough to begin with. Her fully laden rucksack soon became sodden, and her oversized army-issue boots had slipped in the mud and clung to the peat like glue. Then, when the others in the group had pressed on ahead, she had become disoriented and lost. Her drenched map had shredded like blotting paper, and her compass had directed her to the bottom of a vertical cliff. Anger and frustration had got her to where she was now. Why on earth were they putting her through these ridiculous drills? She lacked confidence, but she wanted to learn. Nothing had prepared her for this. She was a doctor! It was not as if she was training to become a member of the infantry or paramilitary, was it? She was not being groomed as an agent in the field, running about the countryside setting up covert sabotage with the resistance. Or perhaps she was. She was beginning to wonder. Near to despair, her spirits had lifted when she'd sighted the croft, slithered down the last of the heather-clad hill and dragged herself through the door.

There, slumped in a comfortable armchair, sat William Fairburn, checking the time on his watch. Eric Anthony Sykes was standing behind him, looking disappointed and impatient. In silence, Liese eased the soaking rucksack off her back and wrung rainwater from the hair clinging to her face.

'That was pathetic,' said Fairburn. 'That trek should have been completed in three and a half hours. It took you six. You had a map and a compass and you still got lost.'

Liese was struggling to peel off her coat, heavy with the rain, and remove her mud-clogged boots. 'I don't care,' she said in frustration. 'I don't know if you derive some sort of sadistic satisfaction from setting out such tasks, gentlemen, but I fail to see the purpose of them. Do you actually have any idea of what I have been asked to take on? I'm sure that if you did, you would realise this is all a complete waste of time. Yours and mine.'

'I don't give a damn about who you are, what you do, or where you're from,' said Fairburn. 'And it's important that I never find out. But believe me, lady, what you are learning here could one day get you out of a tight spot.'

'It could even save your life,' added Sykes.

Liese had been told to keep her proposed mission entirely to herself, but she was still fuming about the macho attitude of this pair. She could at least give them a piece of her mind.

'I don't know what is so special about you two clowns that gives you the right to be quite so beastly. I can understand the need to be fit and healthy. I can see the significance of mastering signalling and radio communications along with some elementary Morse code. But the use of weapons? Demolition techniques? Maps and compasses? Burglary and lock-picking? Unarmed combat? Can you really see little old me getting the better of a gang of Nazi thugs?'

She paused, then continued, 'I'm beginning to think I'm not cut out for this kind of thing. You've got your job to do, I appreciate that, but I'm afraid I'm not very good at it. My heart really isn't in it.'

'We were coming to the same conclusion ourselves,' said Sykes. 'You're one of the worst candidates we've entertained here for some time.'

'Thanks very much. Some entertainment.'

'This is just a preliminary training school. It's a first stage for prospective agents, where we assess your fitness, aptitude and psychological profile. As you are beginning to discover, some people are simply not suited for the role. You might be more of a liability than an asset.'

Sykes picked up the conversation next. 'We know you don't like it, but that's why you've been given little information and why you've met no other candidates outside your group. You're at the stage where you can simply walk away, with nobody any the wiser. You can chuck it all in and go and resume your ordinary life on civvy street.'

To Liese, this sounded inviting.

'Your lack of enthusiasm in learning anything much here has been nothing short of remarkable, Miss Fischl,' said Fairburn. 'Although we both still believe you have potential.'

'And who are you to be the judge of that?'

'You ask who we are. We have, shall we say, special skills, which can save a life.'

'Or take someone else's,' added Sykes.

'I don't think I could ever do that,' Liese said. 'You've already told me how unsuitable I am. I agree. So why am I still here? What possible reason would any of us have for persevering?'

'All we know is that the assignment you have been given is

uniquely suited to you. It seems nobody else is in a position to fulfil it. Clearly, it's also seen as vital for the war effort.'

'Though you may also have a particular reason and incentive of your own.'

Liese looked at the two men, puzzled. She had been rather ambivalent about the ethics of the mission from the start. 'What do you mean?'

'We had notification from Sir Andrew Morrison this morning, while you were out on the mountain,' said Sykes.

'Notification of what? I don't underst—'

'Your father is Professor Rolf Fischl, we understand.'

'Yes. Why? Wait . . . no, don't tell me—' Liese faltered.

'I'm afraid so. I'm sorry,' said Fairburn. 'There's no easy way to say it.'

Liese took a moment to gather her thoughts. 'How?'

'He was apparently brought out of confinement and offered his freedom in return for scientific collaboration with the Nazis. He refused. As a result, he was executed last week in Berlin.'

Liese's knees gave way and her head swam. Fairburn caught her just before she hit the floor.

50

Dunn Institute

The relationship between Professor Florey and Dr Chain was becoming increasingly strained. Where Florey was reserved and unsentimental with a dry sense of humour, Chain was vociferous and dramatic, but sensitive. Perhaps it was to be expected that they would not always see eye to eye. Judging by the raised voices emanating from Florey's office as Grace approached the door, they were at complete loggerheads.

'Grace, thank God you're here,' said Florey, sounding both angry and relieved at the same time. 'You can mediate.'

'You need to tell the professor he is being foolish and naïve,' Chain said, equally impassioned.

Grace was used to acting as the go-between and peace-maker, as such disagreements were now commonplace. In the first two or three years, the two men had got on famously, their shared commitment obscuring any inherent differences in their personalities. But these days, they argued about almost everything.

'I've been urging the professor to patent penicillin immediately.' Chain's cheeks were flushed red. 'Now we know what the drug is capable of, now we know what a difference this could make to the world, we must capitalise on our wonderful endeavour.'

'And I'm trying to tell Dr Chain here that penicillin is not a commodity. It is not something we should be seen to be profiting from, when half the world is dying prematurely from infections it can effectively treat.'

'I don't mean we should be profiting from it personally. But the Dunn Institute certainly should. It is we who have invested our time and effort up until now. It is our brilliance, *your* brilliance, that has got us this far. If we patent penicillin, we can invest in further work on other antibiotics. We are struggling to find industrial partners who will help us produce the drug. You have been flirting with the Americans for some time. Now you are in bed with them, and promising them mould samples and sharing the precious knowledge we have collated over the last few years. We will inevitably lose that commercial edge if we delay.'

'We must rely on the help the US can give us. Without them, I doubt we can ever succeed. Not as quickly as we would wish to, anyway.'

Both men looked as if they were ready for a physical fight.

'Gentlemen! If I may!' Grace said diplomatically. 'I understand what both of you are saying. Both viewpoints have their merits. But calm down. We can't have you killing each other. Otherwise we will never have penicillin.'

The two men sat back down and eyed Grace resentfully, like a pair of scolded schoolboys.

'Professor, as you know, Dr Chain is the son of an industrial chemist. In his world, and in Germany in particular, it's normal to patent everything. Clearly, the revenue generated allows for further research and faster progress. But equally, Dr Chain, you must respect those who fervently believe that such discoveries should not be exploited for monetary gain.'

'That's shortsighted! You talk to me about ethics? You concern yourself with the morality of what is right and wrong? *Mein Gott*! What is right is to protect what we have achieved so far. For this institute and for this country. The country that I have adopted and that has adopted me. What is wrong is to give away everything we have strived for, and, for that matter, as this is a university establishment, what the British people themselves have funded.'

He stopped and looked down at the floor.

'I disagree,' said Florey. 'It is the people of this country and my own country, and other countries, too, that will be harmed if penicillin becomes the subject of patents. The rich would be able to afford it, while the poor as usual would go without.'

'Stuff and nonsense,' said Chain, throwing down the gauntlet once more. 'It is only through mass production that the drug will become affordable for all. If we don't patent penicillin, somebody else will. Either individuals, academies, or other countries. You mark my words. This is inevitable.'

'That's a very jaundiced look at the world, I must say. A cynical one, not shared by many of the colleagues with whom I have spoken.'

'Cynical? Maybe so. But realistic, certainly. You can bring Mrs Burnett in here to talk to me if you like. You can try out your considerable female charms on me, dear lady, but I won't change my mind. Not to patent penicillin is a crass error. If we don't act now, we will be paying for our own drug before you know it.'

'I'm not trying to change your mind, Dr Chain,' said

Grace, 'and it's clear any female charms I might have are wasted on both of you.' The two men looked away.

'May I make a suggestion of my own?'

'Please do,' said Florey with a sigh.

'Take the matter to Mellanby at the MRC, and Sir Henry Dale at the Royal Society. You'd need their approval anyway. Why not see what they have to say?'

'Yes,' said Chain. 'The final decision would not be solely ours anyway.'

'That's a sensible suggestion. I'll go and see them,' said Florey.

'Good,' concluded Grace. 'We can agree on that plan at least. Dr Chain, would you like to come and join me for a cup of tea?'

'Yes, of course,' he said. 'Tea. A nice cup of your best English afternoon tea. That will resolve all the ills of the world in an instant, I'm sure.'

51

Beaulieu, New Forest, Hampshire

Liese completed her third successful parachute jump at Ringway near Manchester and was taken to a 'finishing school' in Beaulieu in the New Forest. The news of her father's death had spurred her on, and now she could pick any lock, use a portable radio, hold her own in a fistfight, and silently kill a man with her Fairbairn Sykes commando knife. Her mission had become a personal one, and she had arrived at Beaulieu with glowing references. She had become adept at surveillance, could lose anybody tailing her, and could embellish any cover story convincingly, if detained by relevant authorities. She was proficient in disguise and knew what to do under duress or torture. Finally, Ernst van Maurik of the air liaison section, had visited her at her holding flat for a very last briefing, to show her the intended dropping point on a map and sort out any equipment she would need. He interrogated her about her new identity and her fictitious past. Then he handed her two sets of pills: Benzedrine to keep her awake, if that should be required, and the 'L' tablet with a little rubber cover. It was the suicide pill which, when bitten down on, would kill a human within fifteen seconds.

'Sleep well, Miss Fischl. Or Doctor Margherita Vogel, as you will be known until the end of the war. I shall be here at seven o'clock tomorrow night to accompany you to the airfield.'

*

The pilot of the Armstrong Whitworth A.W.38 Whitley had completed his task admirably, finding his target in Utrecht with precision and dropping Liese from the plane at exactly the right time on the darkest night of the month. She had parachuted down, buried her silk chute and 'striptease' overalls with the little shovel provided, and made her way undiscovered to the outskirts of town. The practice jumps she had made at Ringway and Manchester had paid off. Fairburn and Sykes would have been proud of her. All she had to do now was lie low until morning when the curfew was over, and blend in with the traffic on her way to her new accommodation. It sounded so easy in theory. Her Swiss identity papers were in her pocket, the portable radio transmitter tucked away discreetly in her case. Hopefully, the Dutch resistance had provided everything she would need at her new lodgings in Wittevrouwenstraat, a short walk from Dr Westerdijk's Centraalbureau voor Schimmelcultures. She was excited, but apprehensive at the same time. She was well aware of the risks, but even more aware of the score she had vowed to settle on account of what had become of her father at the hands of the Nazis.

52

Medical Research Council, London

'Sir Henry Dale and I are in complete agreement,' said Edward Mellanby, the President of the Medical Research Council. 'We find the whole idea of patenting penicillin abhorrent. It smacks of commercialism, which we feel the vast majority of the British scientific community would consider unethical. I've already had your Dr Chain demanding an audience with me about this, Professor Florey, but rest assured he'll not get any further with it.'

Florey at least now felt reassured that a visit from Chain would not come to anything. 'Thank you.'

'Not at all,' Mellanby added dismissively. 'I think the whole issue will soon blow over.' He cleared his throat. 'Two other issues, however, almost certainly won't.'

That grabbed Florey's attention. 'What are they?'

'Firstly, a matter of national security. We have spoken before about the potential for penicillin to offer our country and allies a military advantage. If we can return more wounded men to the front, then your drug provides us with a significant weapon, albeit of a medical bent.'

'I'm certain of it,' said Florey. 'And that is why I implore you to do anything in your power to accelerate and enhance our programme.'

'I'm due to speak with Parke-Davis and Wellcome & Co this very afternoon. If I can get them on board—'

'They're not interested,' Florey interrupted. 'I've asked every pharmaceutical company in the land until I was blue in the face.'

'Or possibly distracted by other pressing issues?'

'It boils down to the same thing. However, you can arrange for me to garner assistance from the Yanks.'

'But you've already been talking to them yourself. And if I may say so, in your *Lancet* publication, you appear to have given the Rockefeller Foundation far more appreciation for their funds than you did us, despite our being your major financial backer.'

Florey knew the latter point was not true, but he was certainly not going to reveal the exact amount of the Rockefeller endowments for fear of alienating Mellanby. 'Unintended, and I apologise. I need to visit them on their own turf. I'd particularly like to look at their fermentation processes. I want to see if I can get them to collaborate with us to secure a greater roll-out of penicillin.'

Mellanby looked at Florey steadily, considering the proposal.

'It's a big ask. With the U-boats sinking so many tons of merchant shipping, an Atlantic crossing in a convoy is highly risky. Tickets for a flight across the water are in huge demand, and besides, a visit would require visas and special permissions at the highest level.'

'Well, get them!' said Florey curtly. 'Without them, you'll never have your strategic military advantage.'

Mellanby agreed that Florey's trip to the US was now essential. Somewhat irritated by the professor's directness, he came to the second issue.

'On a separate matter, your most recent *Lancet* paper on penicillin seems to have piqued the interest of many more people than the first.'

'I hope so. The clinical results of the trials were spectacular, and we need all hands to the pump.'

'Quite so. But not German ones.' Mellanby paused, before continuing, 'It seems that despite the official suspension of scientific publications internationally, your article has been picked up by agencies in Switzerland, and forwarded to interested parties in Germany.'

Florey was momentarily flummoxed. If he did not publish his findings, the pharmaceutical industry would never become involved and the entire project would come to nothing. Surely Britain was already miles ahead of other countries in the game?

'Without the mould itself, they have no raw material with which to work.'

'But they do have the cultures, Professor. I'm sure you're aware that Fleming was sending samples of his mould to scientists all over the world. To the US, to Europe, to Australasia, you name it. Now I think he rather wishes he hadn't.'

'Then let's stop any more cultures being shipped from the central storage at the National Type Collection Laboratory.'

'That decree has already been issued, Professor, but I fear the horse has already bolted. And as I recently learned from a man who took me to one side at the RAC club, British agents will soon be in the field trying to track these bloody samples down.'

Florey could hardly believe it. Secret agents in occupied Europe searching for penicillin. It seemed incredible. One place they would not find it, however, was in the form of spores encrusted in the fabric of his coat.

53

New York to Connecticut, June 1941

The sound of the four Wright GR-2600 Twin Cyclone engines was surprisingly muted and Florey's current experience was proving a lot less turbulent than some of the recent academic meetings he had attended. He relaxed into a luxurious reclining armchair and looked around the compartment again, taking it all in. It seemed incredible that at last his demands had paid off. The Boeing 8-314 Dixie Clipper flying boat had taken off from its base on the Tagus River estuary near Lisbon, on its way to LaGuardia Field in New York City, and the opulence of the surroundings was stunning. At Oxford, Florey had become accustomed to rationed food, austere furnishings, and cold, cramped accommodation. Here in the flying boat, beautiful gold carpets covered the floors of each of the seven huge compartments, the last leading into the passenger lounge, which could be transformed into a plush dining room. Florey was enjoying the short flight to the Azores, where they would refuel. After that, he was planning to use the time on the longer leg towards Bermuda to prepare his pitch to the Rockefeller Foundation. Everything he and his team had worked for depended on the outcome of this mission.

Heatley was already asleep in the chair opposite, so Florey

closed his briefcase and gently set it down. He closed his eyes and reflected on the hectic last few days. The procurement of two tickets for the trip had been a triumph in itself. With national security tighter than a drum, officialdom severe and costs prohibitive, demand was enormous for this escape route to America. With the help of the Ministry of Defence, though, they had managed it. In great secrecy, they had driven to Bristol to catch a blacked-out Vickers Victoria transport plane, whilst carefully protecting the clinical trial results and the phials of freeze-dried mould cultures in the cotton-wool wrappings in Florey's briefcase. The only time it had been out of his sight was when it had been securely locked up in the Lisbon hotel safe.

Lisbon was a delight, a complete contrast to the bombed-out cities of war-torn Britain. The summer sunshine was glorious, the busy restaurants brightly lit, the food varied and plentiful, and the mood of the public cheerful and insouciant. Florey harboured one small regret. Ernst Chain had reacted furiously to their hasty departure, especially when he had discovered that the trip had been planned for some time. Although there were very good reasons for this, which Florey had explained to him, he could not be pacified. He had felt left out and sidelined, and bitterly resented being kept in the dark. In the end, both Florey and Heatley had been desperate to leave and let the rest of the department pick up the pieces. Dr Chain was a brilliant man, of course – indispensable, in fact – but Florey still found handling him a challenge.

As he settled back into his padded seat he finally drifted off into a fitful slumber. Had he known what his German counterpart in Berlin was doing at that very moment, he would not have been able to sleep at all.

*

In Germany's capital city, Dr Schmidt could hardly believe what he was reading. It was like the Allies telling the Third Reich in advance where an invasion might come from.

Florey's second *Lancet* paper confirmed that penicillin was an innovative and safe antibacterial treatment, purported to be more effective than any other. It even supported those claims with data pertaining to human trials and methods of production, although Florey still needed to convince the medical establishment – and the government – to back his research with funding.

Schmidt himself had no such difficulty. He grinned like an alley cat who had got the cream. 'Thank you, Florey,' he said to himself. 'You might as well be working for me.'

54

Royal College of Surgeons, London

Will was becoming as demoralised as everyone else. Usually a cheerful optimist, he was beginning to wonder if he really could make much of a difference. Grace had witnessed his low moods occasionally, and his even rarer outbursts of violent anger, but his persistent gloom was uncharacteristic and was starting to worry her. She was fully occupied with her own work at the Dunn Institute and Radcliffe Infirmary and not a day had passed when Will had not been operating in the surgical theatres or seeing his charity patients in the precious little time he had off. He had never had to deal with so many domestic and road traffic accidents as he had during the blackout: without streetlights and car headlamps, falls and collisions were inevitable. The East End of London had been as good as destroyed. On some days when Will had been called there, he had lost count of the fractured bones he had reset, the dislocations he had reduced, and the spines he had put into traction. And still, mortality from infections remained depressingly high. When the hell was Florey's work on the new antibiotic that Grace kept telling him about ever going to materialise? Progress seemed agonisingly slow and there was no real certainty that anything tangible would come of the research at all.

All around him were glum faces. Food was rationed, clothes in short supply. Fuel was scarce and an air of defeatism seemed to pervade every conversation. Had it not been for his brother-in-law Henry's allocation of petrol for the family farm at Bishop's Cleeve, and Will's special dispensation as a surgeon, he would have had to take his beloved Riley Nine off the road. Fortunately, Henry was able to supply him with just enough to enable him to drive to work and back.

As far as Will knew, Kitty was toiling endlessly as a nurse with the Red Cross in London, coping with the consequences of the air raids, and Jack was risking life and limb defusing unexploded bombs. Grace's brother, Rupert, was running the gauntlet of the U-boat wolfpack attacks in the Atlantic, and Will and Grace's daughter, Emily, was single-handedly flying powerful but untested military aircraft all over the country. Will felt he should have been doing more himself. It was during this time, while on a visit to London, that he was approached in the Royal College of Surgeons by a high-ranking naval officer. Apparently, there was a temporary role that required his technical expertise. Over a beer or two, the potential assignment was fully explained. It would not be easy, and it would be far from comfortable. In fact, it would be inherently dangerous. As another air raid siren sounded somewhere in the distance and they were asked to retire to the basement of the college, Will readily accepted the proposed task.

Later, he told Grace about his decision. 'The Arctic convoys are notoriously hazardous and the casualty rate horrendous,' she had protested. 'Not only are the weather and sea conditions dangerous, but the water and skies are heavily defended. We read about it all the time. Why, Will?'

She cried into his chest as he held her. 'Of all the things to volunteer for, this must be one of the worst. You're in the Army, not the Navy. We need you here. *I* need you here.'

55

New Haven, Connecticut, July 1941

Florey and Heatley's trip to America had been frantic so far. As soon as they had arrived in New York, they had met with the top brass at the Rockefeller Foundation, whose initial interest was to see whether their research funds had been responsibly spent. But after Florey's meticulous and detailed presentation of the facts and the clinical revelations about to be described in his forthcoming *Lancet* article, there were no longer any doubts.

Dr Alan Gregg, the Head of the Foundation's Medical Science Division, had been mesmerised by Florey's account and suggested one particular commercial partner that might be willing to proceed under the supervision of the US government. He knew George Merck, head of his own pharmaceutical company, to be a trustworthy and decent man, and suggested Florey seek him out.

'Just be aware you've got two main government factions in competition with each other. Dr Thomas Parran, the Surgeon General, will be interested in penicillin to improve medical and social services for the general public, whereas Dr Lewis Weed, who heads up the National Academy of Sciences, will want penicillin in the first instance for national defence. The country is increasingly twitchy about becoming embroiled in your war.'

'*Your* war' seems a strange take on the situation, thought Florey. But then the stance held by many of Gregg's compatriots remained strong.

Florey and Heatley had then gone to spend the Independence Day weekend with the professor's old friends, John and Lucia Fulton, in New Haven. The Fultons had welcomed Florey's children, Charles and Paquita, into their home after their evacuation by sea and had been devoted to their welfare as surrogate parents ever since. It was an emotional reunion and was all the more enhanced by the lavish cocktail party thrown by the couple on the fourth of July. Alcohol flowed from the several bars set up in the house and garden, and despite the volume of the music played out by the twenty-strong big band, it could not quite drown out the animated conversation of the dozen or so scientists. Much to the indifference of most of their partners and wives, penicillin was the only subject they could talk about.

'Florey, this is Donald Hendrick,' said John Fulton. 'He is a senator and a friend of mine, who has come all the way from Washington DC to hear more from you.'

Florey shook his hand.

'And this is his fiancée, Amy. I believe you know her sister, Grace?'

'Indeed, I do. A pleasure to meet you, Amy. I have the highest regard for Grace's work. She's an extraordinary woman. She's certainly not afraid to speak her mind.'

'That sounds just like her,' said Amy. 'She never leaves anyone in any doubt about how she feels.' She nudged her soon-to-be husband with her elbow and smiled. 'But she always means well.'

56

HMS *Impulsive*, Barents Sea, Arctic Circle, August 1941

Dr Will Burnett stood on the bow of the ship and sucked in the salty air of the Barents Sea, the vicious gale blowing into his face. As dawn broke, slate-grey clouds scudded by overhead, and leaden squalls of snow fell in thick vertical sheets. He braced himself against the rail as the vessel pitched and corkscrewed and the stiff north-easterly breeze sent columns of white horses crashing down the leeward side of the mountainous dark waves. Although the weather was against him, the surgeon grimly reminded himself of why he was there. He licked the briny spray from his crusted lips and pulled his scarf up to cover his freezing face.

HMS *Impulsive* had left Liverpool for Iceland in mid-August, and, having rounded the North Cape, was now 1,500 miles into its journey towards Archangel. It was a large convoy consisting of twenty-two merchant ships escorted by destroyers, anti-submarine trawlers and a light cruiser. It sailed in six columns abreast, surrounded by the zigzagging naval escorts. They had warned Will that the weather was notoriously bad and unpredictable within the Arctic Circle, but nothing had prepared him for this. The force-nine blizzard was blowing straight off the polar ice cap, and the temperature had fallen to –30 degrees. The sea spray whipping over the bow of the ship quickly turned to ice and in places had built up a coating several feet thick. This had already forced one ship to turn back; Will, with nothing else to do until reaching his destination, had volunteered to help chip away at it. Kitted out in a woolly hat, long johns, a heavy jersey, a sheepskin jerkin, a canvas duffel coat and gloves, he toiled away with a mattock. Despite his size and strength, he made little headway and still felt chilled to the marrow. He had already treated several men for frostbite. Looking at the dark, swirling seas and the network of silvery spindrift on top of the cresting waves, he knew no man would be able to survive in the water for more than two or three minutes.

The *Impulsive* shuddered as it crashed and dived into each oncoming wave, but Will was glad he was on this ship rather than any of the overladen rust-buckets making up the bulk of the slow-moving fleet. The convoy was bringing desperately needed supplies to their Russian allies holding out against the Nazi onslaught on the outskirts of Moscow.

As he hammered away at the sheet ice on deck, Will remained oblivious to the other dangers approaching, such as U-24, one of three German U-boats from the Ulan group based at Trondheim, which had slipped its moorings two days ago and was now at periscope depth half a mile off the starboard bow of its target. It had already sent five ships to the bottom of the sea and hundreds of men to a watery grave. The fog banks had reduced visibility to a few yards, making it impossible for the convoy to stay in formation, and the escorts had found it impossible to keep track of the position of every ship. So the convoy was already scattered when U-24 released its two deadly torpedoes. The wallowing old merchant ship they hit was lifted from the water in a huge explosion, engulfing the vessel and breaking it completely in two. Will immediately felt the *Impulsive* speed up to give chase to the submarine, but there was little hope for the survivors. Stopping to pick them up would only provide the U-boats with another target. As he looked on, one helpless mariner in the choppy, ice-cold water was holding up one arm and waving it in a final defiant expression of black humour. 'Taxi!' he was yelling. 'Taxi!'

Will could only look back at the disappearing figure, the morbid joke already imprinted indelibly on his mind. Ahead of them were another five hundred miles of storms, blizzards and heavy seas. On top of that were the reconnaissance aircraft of the Luftwaffe based at the North Cape, and the constant threat of the German battleship *Tirpitz* and the battlecruiser *Scharnhorst* appearing on the horizon at any time. The Royal Navy were fully aware that several hundred Luftwaffe torpedo and dive bombers had been tasked with sinking as many enemy ships as possible.

Will huddled down into his duffel coat. He picked up the mattock with his stiff, frozen hands, found the heavy hatch door just behind the bridge, and went back inside. Relieved to be out of the wind and in a slightly warmer environment, he descended the galley stairs and made his way to the hold.

57

Beltsville, Maryland

Charles Thom was an interesting man. One of the world's leading experts in moulds and fungi, he was best known for his work on the unique microbiology of dairy products and soil. After talking to countless different people, some from the government, many from industry, and others from the world of academia (most of whom were intellectually invested but devoid of cash), nothing much was happening, so Thom, at the Department of Agriculture's Bureau of Plant Industry, was Florey's next target.

'As our clinical findings so far suggest,' said Florey, 'we need two thousand litres of mould filtrate to treat just a single patient.'

'So a large-scale fermentation process will be the key,' said Thom thoughtfully. 'And there is nobody better placed than the Northern Regional Research Laboratory in Peoria, Illinois. I'll send them a telegram telling them you're on your way. If they can't do it, nobody can.'

*

The *Peoria Rocket* from Chicago was a speedy and comfortable train, and the team at the NRRL engaged immediately.

Florey's hopes were further raised by ethical agreements between them, which prevented any personal gain being derived from any anticipated discoveries, and with any patents accruing being assigned only to the Secretary of Agriculture. They also agreed that any medical publications resulting from such an undertaking would reward all personnel involved with equal credit.

At last, here was the level of cooperation and support Florey had longed for. For the first time, he dared to dream that his long-held ambition might actually materialise. Leaving Heatley in Peoria to work on higher yields together with Dr Andrew J. Moyer, whose wizardry with moulds was apparently on a par with squeezing blood from a stone, Florey left on another tour of high-profile drug companies. Frustratingly, none would commit. Why, they reasoned, would they spend inordinate sums of their own money when the possibility of cheaper synthetic production was just around the corner?

*

A few thousand miles away in Berlin, Dr Schmidt was thinking the very same thing. If the German pharmaceutical industry could only obtain sufficient samples of Fleming's original penicillium notatum strain, there was every chance they could identify the chemical structure of the active compound and synthesise it in bulk. To that end, Jürgen Altmann was already on the hunt, rooting around in research laboratories throughout northern Europe, like a ravenous Dobermann searching for a bone.

58

Archangel, Russia

HMS *Impulsive* finally pulled into port at Archangel on 31 August. It had been a miserable and harrowing voyage. Will realised that Grace had been right to protest; perhaps he should have listened. He tried to convince himself that the enemy would be more concerned about convoys bringing cargo into Russia than ones returning home with their holds empty. Either way, it was a trip to hell and back.

Impulsive had been slightly damaged by dive bombers, but a third of the convoy had been sunk. Will could only imagine the plight of the men who had had to abandon ship and were possibly still being thrown around in their lifeboats, their lives hanging in the balance.

When he came ashore and reached the hospital, he could hardly believe what he was seeing. He had been led to believe that the medical facilities there were rudimentary. As it turned out, that description proved to be too glowing. The conditions were appalling, not to mention unsafe. Peeling paint hung from the bare walls, and damp and mould coated the windowsills and ceilings. The floors were blood-stained and filthy, and a frosty draught blew along the corridors and through the rooms like a wind tunnel. Wounded men shivering in metal-framed beds were huddled under filthy sheets and blankets and the foul odour of gangrene pervaded the atmosphere. One man had suffered severe frostbite in both legs and had to have them amputated without anaesthetic. Unlike others, he at least had survived.

The medical supplies Will had carefully catalogued and organised included anaesthetic, but much more clinical paraphernalia was needed. No wonder the RAMC had been begging someone to make the trip to try to sort it all out.

As Will contemplated the job at hand, he was shaken from his thoughts by a terrible and familiar screeching sound above him. Within seconds, the Stuka dive bombers had dropped their payload on several of the ships still offloading their cargo in the harbour causing explosions, fires and heart-rending cries for help. Will could only look on helplessly and hope that the precious medical supplies had already been offloaded and stored somewhere safe.

*

Meanwhile, in Pennsylvania, Florey was frantically busy trying to attract interest from several major pharmaceutical players. Without the passion and determination of his old friend, Dr Alfred Newton Richards, however, he would be getting nowhere. Richards was chairman of the US Committee on Medical Research in the Office of Scientific Research and Development and carried an awful lot of clout. He regarded Florey very highly and was convinced his friend could bring his plan to fruition with the right kind of help. He had already persuaded four major pharmaceutical companies to show more than a passing interest.

Together, they hoped the financial and political backing of the government might prove too tantalising not to rise to the challenge.

59

Peoria, Illinois

Heatley enjoyed a political debate as much as the next man, but he was already beginning to find Andrew J. Moyers irritating. His home country was embroiled in a life or death struggle, and here was this man, vehemently against any kind of useful support from America.

'If you guys in Europe are so hellbent on war every few years, you should just be left to get on with it,' he said to Heatley in the crowded coffee lounge.

'It's not as if we have much choice.'

'But we do!' Moyer affirmed, rather too abruptly. 'Sending more of our boys across the Atlantic to die on foreign soil just so that Germany or France or Spain can dominate other nations is absurd. Any sensible American just wants to advance our own country, not be stymied by spats across the pond.'

The rest of the group could see Heatley was angered, but to his credit, he retained his composure. 'Spats?' was all he could say in reply.

'Look. We're working together to get your precious penicillin made. Let's not fall out over this. If we get it done, and we *will*, we'll have done our bit towards your war effort.'

It was true. Heatley had been struggling to coax the spores

he had brought with him to germinate, due to adverse climatic conditions in the American Midwest, but with the help of Moyer they had started to make significant progress.

Peoria was located deep in the heart of corn- and wheat-growing country. Corn steep liquor was the sticky gloop left behind after the removal of the kernels and the extraction of cornstarch by evaporation. It was dark brown and tasted of toffee, but because it was so rich in nitrogen, it was an excellent medium for growing mould cultures. More to the point, there was plenty of it. Things were beginning to look more promising, that was for sure. That was the vital thing. Heatley, always the tolerant diplomat, would simply have to try to ignore Moyer's antagonistic views and focus on the task at hand.

60

Pearl Harbor, Hawaii, 7 December 1941

At 7.48 a.m. Hawaiian time, 353 Japanese fighters, torpedo boats and dive-bombers attacked the United States naval base at Pearl Harbor in Honolulu in two devastating, lethal waves. Huge numbers of ships and aircraft were destroyed, thousands of men were killed, and hundreds more were wounded. It was an assault that took America completely by surprise and was described by Franklin D. Roosevelt as 'a date which will live in infamy'. Dr Newton Richards' attempts to bring together the biggest influencers from various US pharmaceutical companies in the noble cause of national defence were dramatically facilitated by these events.

A meeting held in Washington in October had resulted in an agreement to collaborate and expedite the production of penicillin, though little had happened since. The inertia was shattered at the next meeting, held ten days after the Japanese attack and nine days after the country declared war. Now, they all resolved to work independently but to share their findings. One significant person who did not approve of that commitment was Moyer.

Behind the scenes in Peoria, the yield of penicillin was already increasing significantly. Moyer was constantly tinkering with the fermentation process and was finally beginning to produce measurable amounts of sterile, stable penicillin. But the stark reality was that there was still barely enough anywhere in the country to treat a single patient.

*

Back in Oxford, Ernst Chain was feeling rather philosophical. 'Every cloud has a silver lining, Professor Florey,' he said. 'If the attack on Pearl Harbor has finally brought the US into the war and made penicillin production a matter of urgency, then so much the better.'

'It's just a pity it has taken such a terrible event for it to happen.'

It was true, Florey realised, that the attacks launched without warning or declaration of war by the Japanese had incensed the nation's idea of fairness and honour, and the huge loss of life had roused the sleeping giant. It was now the sworn duty of every American citizen to support the war effort and defeat Nazism and the Axis powers. The Allies would benefit enormously, just as they had towards the end of the First World War. There could also be unexpected benefits for another international group of people: the collegiate team currently working on penicillin.

Chain and Florey sat either side of the Marconi 911 Bakelite radio and listened to Churchill's address to Congress.

'Many disappointments and unpleasant surprises await us,' he was saying, describing the Axis powers as: 'Enormous; they are bitter, they are ruthless.'

Now he continued solemnly: 'We are the masters of our fate.' And, as if to capitalise on any remaining support for the isolationist movement, he commented on the American resolve to defeat the Axis powers. 'Here in Washington,' he said, 'I have found an Olympian fortitude . . . the proof of a sure, well-grounded confidence in the final outcome.'

As the Senate chamber erupted into applause, Florey switched off the radio.

'We are in the right hands, I believe,' said Chain. Florey nodded.

'And isn't it ironic? I spent months over there, cap in hand, trying to garner interest and investment in penicillin. Then at the drop of a hat – well, several tons of bombs and torpedoes, to be more accurate – a dozen chief executives from the biggest American pharmaceutical companies get together around the negotiating table and promise to do everything they can to produce it in bulk.'

'Well, it's now a matter of national priority, clearly. The government will be throwing money at them, with the most successful reaping the greatest rewards.'

'I guess I never had that bargaining power.'

'It's called incentivisation, my dear Professor. Personally, I see nothing wrong with it.'

'Well, if it achieves the right results, who are we to complain?'

'We shouldn't. Heatley, on the other hand, has every right to do so.'

'Heatley? Why?'

'Because despite the agreements about publications relating to penicillin having to cite every contributor fairly and equally, Moyer is leaving everybody out, including Heatley, and is publishing entirely under his own name. Heatley's letter is quite explicit.'

Florey paused, thinking. 'Maybe we should get Heatley back here, then. The yields are improving all the time and he's probably done all he can there. He and Moyer never got on particularly well. Let's cut our losses and redouble our efforts here.'

'Very well. And the matter of patents?'

Florey sighed. He had hoped his colleague had forgotten the subject of patents. Apparently not. 'They have given me undertakings. But I still can't envisage Britain ever having to pay the US for the penicillin that we let them have in the first place.'

Chain looked at Florey incredulously.

'We shall just have to wait and see, won't we? But don't say I didn't warn you.'

61

Houses of Parliament, January 1942

'The coalition party as it stands today is doomed,' asserted Marmaduke Trevelyan. 'And you, Fitzwilliam, will vote against it in this vote of no-confidence in the prime minister and his failing government.' The MP for Shropshire had barged into Fitz's office and was looming over his desk, barking orders. As chief whip, he enjoyed exerting his power over his frontbenchers.

Fitz remained where he sat and glared straight back at the bully whilst struggling to control the palpitations and ignore the fleeting stab of pain across the left side of his chest. 'I will not, sir.'

'You'll do as you're bloody well told. Churchill is out of his depth. He did far too little to resist the Japanese and we've already lost the *Prince of Wales* and *Repulse*, not to mention those sixty RAF aircraft right at the start. Malta is being pummelled, Rommel has got Auchinleck on the retreat in Libya, and if he conquers Egypt and the Suez Canal, God help us all. Wake up, Fitzwilliam. It's been a series of disasters and blunders for far too long. He has to go.'

'I disagree.' Fitz looked over at Stephen, who was pretending not to be listening. 'Let me remind you, Trevelyan,' Fitz said, 'Churchill was one of the few politicians who spoke about the alarming growth of the Nazi party and the threat it posed. Almost single-handedly, he warned of the foolhardiness of trying to appease a man like Hitler. All his forebodings have proved to be well founded. I'd say he saved us in the nick of time.'

'It hasn't done us much good in the long run, has it?'

'We need a figurehead, Trevelyan, and a man who can lead the people. Someone who can raise morale and provide hope, even in times of peril and strife. *Especially* then, in fact.'

'The man's a loose cannon. He is impulsive, irascible and arrogant. He's often the worse for wear with drink, and he won't even listen to his own chiefs of staff.'

'Come on, Trevelyan. You've never liked him. You saw him as a class traitor because he supported social reforms and the redistribution of wealth, and you hated him for it. He even had the humanity and the philanthropy to vote for unemployment benefits and old age pensions. I, for one, greatly admire him for it. We need consistency and strength right now. That's my position.'

Trevelyan was visibly losing patience as Fitz continued. 'Churchill and the coalition still offer the best option available. I will not put my marker on "for" in a vote of no-confidence.'

'I haven't come here to ask you, Fitz. I've come here to tell you.'

Fitz glared at his opponent, his heart lurching inside his chest with frequent ectopic beats.

'I'm sorry, Trevelyan, but I'm not prepared to compromise my principles.'

'How very noble of you.' Trevelyan leaned across the desk, resting his hands in the middle of it, and thrust his face in front of Fitz's. 'I don't suppose you're prepared to sacrifice your private proclivities, either.'

Fitz narrowed his eyes. 'What do you mean by that?'

Trevelyan straightened up and adjusted his tie theatrically. 'Look, this is a bit awkward, old boy, but a newspaper friend of mine is sniffing around with some sort of story about your rather . . . shall we say . . . *close* relationship with young Stephen over there.'

Stephen looked up sharply from his paperwork.

'What was the word he used? Not close . . . er . . . *intimate.* Yes, that was it. Your rather intimate relationship with your political assistant. Your dashing, young, *male* political assistant.' The chief whip grinned. He was rather pleased with himself. Both the insinuation and the threat were obvious and crude.

'Look,' he continued, 'sometimes in politics, your own personal views must be subjugated to the greater good. For the party. You'll come to learn this. You've come a long way in a short time in your political career, Fitzwilliam. It would be a shame to throw it all away as a result of some . . . salacious intrigue and scandal.'

Fitzwilliam was shaking his head.

'But luckily for you, I may be in a position to help. Let me put it this way,' Trevelyan continued. 'I think if I could count on your change of heart about this vote of no-confidence and the withdrawal of your support for the prime minister, I believe I could make the whole thing go away.'

Fitz was about to reply but Stephen beat him to it. 'A man with a reputation like yours, Trevelyan, should be careful about making idle threats.'

Trevelyan whirled around and stood up even straighter. 'Excuse me? Was I speaking to you? It's Robinson, isn't it? Stephen Robinson? I'll thank you to remember your place. This is a private matter between Fitzwilliam and me.'

'As my name was also mentioned in your veiled insinuation, it's a matter for me, too.'

'As a mere assistant, do you really think *your* reputation is something anyone would be remotely interested in reading about?'

'I'll tell you what I think, Trevelyan. I think people in glass houses should think twice before throwing stones.'

Trevelyan paused. 'Meaning?'

'Meaning that a married man of your standing, who publicly claims to champion family values, should probably not be regularly consorting with the wife of a decorated Army officer currently serving in Libya and fighting valiantly for his country.'

Trevelyan had turned pale. He was temporarily lost for words.

'I have no idea what—'

'I'm sure Mrs Marjorie Watson,' Stephen interrupted, 'would be horrified if her good name was besmirched alongside your own. I don't think the British public would think very much of such hypocritical and caddish behaviour in a senior politician, do you?'

'Nobody would believe—'

'My brother certainly believes it. He works on the news desk at the *News of the World*. He has, shall we say, all the evidence he needs, photographic and otherwise. Quite a scoop, I'd say. He may only be a mere "assistant" like me, but he happens to be the assistant of William Emsley Carr, the editor.'

Trevelyan had turned purple in the face at the thought that this impertinent upstart seemed to know about his affair. If the truth got out, he would be finished. The reason he had come to see Fitzwilliam paled into insignificance.

'You, sir, are just an impudent nobody.'

'Impudent, perhaps. But better to be impudent than imprudent, don't you think?'

'This is nothing but blackmail,' Trevelyan spluttered.

'Let's just call it insurance. You retract your threats and vile insinuations about Fitz, and I will ensure my brother keeps his story and photos locked away in his safe.'

Trevelyan was outmanoeuvred. 'For how long?'

'Indefinitely. You have my word.'

Trevelyan's face was the picture of hatred and fury. 'Vote how you damn well like, Tustin-Pennington,' he spat. 'If Churchill stays in power, we're all buggered one way or another.' He swivelled on his heel and left the room, slamming the door behind him.

'Charming man,' said Stephen, grinning.

'That was quite brilliant! How the hell did you know of his affair?'

'As I said: my brother. He's a taxi driver. Trevelyan has been foolish enough to regularly book him every Tuesday and Thursday evening to ferry him from his private club to her place, with no return booking. My brother recognised him, even though he tries to disguise himself with a hat, scarf and spectacles.'

'But I thought you said your brother worked at the *News of the World*.'

'I did. Total bluff, of course. The only evidence is hearsay, but it seemed to do the trick!'

'I believe it did.' Fitz came over to his assistant with a huge smile on his face and put a hand on each of Stephen's shoulders. His pulse rate was steady again. 'Thank you, Stephen. As a game of political chess, that was the fastest checkmate I've ever seen.'

'Fool's mate, I think they call it.'

'I just love . . . I love the way you handled that!'

'My pleasure,' said Stephen, looking at Fitz adoringly. 'That's what I'm here for, isn't it?'

62

Dunn Institute, February 1942

Ernst Chain and Gordon Sanders had set up the largest penicillin extraction plant in Britain, housed in the Dunn Institute's animal autopsy room. Sanders shared Heatley's genius at improvisation, and the machinery used included steam-heated dustbins functioning as stills, dairy farming equipment, and even a household bath to act as a reservoir for crude mould filtrate. Grace was suitably impressed with the ingenious set-up, but had become increasingly concerned about the deteriorating health of the six penicillin girls who worked there. They were all suffering from anaemia and infections, due to low white blood cell counts. Despite the women having worn protective equipment, the problem had started when the team had substituted amyl acetate for ether because it was less flammable and therefore less dangerous. Once Grace had made Florey aware of the problem, he'd immediately instigated regular health checks for them and a strict rota system to reduce their exposure. The extraction plant, despite still being rudimentary and tiny compared to the American facilities, was now producing a thousand times more penicillin than previous contraptions, but that was still barely enough to conduct even small-scale clinical trials. The Americans had agreed to send Florey a kilogram of penicillin in return for the vital research information and data he and his team had painstakingly collated at Oxford. So far, he had received just a paltry five grams, with no promise of more.

*

As usual, Grace had turned down Professor Florey's offer of a cigarette and was wondering why he had sent for her.

It was a cold, overcast day and the office was chill and damp. It was not what the Australian Florey would have chosen, but the institute did not have the funds to turn on the heating. 'I received this letter from John Fulton in the States,' he said, gesturing to the chair opposite him. 'I wanted to read it to you.'

'John Fulton? Of the Fulton family my sister Amy has become friends with?'

'The same. It starts . . .' he began.

Dear Professor Florey,

I trust this letter finds you in good health and that your work is advancing satisfactorily. I had to tell you myself about a happy and fortuitous event born out of sheer coincidence and serendipity. You know what they say about one person's misfortune being another's joy? Well, I was unfortunate enough to contract a viral infection severe enough to have to be admitted to my local hospital in Yale. My doctor told me in confidence about another patient next door, who was dying, and asked me if I could help obtain any penicillin. Long story short, I telephoned Heatley, who approached Merck. Merck said that any use of their supply was decided by Richards, and Richards said I had to approach the Chair of the Committee on Chemotherapy. After describing the case, we got hold of 5.5g of penicillin and Mrs Anne Miller became the first ever recipient in America. I cannot describe how dramatic the result was! On 12 March, this lady was at death's door and almost all the way through it. Within 24 hours of starting treatment, her temperature was normal and she was considerably restored. So we bombarded every single establishment we could think of for more supplies and continued. You can guess the rest. By April, she had made an astonishing and complete recovery. The excitement here is indescribable. Suffice to say, the incentive to accelerate further penicillin production has been ramped up a thousand-fold. Exciting times, my dear friend. Please look after yourself and I will write again with more news of the family and children when I'm feeling better. Lucia tells me they are flourishing and have made lots of good friends locally.

Yours as always, John.

'They didn't make the mistake we made with Albert Alexander, did they?' said Grace airily.

'That wasn't a mistake. We simply didn't have enough of the stuff.'

'But it taught us the importance of extending the treatment for long enough,' she said.

'Not least because we now know that too short a course can potentially lead to the development of antimicrobial resistance. Gardner demonstrated that. What is that quote? "That which does not kill us makes us stronger"?'

'Nietzsche. From his book *Twilight of the Idols*. Obviously, the same rules apply to bugs.'

'Yet even America, with its vast resources, had to scramble for enough penicillin to treat their first patient.'

'First clinical trial patient, anyway,' corrected Grace.

'What do you mean?'

'Apparently, almost unknown to anyone until recently, a Dr Martin Dawson in New York was using an extract from

Fleming's mould on patients with subacute bacterial endocarditis as far back as October 1940. So I suppose his people were in fact the first ever treated.'

Florey was stunned. It was the first he had heard of it. 'With what results?'

'Both patients died.'

'Perhaps he didn't have enough of the stuff, either.'

'Perhaps. It's much more likely that whatever he was producing was too diluted or impure, and possibly toxic.'

Florey crushed out his cigarette in the ashtray. 'Let's not make the same mistake. However much we can muster must be pure as well as potent. Thank you, Grace. You are a good listener. What's your lecture on this afternoon?'

'Polio and avoiding a lifetime in the iron lung.'

'Very good. I might come along myself.'

'Please don't. You'll make me nervous!'

63

St Mary's Hospital, London

Florey returned from a visit to the laboratory to find the telephone ringing on his desk. Taking it off the hook, he was surprised to find it was Alexander Fleming on the line. He had hardly had any contact with the man since he had last invited himself up to Oxford to have a look around, out of curiosity. Since then, he had shown no interest.

'Good day to you, Professor Florey,' he began in his soft Scottish brogue. 'I wondered if I might call upon you for a favour.'

Florey was taken off guard for a moment, and even more so when Fleming continued, 'I understand you are achieving remarkable results with my penicillin.'

'*My* penicillin?' thought Florey. I hardly think so. You have contributed nothing since you abandoned work on your mould years ago.

'How can I help?'

'A friend of mine by the name of Harry Lambert is lying in a hospital bed here at St Mary's with clinical meningism, which has failed to respond to anything we have thrown at him. He's a fifty-two-year-old man who is well worth trying to save.'

Florey considered his words carefully. 'The penicillin we

have here is in short supply, Dr Fleming. You say meningism. Is there a definitive diagnosis? How do we know he might respond?'

'His physician asked me to test a sample of his cerebrospinal fluid. I cultured it and it grew streptococcus.'

Florey waited for more.

'Interestingly, when I cultured the bacteria with sulpha drugs, I found them unresponsive.'

'Explaining the patient's failure to respond to his treatment,' said Florey.

'Precisely. But when I cultured them with some of my remaining crude mould juice, the streptococci were killed instantly. You can probably guess what I'm asking.'

Florey was conflicted. He did not enjoy an easy relationship with this man, but a gravely ill patient who was a good candidate for a trial of the novel treatment and could possibly be saved could not be ignored. Out of professional courtesy and etiquette it would have been churlish to turn down Fleming's polite request. 'I can hardly refuse. I'll collect what I can find and bring it down to London immediately.'

If a thank you was expected, it was not forthcoming. There was a sharp click at the end of the line and the phone went dead. Florey put the handset back in its cradle and frowned. He had a strange feeling that events were beginning to spiral out of his control.

*

Florey stepped off the train at Paddington the next morning and walked the five minutes around the corner into Praed Street and through the main doors of St Mary's Hospital.

Within the hour, he had handed over the goods and advised Alexander Fleming how to calculate the dosage. Any differences between the two men were easily forgotten in the interests of treating such a sick patient and the meeting, albeit brief, was cordial and respectful. Florey was back on the return train to Oxford within the hour.

*

A week after starting treatment with the intravenous penicillin injections, Harry Lambert showed no signs of improvement and remained gravely ill. His friend, and now his personal doctor, Alexander Fleming, hypothesised that since the symptoms predominantly pointed towards a form of meningitis, it would be worth injecting the drug directly into the spinal canal by lumbar puncture. He had almost no clinical experience with penicillin, so he telephoned Florey for his opinion.

'I hesitate to say,' was the response. 'We have no data on the efficacy or safety of such administration. Let me carry out a test on one of our rabbits first and I'll let you know the results.'

Fleming saw the logic in this and agreed. On his next visit to the patient, though, he realised that a decision could not wait. The man's condition was deteriorating rapidly. With nothing to lose, he went ahead anyway with the spinal injection. Six hours later, sitting at his workbench back in his cramped laboratory, Fleming's telephone rang. It was Professor Florey.

'Don't go ahead with the lumbar puncture,' he said flatly. 'Our rabbit died almost immediately.'

64

Dunn Institute, August 1942

On 17 August, Professor Florey posted five letters begging for more funds to pay for staff salaries and equipment, and took receipt of the incoming mail from his secretary. The topmost letter was postmarked London. Fleming had written:

> *I am rather a pessimist, but it really seems to me that Lambert (the penicillin patient) is going to recover. No temperature, brighter in every way, pulse better. When you saw him he was a dying man. When you see him on Tuesday you will (unless things change) see an enormous difference.*

Apparently, four further spinal injections had been given, as well as some intramuscular shots. The results in the second letter were even more satisfactory.

> *Temperature normal, blood count normal. The only thing he suffers from now is headaches. I am sending you back 4cc of the penicillin. This is all I have. We are all very grateful here for your kindness in letting us have some of your supply, which has undoubtedly saved the man's life.*

Florey was thrilled to hear such positive news and reflected on how much of a coincidence it was that he had been able to come to the aid of the man who had tripped over the curious properties of penicillium notatum all those years ago. However, the elusive and somewhat grudging mutual respect they had earned for one another was to prove short-lived.

The news of Harry Lambert's astonishing recovery was leaked to the press and bedlam ensued. Every newspaper and publication wanted to cover the story. Journalists flocked to St Mary's Hospital in search of more information. What they could not immediately glean, they embellished with considerable poetic licence.

Florey was fuming. Never had he imagined that his own sense of fairness and the spirit of scientific collaboration would be so blatantly steamrollered by another man and another medical establishment.

That Lambert had made a remarkable recovery was wonderful news. For the man himself, anyway. But the coverage printed in the newspapers in the days following his recovery was less than wonderful. The glory afforded solely to Alexander Fleming and St Mary's Hospital was a travesty, given the efforts and carefully monitored trials that had been run by the Oxford group. Lambert was the only patient that had ever been treated at St Mary's, and only then as a favour. Fleming had done nothing to extract or purify penicillin, nor had he carried out any animal studies or clinical trials on patients. Now the London press were heralding him a hero who would single-handedly save mankind.

There were good reasons why Florey had confined his team's work to the scientific press only, and Fleming and his acolytes had spectacularly failed to understand this. Now Grace, Chain, Gardner and Heatley were all standing in Florey's office leafing through the various publications.

'Look at this one,' said Chain. 'It's the *News Chronicle* from Friday. It talks about the miracle of mouldy cheese . . . the fungus that will cure infection. Then it exhorts the government to pursue the industrial production of penicillin.'

'And this one,' added Heatley, 'in the *Sunday Express*. "New drug will revolutionise the treatment of infected wounds." '

'And all of them give the credit entirely to that man Fleming,' added Gardner bitterly.

' "Professor's great cure discovery",' this rag says, and here, as we might have expected, in the *Glasgow Herald*: "Scottish Professor's discovery".'

'The man who didn't even realise what he'd discovered,' said Grace.

'Let me read you this,' said Florey. 'It's a letter printed in today's *Times*, from none other than that bigoted egomaniac Almroth Wright.'

Sir, in the leading article on penicillin in your issue yesterday, you refrain from putting the laurel wreath for this discovery around anybody's brow. I would, with your permission, supplement your article by pointing out that, on the principle of 'palmam qui meruit ferat' (in essence: honour to one who earns it), it should be decreed to Professor Alexander Fleming of this research laboratory. For he is the discoverer of penicillin and was the author also of the original suggestion that this substance might prove to have important applications in medicine.

I am, sir, yours faithfully,
Almroth Wright, Inoculation Department, St Mary's Hospital,
Paddington, W.2, August 28.

'How very perverse,' Grace said. 'Whilst I was at St Mary's twelve years ago, Wright publicly stated he saw no potential value in penicillin whatsoever. He even got Fleming to remove any suggestion of the idea from his original paper!'

Chain sighed. 'And now these same people in London want to usurp our achievement.'

'He's in everything from *Tit Bits* to *Picture Post*, which names him "Man of the Year". The *Evening Standard* has a lengthy interview with him and the *News Chronicle* a lovely photo and four columns all about him and his brilliance.'

'We must correct these distortions immediately,' said Chain, fiercely protective of the team. 'I find it intolerable that the popular press can so badly misrepresent the true facts.'

'How, exactly?' said Florey. 'By saying that we are solely responsible for the production of this life-saving medicine?'

'Why not? It's the truth, after all!'

'And encourage every Tom, Dick and Harry who is sick or has a sick relative or friend to come to Oxford with their begging bowls for supplies we don't have? When we still need to fully evaluate the efficacy and safety of the drug? I have already received pleading requests from as far afield as Australia, Moscow and Saskatchewan.'

'That's a good point,' said Grace. 'We shouldn't be offering false hope. Here's what the *Daily Mail* has to say: "Experiments in the laboratory at St Mary's Hospital Paddington are being made with a substance called penicillin, which may become the most valuable drug of the war and one of the most important medical discoveries of all time." It goes on to say that Professor Fleming hopes it will soon be possible to produce it on a commercial scale. He's hardly shown any interest in penicillin since 1928, and now he tells the world it will soon be available to everyone.'

'We cannot permit that misconception to endure,' said

Chain. 'Surely we can address the issue of where the credit is really due?'

'Wait,' said Florey. 'We all know we cannot currently satisfy demand. The newspapers will ignore that, and we'll risk being regarded by the public as obstructive and incapable. Having rival reporters insisting on interviews and fabricating stories will only distract our researchers and hamper our work. Remember what happened to my predecessor, Dreyer. He thought he had found a vaccine to prevent tuberculosis in humans, he published his results prematurely, and they turned out to be erroneous. It ruined his reputation, and for a while, the standing of the Dunn Institute itself. We cannot allow that to happen again.'

It was Heatley's turn to join in. 'Isn't it also the case that the GMC strongly disapproves of doctors' self-promotion and aggrandisement? I've heard of many a doctor actually being struck off the medical register for such things.'

'So how do Fleming and Wright get away with it?'

'Friends in high places, I imagine,' said Florey.

'We surely must refrain from saying nothing,' said Chain, 'and be prepared to accommodate briefings with the press, if for no other reason than to protect the financial backing we will need for further research. Our work is not yet finished.'

The group looked to Florey for his response. 'Let me mull it over,' he said finally. 'It's a double-edged sword, as you can see.'

The others sidled slowly out of the room, leaving their director to think. He did not need to, however. He had no intention of consorting with the gutter press.

65

Medical Research Council, September 1942

It was the opinion of Professor Mellanby and Sir Henry Dale that despite what the newspapers were telling the general public, the scientific community was fully cognisant of who really deserved the credit. They believed the truth would out, and were trying to reassure Florey that all would be well, reluctant as they were to allow an unseemly spat between eminent members of their own highly regarded profession. After the first flurry of publicity in early September, one such eminent scientist attempted to correct the situation with his own letter to *The Times*.

> *Sir, now that Sir Almroth Wright has so rightly drawn attention to the fact that penicillin was discovered by Professor Alexander Fleming and has crowned him with a laurel wreath, a bouquet at least, and a handsome one, should be presented to Professor H. W. Florey of the School of Pathology of this university. Toxic substances are produced by the mould alongside penicillin and Florey was the first to separate 'therapeutic' penicillin and to demonstrate its value clinically. He and his team of collaborators, assisted by the Medical Research Council, have shown that penicillin is a practical proposition.*
>
> *I am, sir, your obedient servant, Robert Robinson,*
> *Dyson Perrins laboratory, Oxford University, August 31.*

But the letter had made no difference. The only name on everybody's lips was Alexander Fleming's. Whilst by nature Fleming was a reserved man, he obviously rather enjoyed the unprecedented publicity around his discovery, and although he might not have sought it, nor did he offer much resistance to the numerous offers for interviews. To add insult to injury, he had privately told Florey that he deplored the level of press attention he was receiving, while doing precious little to avoid it. Whether he truly loved or loathed it, the public relations machine and political interests of St Mary's Hospital were now in full cry. Fleming was a national icon.

In the weeks that followed, the Oxford team became even more frustrated. They were decent people who were not out to seek glory, but simply some recognition for their efforts and travails.

The pressure from his own colleagues to do more to apprise the public of the truth was unremitting, so in December, Florey wrote to Sir Henry Dale, President of the Royal Society, with the facts, and Edward Mellanby of the MRC sent a reply that was unfavourable to say the least. It pointed out that Alexander Fleming was currently a candidate for election to the Fellowship of the Society and Florey was a Member of the Council who would therefore have to act as a judge. The president insisted that Florey refrain from publishing anything that might be seen as contradicting or refuting anything Fleming had said. Florey was livid. He lit a cigarette, training his match over the corner of the letter. He watched the rest of it burn away in his ashtray.

Once again, it looked as if his silence would only enhance Fleming's own standing and reputation.

66

Old Ebbitt Grill, Washington, June 1943

Oxford's supply of penicillin had been diverted to North Africa and Italy for clinical trials in the Army. Little or none would now be available for civilians – not in England, at least. On the other side of the Atlantic, though, things were dramatically different. After Pearl Harbor and the encouraging results of clinical trials of penicillin in the Pacific, it was obvious that production must be increased.

In the first five months of 1943, 400 million units of penicillin had been produced, which was encouraging, but still only sufficient to treat about 180 serious cases. In the seven months that followed, though, 20.5 billion units were made available, and by June, production had increased to 200 billion units every month.

Donald Hendrick was telling his wife all about these exciting developments over a romantic candlelit dinner one evening at the Old Ebbitt Grill in Washington.

'What's been holding production back all this time?' asked Amy.

'It was an engineering issue, really. The deep fermentation process on such a large scale proved to be a huge challenge.'

Amy pretended to look interested. She had perfected a

convincing facial expression that gave the appearance of intense concentration while all the time she could be thinking of something else. In this instance, it was the latest sunback dress created by Claire McCardell, which was flying off the shelves at Dior.

Donald persevered. 'A guy called Raper at the North Regional Research Laboratory in Peoria is their top mycologist.'

'Mycologist? Is that like a gynaecologist?'

'Not really. This guy's an expert in fungi.'

'Golly.' She took another sip of her sauvignon blanc and looked around the room in case anything more interesting was happening.

'Yes. His team worked around the clock seven days a week. They looked at soil samples from all around the world.'

Amy stirred her softshell crab chowder and gestured at the waiter to bring her some croutons. 'Uh-huh.'

'Then – and you won't believe this, Amy – one day, his assistant, a woman called Mary Hunt, came back from the local market with a decaying cantaloupe melon, which happened to be carrying a strain of mould so powerful that in terms of producing penicillin it eclipsed any other strain researchers had ever used. All of our penicillin now derives from it.'

Amy blew on her spoon to cool the chowder. 'Good for her. You can always count on a woman for the shopping. And what did Mary get out of it, apart from a rotten fruit salad and a receipt?'

'Just a rather memorable sobriquet, as it happens.'

'A what?'

'An epithet. Nickname. They call her Mouldy Mary now.'

'Charming! Maybe she should see a gynaecologist after all.'

Donald laughed. 'Maybe she should. Thing is, the military soon realised the production of penicillin would give our forces a significant edge in the war. We'll have it ready for the invasion, you mark my words.'

'The invasion? What invasion is that?'

Donald worried about Amy's disinterest in politics and world affairs. Her family, after all, were heavily involved. But he loved her anyway, and figured her nonchalance about his career was exactly matched by his indifference about her own world of cosmetics and fashion.

'The invasion of Europe, Amy. Whenever that may be. But everyone in Washington's hoping it will be a turning point in the war. And it can't come a moment too soon.'

'Let's hope my croutons come soon, as well,' she replied glibly. 'The waiter's taking forever.'

67

Woolworths Department Store, Battersea

The unexploded bomb had dropped straight through the roof of Woolworths, crashed through three floors, and come to rest in the confectionery area on the ground floor. It had killed a shop assistant and one of the customers on the way down.

The store had been rapidly evacuated, and Jack and his bomb disposal team had cordoned off a wide area around the site. With the aid of one of Will's stethoscopes, Jack had listened for any ticking sounds coming from inside, but had reassured himself that any timer designed to detonate a delayed explosion was either absent or non-operative. Jack had hauled himself up on to the bomb and was now sitting astride it, its pointed business end jutting out in front of him between his legs. The bomb was roughly cylindrical, at least six feet long and two feet wide. His trusted sergeant and best friend, Huwie Moss, whistled through his teeth. Jack seemed to be in something of a rush.

'Steady now,' Huwie said. 'It's not a race. You might want to slow down getting those screws out of the hatch cover.'

Jack knew full well that anything could set the bomb off. He also knew some of them were booby-trapped. Too rapid a movement here, too great a vibration there, and they were goners. Bizarrely, the more devices he dealt with, the less worried he became. He was also becoming increasingly impatient in his approach generally, when patience and care were logical prerequisites in this line of work.

He and Huwie had developed an almost telepathic understanding. They both worked hard and played hard, offsetting the life-or-death stresses of their work in all sorts of nefarious ways when their shift was over. There was not much they would not do for each other. For that reason alone, Jack slowed down a bit.

'This fucker is tight,' Jack said, leaning hard into the screwdriver and twisting.

'Want me to have a go?'

'Nah, you're all right. Just give us a sec. I'll give it a tap with the claw hammer.'

'Really? Is that wise?'

'What would you suggest, Einstein?'

'You're the boss. I've just never seen you do that before.'

'Never had to. Pass it over, would you?' Without hesitation, but taking care not to drop or scrape the metal tool against the bomb casing, Huwie placed the instrument in the palm of Jack's right hand. Jack held the little hammer an inch above the top of the screwdriver and turned to grin at his friend.

'Nice knowing you, mate,' he said, and before Huwie could respond, he brought the hammer down on to the screwdriver with a delicate tap. The last obstinate screw finally turned, and within a minute, he had removed the hatch cover. 'Fuck me, look at this,' he whispered. 'Frigging wires everywhere. And the bastards are all the same colour. Every single wire is red.'

'Aren't we the lucky ones!'

'It's what we get paid for, Huwie.'

'Yeah. Posthumously, probably.'

Jack was still fiddling with the innards of the thousand-pound bomb and his voice echoed slightly from within. 'Well, you can't take it with you, old son.'

'Why'd you think I spend it so fast?'

Jack threw him a laconic look and resumed what he was doing. 'Pass me the cutters, would you?' Huwie did as he was bid.

'Which wire are you cutting?'

'The red one.'

'You said they're all fucking red!'

'They are,' said Jack as Huwie registered the sound of a snip, 'but this is the only one attached to the detonator.' He lifted the little black box towards the hatch cover, intending to pass it to his friend, but it snagged. There was another red wire attached to the hidden side. Jack looked surprised.

'That was lucky,' he said matter-of-factly. The device was safe now.

Huwie was horrified. Jack should have checked. If he'd cut the wrong one, they'd have been blown to smithereens. Yet he did not seem perturbed in the slightest. In fact, he had walked away from the bomb and was helping himself to jelly beans, lemon sherbets and bars of chocolate, which had been locked away in a glass cabinet. Luckily for them, that glass cabinet had been smashed to bits by the fallout from the bomb.

'Come on, Huwie. Help yourself. This stuff's usually rationed, but who's gonna know? Fill your boots.'

Shaking his head in disbelief, Huwie joined him. He picked up a handful of sweets and casually scanned the labels. Among other things, there were Liquorice Bluebirds, Fruit

Salads, Chewies and Sherbet Fountains. There was also a packet of his favourite extra strong mints.

'Here you go, Jack. Just the job. A packet of Glacier Gob Grenades.' He threw the packet over.

Catching them in one hand, Jack replied, 'What you need, my old fruit, is chocolate. It might make you a little sweeter.'

Huwie bit off a chunk of Cadbury Dairy Milk and savoured it as he studied Jack. He was sitting with his eyes closed and his back to the confectionery counter. He was away with the fairies. He was his own man: confident, although some would have said cocky. But up to now, he had always been entirely professional and skilled at what he had chosen to do. Lately, though, he seemed different, a little distracted. Maybe Huwie was imagining it. Maybe Jack was taking the piss, deliberately playing the fool to wind him up. It would not have been the first time. But deep down, he knew something was not quite right.

Crumpling the Dairy Milk wrapper in his fist and throwing it over his shoulder, Huwie stood up and patted the casing of the bomb. 'I'll get the other buggers in now, to get this bastard removed. They can carry out a nice, controlled explosion to everyone's satisfaction.'

Three pints of watered-down ale later, enjoyed at the Ship Inn by Wandsworth Bridge, the two men parted and Jack strode off towards Rosie's place in Balham. The beer had helped but there was nothing quite like a rampant all-nighter with an adventurous and willing girl like Rosie to help relieve the tension of bomb disposal.

68

Medizinische Forschungseinrichtung Facility, Berlin

Jürgen Altmann was furious. For months, he had been frustrated by the lack of progress in obtaining the mould samples for Dr Schmidt in Berlin. The man was now blaming him personally. 'They are pulling the wool over your eyes, Altmann,' he had said mockingly. 'They are taking you for a fool.'

'But what do you expect, Herr Doctor? I'm not a medical man. I can only take what they give me.'

'They give you what they are happy for you to take.'

The gaunt, bespectacled man, in his long white coat, crept over to Altmann and sneered.

'Do you think that Professor Fleming would have sent just any old mould to the most famous institute in the world for fungal material? He would have staked his professional reputation on samples that were guaranteed to produce penicillin. They are palming you off with rubbish. And you are failing to do what you have been asked. Perhaps I should let Standartenführer Hermann Pister know.'

For Altmann, this was a slap in the face. For a man who had been awarded the Iron Cross, an unforgivable insult. But Schmidt had the Führer's ear, so he resisted the urge to remonstrate and forced himself to adopt a more deferential tone.

'I'm sure there is no need for that, Professor. I apologise. You are right. What other strategy can I pursue?'

'You can stop requesting and start demanding. I don't want just the few random samples they provide anymore. I want it all. Everything they have in Utrecht and everything from the Institut Pasteur. Bring it all to me and I'll take it from there. And take Dr Berger and Roth with you to ensure you don't fuck it up whilst transporting it. Dismissed.'

Fuming, Altmann turned on his heels and left. That arrogant bastard. Who is he to talk to me like that? Altmann thought. Schmidt was nothing like the doctors he had worked for at Hinzert concentration camp. They had welcomed his participation in their innovative experiments. He had enjoyed every second.

69

Institut Pasteur, Paris

The Nazis were intent on tracking down original samples from Alexander Fleming's mould in France, and suspected some was held at the Institut Pasteur on the Rue du Tot. The Institut had developed a new age of preventative medicine, with vaccines for numerous diseases including TB, diphtheria, tetanus, yellow fever and polio. Kitty had been dropped by air into France, with instructions to thwart the enemy using whatever methods she could. There was still no organised resistance movement in the Vichy-held capital and there were far too many collaborators and defeatists to make seeking help a safe strategy. In reality, Kitty was acting alone and had to remain patient and cautious. The Germans were everywhere. It had taken four months of local exploration to secure an appointment as librarian at the Institut. The fact that many of the male employees had been recruited into the French army and then killed or imprisoned in the earlier fighting had made it easier for her. She had been offered other roles elsewhere but had always found a credible reason not to take them on. She was where she needed to be.

Soon after starting work there, she realised that the Nazis' principal interests in the Institut related to the provision of serums and vaccines for their troops. They appeared so confident in the superiority of their own scientific knowledge that they seemed disinterested in other research, so only one German officer proved to be a constant thorn in the Institut's side: Jürgen Altmann. He and his men had trashed their laboratories several times in their search for samples, but had so far come away with nothing.

Kitty needed to stay on and observe. Someone at the Institut had stolen a culture of salmonella organisms and with an accomplice had contaminated a large supply of butter distributed to German troops. An epidemic of typhoid had swept through their ranks, hospitalising hundreds. But when a number of civilians also came down with the illness, the original source of contamination became clear. Two biologists at the Institut, a Dr Wolman and his wife, and three laboratory assistants, were arrested and dispatched to a concentration camp. Apart from that, Kitty was sure the Institut Pasteur posed little or no threat in providing the enemy with a source of penicillin. As far as she could ascertain, none of the hospitals had any, and there was none to be found at the Rue du Tot. But Altmann was relentless. The next place the Germans would search would be the Netherlands, where Liese was now stationed.

*

Liese, now known locally as Dr Margherita Vogel, had been warmly welcomed at the Centraalbureau de Schimmelcultures by Dr Johanna Westerdijk, who, like the majority of Dutch civilians, was doing everything possible to resist the Nazis. Since the invasion of the Netherlands in May 1940, life had been utterly miserable. Three years later, the occupying forces had a stranglehold on most of Europe, but the fortunes of war were gradually changing. The outcome hung in the balance and every small contribution towards bringing the war to an end was vital. Preventing the Germans from getting their hands on penicillin was part of it.

Liese's relationship with Westerdijk had flourished from the start. The director of the bureau was just as impressed by Frau Vogel's courage and commitment as Liese was with Westerdijk's exceptional leadership. She had taken on the foreign bacteriologist at the expense of several of her own colleagues, knowing that there were more important reasons for this particular appointment. She did not know the details, but as time went on, she had reached her own conclusions and was happy to assist Margherita in any covert way she could. She suspected she was some sort of agent, yet she would not ask too many questions. For her part, Liese greatly admired Johanna's work at the bureau, and had learned a great deal from her. Here, she had overseen the largest collection of fungal samples in the world.

The doctors had agreed on two fundamentals at the outset. First, they would continue to strive to produce greater yields of penicillin, and secondly, they would do anything to ensure it never fell into enemy hands. The Nazis might obtain it independently from the Institut Pasteur in Paris, but they were determined it would not reach them from Utrecht. They knew Dr Schmidt in Berlin was desperate to get hold of Westerdijk's mould cultures for his own research, and had sent a particularly nasty SS officer by the name of Jürgen Altmann several times to fetch it. But so far, the two women had thwarted him. Four times Altmann had requested samples, and on each occasion, he had left with cultures that the two women had ensured were quite incapable of producing penicillin. It was the wrong strain of fungus and they had deliberately rendered it biologically unproductive. But the Germans were never going to give up. They knew that the production of penicillin was a potential game-changer, regardless of the slow, frustrating process of obtaining it.

'I had another visit from Altmann,' said Johanna one morning.

'That foul man,' said Liese. 'He makes my skin crawl.'

'Mine, too. He undresses me with his eyes but at the same time wants to kill me.'

'He's a bully, that's all. Just like the rest of them.' Her mind once again wandered back to the fate of her father and she was reminded of her purpose for being here. 'What did he want?'

'The usual thing. More samples. But he was more insistent this time. More threatening. The loss of their Berlin facility has obviously incensed them. They need to start again, and Altmann is more desperate than ever. He marched into the lab with two other soldiers. He has no respect for our work here at all, nor our history. He just wants to steal whatever we have produced, which is especially annoying considering how long it's taken us to even get this far!'

'Did he leave satisfied?'

'I gave him more of the useless stuff as he was never going to agree to leave empty-handed. But I fear they are on to us. His look. His expression. And something else . . . Altmann said: "Dr Schmidt is no fool, and I may not be a scientist myself, but I don't need a microscope to discover treachery." '

'What do you think he meant?' asked Liese.

'I don't know. But he's clearly suspicious. More so than ever. God help us if he ever catches us out.'

'He won't. You put me in sole charge of the samples, remember?'

'What shall we do?'

'Fleming's original strains are hidden away here. It's becoming too risky to keep them. Sooner or later, Altmann will take matters into his own hands, and if he finds them, he'll take it all back to Berlin, lock, stock and barrel.'

'And discover that we've been deceiving them.' For the first time, Johanna Westerdijk looked scared.

'That's not going to happen,' said Liese. 'Tomorrow, I'm sending our original samples to Delft. It's a yeast and spirit factory. It's familiar with handling moulds and is less likely to come under Nazi scrutiny.'

'Is it safe?'

'I believe so. The only German officer stationed there seems totally uninterested in what goes on inside, and since we ply him with spirits on a regular basis, he's half-cut most of the time. Apparently, he's very fond of the schnapps.'

'All right. I will carry on here as if nothing has happened. It would raise questions if I were to leave. But Margherita, I'd like you to carry on our work over there in Delft. Continue the research and find ways to increase the yield. Your skills are equal to mine, and Andries Querido will assist you.'

'Querido?'

'He's employed there as a part-time adviser. His Jewish ancestry forbids him from working full-time, but he's shrewd. I spoke to him last night and he has an article for us that he believes we will find useful. It's a copy of a Swiss medical journal setting out the successful progress our allies are making in penicillin production. So this, too, must remain under lock and key.'

Liese realised Johanna was trusting part of her life's work to her and was flattered. Here was another person she dare not let down. 'When will I start?'

'As soon as you can pack. I'll have the samples and a car waiting for you tonight.'

70

Medizinische Forschungseinrichtung Facility, Berlin

As Dr Schmidt had predicted, Doctors Berger and Roth had been more astute than Altmann and had insisted that Kitty accompany them with the samples to the dedicated penicillin facility in Berlin. They believed that as she was responsible for labelling, categorising and identifying them, she was the best qualified to transport them in their current state of incubation. Kitty was relieved she did not have to face travelling alone with Altmann, and apart from a few unscheduled delays and regular identity checks, the train journey had been relatively uneventful. She was fearful every time an SS officer had boarded the train, but so far her forged documents had stood her in good stead.

Her relative sense of calm was shattered when she arrived at Schmidt's laboratories. As far as she had believed, the Germans were a long way behind the British in their quest for penicillin production. The Oxford group's progress had been painstakingly slow, but here in this vast complex, progress had been accelerating apace. She peeped through the door from the office leading into the warehouse. In front of her stood four giant silos, each the size of a two-storey house, and hundreds of glass containers full of a fine grey powder were stacked on metal shelving along the walls. *This must be penicillin!* What else could it be? For a moment, she was stunned. This was her worst nightmare come true. A nightmare she somehow had to share with the Special Operations Executive in London. A thought struck her. Why had they allowed her to see this? Did they assume she would know what she was looking at? Would that not make her a security risk and expendable? A shiver passed through her.

For an hour or so, while the men talked in hushed voices, she was uncertain what to do. She picked up a magazine and pretended to flick through the pages. The men returned.

'The biggest problem has been the issue of toxicity. Initially, the contaminants in the compound precluded its therapeutic use,' said Schmidt.

'And now?' asked Altmann.

Schmidt laughed. 'Thanks to your endless supply of unsuspecting human guinea pigs from the camps, Herr Altmann, and especially the identical twins who acted as ideal controls in our trial work, we were able to, shall we say, expedite the research.'

Kitty realised it was not only medical ethics that had been sacrificed. Countless prisoners and detainees had had experiments forced upon them and had most likely died as a result. *Murdered.* The thought appalled her. She could hardly believe they were having this discussion in front of her. Why?

Altmann had clearly never realised she could speak fluent German since she had only ever spoken to him in French through a translator. It seemed he was arrogant and naïve enough to believe she was what she claimed to be, a secretary acting the role of lab assistant, there simply to locate numbered samples. A woman capable of speaking only in her native French tongue.

Curtly, he dismissed her, telling her to return to Paris

forthwith. She donned her coat, and on shaky legs, made her way towards the exit, half expecting to be detained at any moment. Yet she was not. With a thumping heart and growing nausea, she left the building and sought the sanctuary of a nearby park. She had to get news to London. Everything depended on it. She remembered the address in Berlin Matthias had given her. SOE had deployed him there six months previously to work with the dwindling ranks of the German resistance. She prayed to God that her Spanish friend was still there. Visualising the map of Berlin in her head, she carried on walking. Matthias would help find people capable of sending the vital message to the SOE, and that message would need to include the precise geographical coordinates of the factory. Either that, or she would have to return to Paris to do it herself. There was no guarantee she would not be stopped on the way.

71

St Ermin's Hotel, London

Sir Andrew Morrison's worst nightmare had come true. Without knowing for sure who the minister in front of them really was, or the exact role he fulfilled, Florey and Mellanby had reluctantly confirmed that Kitty's latest decoded message was almost certainly credible. It was not beyond the realms of possibility that the Germans had produced penicillin in bulk. They had infinitely more resources, and very likely all the raw materials required. Florey had been shocked. He had prided himself on his team winning the race and yet they were still some considerable distance from the finishing line. Could the Nazis really be so far ahead of them? Mellanby was simply embarrassed, having repeatedly assured Sir Andrew that nobody else was even a comparable competitor.

'Well, redouble your efforts, then, gentlemen,' the Director of the SOE had said before dismissing them. 'And do everything in your power to speed up your progress. We can't know for sure what the Nazis do or don't have, but whatever the situation, we're going to need your penicillin as soon as possible. Our troops depend on it.'

Now the two men had left, Andrew sat at his desk in

contemplation. After a minute or two, he reached forward and picked up the telephone.

'Get me the Chief of the Air Staff, would you?' he asked his secretary. 'That's right. Charles Portal, at bomber command.'

72

Tripoli, June 1943

Florey remained frustrated that the patients being referred to them all had festering wounds that were weeks or months old and had not responded to sulphonamides. What the professor really wanted was fresh cases where acute wounds could be managed and treated much earlier to give his penicillin a greater chance of success. Grace concurred. She knew that waiting for wounded soldiers to be transferred to a rear base hospital and then having their injuries sewed up with debris still present was costing lives. Florey suggested they try sprinkling penicillin as a calcium salt directly into wounds as a surface dressing before sewing them up, while leaving inside a little rubber drain tube to allow further doses of penicillin solution. It proved to be an inspired idea.

Patients needed to be carefully selected for the trial. Abdominal wounds contaminated by gut microorganisms would be resistant to the therapeutic effects of penicillin, whereas compound fractures, soft tissue injuries and septicaemia would be more likely to respond.

During the next three months, despite their limited supplies, they conducted further trials on this basis. Will toiled relentlessly with the surgical aspects, and Grace matched his work ethic in her makeshift laboratory, identifying the causative germs and assessing the most suitable methods of treatment. By July, they had worked out how best to use penicillin in the field, and whereabouts in the Army's deployment it could be used to the best possible advantage.

Now, with the 8th Army's desert campaign won and the 1st Army ready to begin the invasion of Sicily on 10 July, the military needed a surgeon old enough to have had experience with the failure of sulphonamides and other antiseptic drugs, but young enough to be able to wade ashore in the chaos and mayhem of the invasion. In addition, they wanted a bacteriologist, an expert who could work hand-in-hand with the surgeon. Will and Grace had fallen over themselves to volunteer.

73

Medizinische Forschungseinrichtung Facility, Berlin

Kitty's instructions from the Special Operations Executive had been specific. Anything she could do to help pinpoint the location of Dr Schmidt's pharmaceutical facility on the outskirts of Berlin would be vital. She and Matthias had packed his old canvas-roofed Citroen van with enough straw bales soaked in diesel to burn for some time. Long enough, they hoped, to be visible from the sky. Vehicles were forbidden to drive at night with headlights in the blackout, so at 4 p.m., they had parked the van on the street outside the factory. While Kitty distracted the sentries on guard by ostentatiously applying her make-up, Matthias let down the front offside tyre. When the soldiers came to take a look, they assumed it was a puncture and were told by the car's occupants they would return later with a jack and a spare wheel.

At 10.50 p.m. precisely, Kitty and Matthias returned with the equipment. As Matthias proceeded to change the wheel, Kitty lit firelighters in a cavity beneath the lowest of the straw bales in the back of the van. At 10.52, some pistol shots rang out around the corner and the two sentries dashed off to investigate. Kitty and Matthias downed tools and made themselves scarce.

Within five minutes, the fire was raging inside the van,

and soon, the flames, which had melted the fabric roof, were shooting ten feet into the air. The splitting and crackling of the fire all but drowned out the distant drone of the approaching Pathfinder bombers.

In the cockpit thousands of feet above, the pilot looked down at the heavy cloud cover; any expected beacons from the ground would be totally invisible. It had been a long shot, anyway, a small fire from such a distance. All he could see was the diffused glow from the serried banks of searchlights below, which was no help whatsoever.

The new H2S Mark II radar system used by Bomber Command worked on the basis that different objects had different radar signatures: water, open land and built-up areas all produced distinct returns. The twenty-two-year-old pilot was praying that the coordinates he had been given were accurate, and that he was nearly over the target. The first group of planes had sky-marked the area in front of him using parachute flares and target indicators. The second group had followed that flight path and were dropping incendiary bombs that would burn large and bright. Since he was unable to see the target itself, the bomb aimer readied himself to drop his bomb load bang in the centre of the target markers, the 'mean point of impact', as it was known.

At 11.04 p.m., the first of five massive bombs crashed through the factory roof, blowing out the wall and installations in a tremendous eruption of sound and fire. It was all over within a minute. Several of the Pathfinders had been badly damaged by flak, and two others had been shot down by enemy fighters. By the time they had set a course for home, and on constant lookout for further enemy attacks, Dr Schmidt's penicillin factory had ceased to exist.

74

Sicily, 10 July 1943

Will sprang from the landing craft at Sugar Beach with the rest of the assault team. The sky was black with Allied aircraft. In the front, he could make out Dakotas, Halifaxes and Albemarles, with several Waco and Horsa gliders following behind. Grace remained onboard the packet boat *St David*, which had been converted into a hospital ship and was now stationed five miles offshore.

As Will approached the barbed wire in front of him, two soldiers a few metres to his left were thrown into the air by a landmine. One lost a foot, the other his life.

The enemy fired flares into the air to light up the beach while soldiers of the British 1st Army put up a smokescreen. When the bombing and hand-to-hand fighting started in earnest, the numbers of casualties mounted dramatically and Will found himself working flat out.

The next few hours were frantic. Injuries were caused by all kinds of ordnance: road mines, S-mines, mortar bombs and snipers. There were civilian casualties, too, local children who had been caught up in it all: collateral damage from falling masonry, or who had been unlucky enough to step on mines when running for shelter.

Will did what he could to treat the wounded. He stemmed

haemorrhages, reduced fractures and dislocations, took out ruptured spleens and administered morphine to dying men. Later, he organised the transfer of the most severely wounded to the *St David*, where facilities were reasonably good, and the resuscitation equipment was exceptional, with oxygen and plasma at every bedside. Army nurses were working around the clock, and Will himself was ready to donate blood if needed. Plasma was useful and undoubtedly saved lives, but in Will's experience, it was best for closed injuries and shock, where there was never very much external blood loss. Where haemorrhage was extreme, there was no substitute for whole blood.

The immediate problem was ferrying the wounded to the ship. At anchor five miles off the coast and hidden by a smokescreen, it could be difficult to find. The sea was rough, too, and the flat-bottomed boats rose and slapped down again on the turbulent surface. Will later regretted not keeping some of the wounded in a local bivouac on shore, but the existing arrangement was still a useful stepping-stone towards eventual transfer to Tripoli.

*

A fortnight later, with Sicily fully in Allied hands, Grace had established the 5th Mobile Bacteriological Laboratory onshore and was able to assist the 8th Army surgeons with many of their patients. At midnight on 28 July, she finally sat down for a break and realised she had not seen Will for nine days. Three different casualty clearing stations – each with well-trained, experienced surgeons – and several field surgical units meant he could be anywhere.

When she woke at seven o'clock the following morning and

threw open the flaps of her canvas tent, she saw him standing there in front of her. He looked as weary as she felt. She ran over to him and hugged him tightly. 'Where the hell have you been?' she said. 'I've been worried sick about you!'

'Doing what your boss told me to do. I've been busy selecting patients for the penicillin trial. The 8th Army surgeons are incredibly impressed with the results, Grace. They see clean wounds ready for surgery at the forward base hospital, and are achieving magnificent results. They say they've never seen anything like it. Once we have enough of it, penicillin is going to become the routine treatment of choice.'

'So which patients has he been selecting for the trial?'

'Mainly British casualties.'

'Why? There are Americans and Canadians here, too.'

'I know. But they would likely be harder to follow-up with later on for the research. I promise they are still being well looked after.'

'And the Italians?'

'Italians, too. We were asked not to treat any enemy casualties and there's an embargo on treating venereal disease, as well. You know how rife that is.'

'Venereal disease responds very well to penicillin, though.'

'So it does. And Churchill might very well argue that it gets otherwise healthy soldiers back to the frontline more quickly than treating the wounded. But I couldn't in all conscience leave a wounded enemy soldier to die when I could treat him.'

'That's why I love my husband, you know. A man with sound clinical judgement and a sound moral conscience.'

'We all took the oath, didn't we?'

'We did.' Grace smiled and gave Will a kiss. Then she momentarily reverted to her professional role. 'And here's the thing about venereal disease,' she said. 'I think the reason it's so widespread is because I've been told the girls in the North African brothels have all been regularly taking sulphonamides as a preventative measure.'

'And?'

'They are not very effective against gonorrhoea, and I believe it has led to antibiotic resistance. Abrahams and Chain identified the problem back in Oxford some time ago. If we're going to use penicillin or any other antibiotic, we have to use it sparingly and selectively.'

Will nodded. 'Makes sense. But good luck with that. From what I can see, the Americans are ramping up production like it's going out of fashion. And I see no prospect of them stopping.'

'Maybe. But we'll certainly need more, both during and after the war. After that, we'll have to see.'

75

Operation Overlord, Juno Beach, 6 June 1944

The weather was against them, but at least the tides were reasonably favourable. Ned San Grefria lurched and smashed against the bare metal sides of the flat-bottomed landing craft as it approached the beach rolling and pitching in the rough water. The stench was nauseating; soldiers were throwing up from a combination of fear and seasickness. He just wanted to get out. Anything had to be better than this.

Salt spray from a giant wave cascaded over the bow, and as the motor surged then died, the landing craft juddered to a halt in the sand and the bow door dropped open. Several men in front of him were thrown back amidst a fusillade of machine-gun fire, but some managed to rush forward unscathed, dodging obstacles, anti-tank walls and barbed wire as they ran. Ned felt something bite his upper arm and leg, but the adrenaline was pumping and spurred him on. It was just like it had been in Teruel and at the Ebro in Spain. The fury in him seemed to endow him with strength. He leapt over the wire and rolled. Springing up again, he sprinted to the foot of the cliff and the relative shelter from the gunfire and crouched. He had outrun so many of the other men that he had become isolated, but infinitely safer.

The clusters of men advancing side by side were easy targets for the gunners and snipers in the pillboxes. They did not even need to aim; a sweep of the beach below could take out dozens of men at a time. Ned looked behind him at the slaughter. He saw men thrown into the air by landmines and others torn into pieces by the fire coming from the artillery batteries and the machine-gun nests in the concrete bunkers.

Fourteen thousand Canadian troops from the 3rd Canadian Infantry Division and the 2nd Canadian Armoured Brigade would be coming ashore here, and Ned wondered how many would survive. The beach in front of them stretched eight kilometres from Saint-Aubin-sur-Mer to Graye-sur-Mer and the whole coastline was heavily defended by fanatical elite troops of the 12th SS Panzer Division. The Canadian objective was to establish a foothold and then push inland towards the city of Caen. Yet their incursion here in this part of Normandy would be defended to the death.

They dare not fail. No matter the scale of the casualties, there was no means of retreat or escape. There was no going back. As Ned looked about him, the bile rose in his throat. Without a second thought, he started to scale the cliff, his rifle hanging over his shoulder and his grenades swinging freely from his belt. He ignored the pain in his limbs, and whilst the blood on his hands made his grip on the rocks slippery, attending to his injuries would have to wait. Like every other soldier, he carried a small emergency medical pack, but there were dozens of men behind him who, by the look of them, would have much greater need of the penicillin he carried than he did.

*

Farther to the west and two miles offshore from Courseulles, Will had been patiently waiting in an LST – a tank landing ship. Pitching, seesawing up and down and side to side in the heavy swell, he wondered how many more times he would find himself serving his country and tending the wounded at sea, instead of on land. First it had been the frozen hell of the Arctic convoy, then the emergency operations in the hospital ship *St David* during the invasion of Sicily.

He had been waiting for the first of the wounded to arrive in the DUKW boat-trucks. Known to the troops as ducks, they were the US military's amphibious modifications of two-and-a-half-ton trucks, and could transport goods and troops over both land and sea.

Each LST could carry up to 300 men, and was generously equipped with stretchers, blankets, blood, plasma and tons of other medical supplies. As the first duck came alongside, Will wondered if they would be enough. Many men had suffered burns, open fractures, and several were in shock after their limbs had been blown off, their flesh hanging in festoons below their shattered bones. Some were bleeding out right in front of his eyes.

As he helped lift the wounded from the smaller boats, he felt a rush of air from an enormous explosion. Another LST had struck a mine and was sinking fast. There were hundreds of men on that ship, none of whom would be capable of swimming far or fast enough to get help.

Will knew this was not a time for hesitation or reflection. These soldiers needed immediate treatment and evacuation to the south coast of England. Around forty specially equipped hospital trains would be waiting, and dozens of hastily constructed general hospitals across the south and west of the country would be ready to put them back together.

The wounds inflicted by the enemy were often ragged and contaminated already. Open gashes were full of sand, shrapnel, and bullets lodged in tissue. And fragments of dirty clothing were melted on to burnt flesh.

As he examined the injured one by one, he thanked the god he did not usually believe in for penicillin. He had seen in Tripoli and Salerno the magic, therapeutic powers it seemed to possess. The plentiful supply he now had at his disposal would save thousands of lives.

76

SOE, London, September 1944

After the liberation of Paris in August, Kitty had been recalled to London for an audience with the Special Operations Executive. Just like the Germans and the Japanese, the French had been largely unsuccessful, producing no more than a few grams of penicillin, and Kitty had helped to keep it that way. She had also ensured that no useful material from Paris ever found its way to Berlin, and that whatever Dr Schmidt's lab had produced, and housed in those four vast silos, had been destroyed by the RAF. The situation in the Netherlands, though, was still uncertain, and there were many battles to be fought. In Fitzrovia, Sir Andrew Morrison at SOE headquarters welcomed Kitty warmly and thanked her for her role so far.

'There's one more task I'd like you to consider,' he began. 'Most of the Netherlands is still under Nazi control and it may take several more months before she is liberated. Liese is still there, and her last messages reported considerable success with penicillin in Delft. However, communication with her has recently ceased, and ciphers we have intercepted suggest the enemy is about to raid the facility.'

'Is Liese in any danger herself, sir? As you know, she is a dear friend.'

'She has always been in danger. As you have all been. And what I'm asking you to do now will return you to the fray. The Nazis are more desperate than ever.'

'What is it you need?'

'Liese has served her purpose admirably but the net is closing in. Besides, the Allies have the advantage now, in terms of penicillin. Every soldier has access to treatment, and we can return the wounded much more quickly to the frontlines than the Germans can. As far as we know, they still have virtually none, unless they lay their hands on the materials at Delft. We need Liese out and any materials destroyed.'

'I understand, sir.'

Kitty was struggling with a guilty conscience. She had put Liese in the firing line by suggesting her recruitment to the SOE.

Morrison knew he could be sending this young woman to her death, but could not allow himself to dwell on it. 'You already have your ID papers and a French passport. When can you be ready?'

'I would need a few hours, sir.'

'Fine. I've asked for the aircraft to be made ready for take-off at ten o'clock this evening. I'll send a car for you and meet you at RAF Northolt for a final briefing.'

77

RAF Caister, Lincolnshire

The final assembly of dozens of Supermarine aircraft was still taking place inside the factory when Emily had arrived to fly a finished machine up to RAF Duxford. She had taken off from the airstrip outside the factory at Eastleigh at around four o'clock in the afternoon, in clear blue skies. It was intended to be a short flight, and she was already familiar with the controls of the Hawker Hurricane. She had no need for the little book of notes and instructions intended for novices. An hour into the journey, though, weather conditions had changed dramatically. Two opposing fronts had collided, and now heavy clouds were rolling in from the east, blanketing everything below. Fog enveloped the ground over much of Cambridgeshire and Lincolnshire, and visibility was poor. The map on her lap was useless as she could not make out a single landmark on the ground, let alone identify and follow a familiar road or river. Her compass had directed her in roughly the right direction, but where the hell was her destination?

She had circled for a while, hoping to see through a gap in the clouds, but had found none. She was unusually worried. She was responsible for this brand-new aircraft and felt duty-bound to deliver it safely. It did not help that the radio did not seem to function, but that was nothing unusual. These planes coming straight from the production line often had little faults that needed ironing out, and that was part and parcel of the job. After another thirty minutes or so, her fuel was running low and she was now completely lost. She would have to descend below the cloud base and take her chances in the fog. If there were hills, chimneys, or radio masts lurking within, so be it. She had no choice.

Her compass told her she was flying south again so she reasoned she must have flown over Duxford some time ago. Now, looking up, she saw a spindly black speck coming towards her. Approaching fast, it became bigger and bigger until it morphed into the unmistakable shape of an RAF Spitfire. If Emily could only signal her distress to the pilot, maybe she could secure some assistance. Instinctively, she manipulated the joystick and foot pedals to waggle her wings. She had heard that combat pilots often did that after a 'kill'. But the Spitfire held fast to its course and flew straight past. Perhaps the pilot had not even seen her. She banked the Hurricane into a steep left turn and looked to see where the Spitfire might have gone. As she straightened, there was no sign of it. Through the cockpit she searched the sky in front and above. To the left and right of her as well, craning her neck. Nothing. She resigned herself to attempting a blind landing. Then, not a plane's width away from her, the Spitfire appeared by her side, the pilot looking across inquisitively.

Emily opened the cockpit canopy slightly and pulled off her helmet so that her long hair streamed out behind her. Then she held up her map and shrugged her shoulders, hoping her knight in shining armour would understand she was a female pilot with the ATA and flying without navigational instruments. The other pilot held up his radio transmitter and began speaking into it. Emily held up her own and theatrically drew her hand across her throat. He understood immediately. Her radio was dead. He nodded and indicated that Emily should follow him. Relieved, she snuck in behind him, flying about fifty yards in his slipstream. The weather was becoming even worse and she could not afford to lose him.

After a few minutes, the Spitfire entered a shallow dive, not veering off course for a moment. Within moments, Emily's Hurricane was engulfed in a blanket of dense cloud and she could see nothing at all. She was being bounced about in the turbulence and flying blind. She had lost sight of her escort, and could only hope that by holding the same course and speed, she would avoid a collision. After a minute, the cloud dispersed, and a hundred feet below she could make out the dim lights of the airstrip. She dropped the undercarriage and followed the Spitfire in before taxiing to a halt on the grass by the hangar. Taking off her goggles, she threw her head back in relief. She stepped out on to the wing and eased herself down to the ground.

A tall, rather burly man in uniform was waiting for her, his insignia identifying him as a chief engineer. 'Wrong airfield, I fear, madam,' he said sarcastically. 'But to be fair, you did quite well to get the kite down in one piece in this weather!'

'Well, you know we women can't read maps,' she shot back indignantly, still pumped full of adrenaline. 'Without that chap over there, I'm not sure I would have got down at all. Who is he?'

The chief engineer looked across at the Spitfire pilot, who was taking off his helmet and inspecting a number of bullet holes along his fuselage, and several chunks missing from the horizontal stabilisers on the tailplane, which had obviously been shot away. He still had his back to her, so she casually strolled over and placed a hand gently on his shoulder. With a huge grin on his handsome face, he turned to look at her. 'Ah,' he said, laughing, 'my maiden in distress.'

'Thank you,' she replied, 'for coming to my rescue.'

The pilot studied her for a few seconds, mesmerised. He thought she was utterly beautiful.

'I'm glad I was able to help. Right place, right time, I fancy.'

Emily was smiling back. 'I couldn't agree more.'

'My name's Bembe,' he added. 'Bembe Paul. Originally from Castries in Saint Lucia. Now with 19 Squadron, Duxford.'

Emily could not believe her luck. Duxford? Had she reached her intended destination after all? 'I'm Emily. So this is Duxford?'

'No. This is Biggin Hill. But what's seventy miles between friends? My Spit's rather shot up, so I felt it prudent to land where I could. Especially in this weather.'

'Any port in a storm, I guess. But it was very lucky for me that you happened along.'

'Now it's my turn to agree with you.' He smiled again. 'Look. I'll need a quick debriefing in the officer's mess, but after that, may I take you out for dinner? You won't be able to fly on to Duxford until at least tomorrow, so it would be my pleasure.'

'Only if I pay,' said Emily. 'It's the least I can do after what you just did!'

'Pay? What with?' He laughed. 'It doesn't look like you carry a lot of spare cash in your flying suit.'

Emily felt foolish. She'd not even thought about the fact

that she had brought nothing with her and had nothing to change into. But she was not really thinking straight. She had just come through quite a challenging ordeal and had still not quite recovered.

78

Neringstraat, Delft

At the little apartment in Engelsestraat, Kitty had made contact with Liese just in time. It had been an emotional reunion, but as they had not had long to catch up on their news, they shared most of it as they hurried to the facility in Neringstraat.

'The officer outside will only allow entry to authorised personnel, Kitty. I know what I've got to do. Go and buy coffee in the university café on the other side of the street, and wait for me there. Ask for café noir.'

'I don't like café noir.'

'You have to here. Milk has been rationed for some time. There are informers everywhere, and anyone not knowing that would be a giveaway.'

Kitty nodded. 'Take care, then, Dr Vogel. Get in and get out. Then we run.'

Liese gave Kitty a hug and a huge smile. 'Make it two coffees. I'll be back before you know it.'

She crossed the street, showed her pass to the sentry, and entered the building. Kitty found a table outside the café and sat down. Moments later, a cavalcade of military vehicles screeched to a halt opposite and a dozen soldiers and SS men ran up the steps of Liese's building and barged past the guard. One of them, the leader it seemed, looked particularly angry. As he turned to gesture to his men, she recognised his face immediately. *Altmann.* Kitty felt exposed and helpless. Liese was trapped inside, and as yet unaware of her desperate situation. What could she do? How could she help? It was impossible. All she could do was to sit and wait. And hope.

*

Inside the spacious laboratory, the equipment and apparatus were performing nicely. In today's batch there was enough of the antibiotic being collected to treat at least 140 patients. The technique Liese had been perfecting was now reaping dividends, and in a few more weeks, this quantity could increase a hundredfold. She took a quick last look around the room at the results of her last two years' work. Then she picked up a two-litre can of amyl acetate and poured the flammable solvent over every inch of the workspace. After emptying four more in the same way, every sample in the room was drenched in the fluid and the strong smell of bananas and apples assailed her nostrils and made her eyes water. She was reaching for the matches and the Bunsen burner just as she heard the crashing of the outer door and the sound of jackboots running towards her. She lit the match, turned on the gas, and trained the Bunsen burner towards the nearest pool of liquid. Just as the men appeared at the door of the lab, a huge whoosh of flame engulfed the room and the lab exploded in a shower of wood and glass.

*

Confused and shaken by the dramatic events across the street, Kitty frantically tried to collect her thoughts. Flames were billowing out of the third-floor windows, and shards of glass were cascading down on to the pavement below. She and several other customers sitting outside the café quickly took refuge inside. A fire truck with its bell clanging loudly roared up outside the building opposite, whereupon an extendable ladder and hoses were ratcheted upwards towards the blaze. Several military vehicles drew up at either end of the thoroughfare, discharging soldiers who were shouting and running in every direction.

The café door burst open and an officious-looking SS officer, dressed in a long black leather trench coat and peaked cap, stepped inside, followed by half a dozen of his henchmen. The officer surveyed the room and brandished his pistol. He was obviously looking for somebody in particular. Kitty's heart was racing but she dare not show any fear. He strode between a number of tables and swiftly marched to the back of the room.

A young woman about Kitty's age, with a similar hairstyle, was forcibly lifted from her chair and manhandled to the bar in the centre of the café.

'Your papers,' he demanded, as the other men circled her. Protesting meekly, she drew them out of the inside pocket of her jacket, a tan-coloured jacket similar to the one Kitty was still wearing under the long overcoat Liese had lent her to keep her warm while sitting outside.

It occurred to Kitty that somebody must have spotted two women approaching the steps of the research laboratory, noticing that only one of them had gone inside. Their descriptions must have been given to the police, and what was happening in front of her was a case of mistaken identity. The Gestapo officer, in his eagerness to make an arrest, had jumped to conclusions.

Under the table, Kitty surreptitiously fastened three more buttons at the front of the overcoat.

The SS officer took the woman by the arm to the window of the café, and pointed to the men across the way who were trying to interrogate another woman, lying apparently immobile on a stretcher.

'You know this woman?' he yelled.

'N-no,' stuttered the accused. 'How would I know her? No, I—'

'But you were seen walking together just a few moments ago, were you not?'

'No. I came here on my own. I'm waiting for my daughter to join me. I—'

'The description was very clear. And where do we find you? Enjoying your coffee and biscuits whilst acting as a lookout for your friend.'

'That's absurd. I only came—'

'Silence!' he barked. 'You can tell me everything in good time. Meanwhile, I shall take care of your papers, Miss . . .'

'Sievers. Mrs Sievers.'

The woman seemed more terrified than ever. The SS man's eyes narrowed. He drew closer to her so that his face was just inches from hers.

'Sievers,' he repeated questioningly, as if slowly mulling the name over in his mind.

'Not Herrou? Not Dominique Herrou?'

'No. No, I'm Sievers. Mrs Marit Sievers.'

A stab of adrenaline shot through Kitty's belly like a dart. They knew her name. They were aware of her fake identity.

Abruptly, the officer turned on his heel and gestured to his men. 'Take her away.'

Two men bundled the trembling woman outside and into the back of a Mercedes staff car. The SS officer followed them out and jumped into the passenger seat before the vehicle drove off. Two remaining soldiers glanced around the room then strolled up to the bar and ordered two coffees.

A well-dressed older lady, with a friendly, moon-shaped face, spectacles and a walking cane, took Kitty's arm and squeezed it under the table. 'We'd better be getting home, then, I suppose,' she said. 'All this excitement has quite disturbed me. And Henri will be waiting for his lunch and wondering where on earth we've got to.'

She stood, still gripping Kitty's forearm, and ushered her out of the door and towards her car. As they exited, a young soldier waiting dutifully outside nodded at them and wished them 'Good day'.

'As your aunt . . .' the woman kept saying in a loud voice as they walked to her old Citroën Traction Avent parked around the corner. Once safely inside the car and on their way, Mrs van der Meer introduced herself at last. 'But call me Doortje, and you are, I think . . . the Miss Herrou the Boche were looking for?'

Kitty gave a little nod and examined her rescuer more closely. She had a kind face, with warm brown eyes, and puffy jowls that wobbled as she spoke. It gave her a distinctly innocent appearance, and Kitty realised she now had to trust her, just as the Germans had.

'You were undoubtedly my saviour back there.'

'We all have to look after each other.'

'You took an enormous risk.'

Doortje shrugged. 'There are risks everywhere.' She took the next bend rather too rapidly but quickly corrected her steering. 'I used to be a decent poker player when I was younger. The greater the stakes, the greater the fun.'

'Fun?'

'Everywhere you look, there's plenty of drama. At my age, you have to find excitement where you can.'

If it was a joke, there was only the slightest hint of a smile.

'And your friend?'

Kitty stared through the windscreen at the flat landscape ahead. Despite her own predicament, she had not forgotten about Liese. She had spectacularly succeeded in her task, but at what cost? Kitty had not been able to see whether Liese was badly injured. She kept asking herself if she could have done more to help. Were they interrogating her right now? Was she even alive? Kitty, with tears brimming in her eyes, looked back at her driver but said nothing.

79

SS Führungshauptamt, Delft

Altmann relished the challenge of an interrogation. It was a unique opportunity to pit his wits against someone who had everything to lose. He had carte blanche to torment his captor psychologically, and then, if that failed, he could always resort to physical torture. He enjoyed that part of it. He loved the sound of breaking bone, the sight of spurting blood, the cries of anguish.

Initially, his interrogation of Liese appeared low key. 'I can only admire your courage,' he had begun. 'You are a very brave woman, and I must respect your patriotic duty to your country – England, I believe, not The Netherlands.' He had not discovered the woman's true identity, but it would not take him long to do so.

'Your scientific principles are admirable, but you must see that resistance is futile. I'm told that penicillin is a substance which will soon be produced for the benefit of the whole of mankind. It's just a question of who first manages to make it widely available. As a doctor, don't you want to leave that as part of your legacy?'

He let the question hang. But Liese had been well-trained by the SOE. She would tell them nothing. They had already found the suicide 'L' tablet in the elastic lining of her underwear, so there would be no quick solution even if she had wanted it. The more she resisted, the more impatient Altmann became. The little control he feigned to possess was not working.

'We know about your fellow collaborator,' he explained, exasperated. 'We know what you have tried and failed to achieve. It is of no consequence.' Altmann then claimed the Nazis had already synthesised penicillin at their research facility in Berlin, but Liese knew that the facility and everything within it had been destroyed. Altmann was bluffing, and that gave her a grim sense of satisfaction.

At first, she did not know which scientists he was referring to. Did he mean Westerdijk, or Kitty? But she waited – the more her interrogator droned on, the more he gave away – and soon it became obvious that Westerdijk was in the clear. Keeping her in the dark about her own background had been the right decision. It was Kitty they were after, and clearly she had escaped their clutches for now and was still in hiding.

The Nazi scrutinised the woman in front of him. Because of her actions, he had failed in his mission – what consequences might he face as a result? The SS were becoming ever more unforgiving and ruthless with each day. This woman had carried out her sabotage, and now Germany was back to square one with the hunt for penicillin. Altmann would torture her just for the hell of it. What was there to lose? She might give them information and she might not. It was irrelevant now. He would have her shot anyway.

80

The Dove Public House, Hammersmith

Will was sitting at a beer-stained table in The Dove, an eighteenth-century building overlooking the River Thames, wondering how much longer Jack would be. It had been a while since the two brothers had been able to arrange a get-together, and Will had a feeling there might be something on Jack's mind. He had been worried about him for some time, so he had taken the trouble to arrive early. Jack was never the best at keeping in touch with family, but he had become increasingly remote. And whenever he *was* in contact, he'd seemed distracted and even moodier than usual.

The door crashed open and someone barged in, bumping into a startled young woman on her way out. It was Jack, squinting in the dim, smoky light, trying to spy his brother among all the other customers. He raised a shaky hand when he saw him and walked jerkily towards Will, his feet slapping down unusually firmly on the sticky pub floor.

'Be with you in a trice, young brother,' he said, 'just need to siphon the python before I piss myself.'

As Will watched him walk towards the restrooms, he came to a terrible realisation. Perhaps the pressure of working in bomb disposal was finally catching up with Jack. Perhaps his latest squeeze had had enough of his philandering behaviour. Or perhaps he was back on the cocaine or the heroin. The knowledge his late, great mentor and teacher Dr Bradstock had imparted to him during his clinical apprenticeship came flooding back, and for a minute or two, his memories took him back to the Hammersmith Hospital and Jack's amazing recovery from syphilis ten years earlier.

'So, young Will,' Jack said as he rejoined his brother at the table. 'How's tricks?'

'I'm fine, Jack. Just fine. But how are things with you?'

'They'd be one hell of a lot better if I had a pint of stout in front of me.'

'God, I'm sorry. Let me get you one.'

As Will stood waiting to be served, he looked back and saw Jack slumped in his chair, his head bowed and his body crumpled. He grabbed the glass of dark ale and returned to the table. 'There you are.'

Jack took the glass and downed three quarters of it in one go. He looked up at Will with a resigned expression on his face and wiped his lips. 'I'm fucked.'

Will looked back at him and waited.

'I can't feel my feet, which means I'm walking oddly. I've pins and needles in my hands and it's a wonder I can even hold this glass without spilling anything. My vision's getting blurry and my joints are stiff as hell. If I'm being honest, the only thing that isn't stiff is my todger. And that, brother, as you know, is my raison d'être.'

Since Will was still listening but not volunteering a reply, Jack continued. 'Look at this,' he said, pulling a lighted candle in the centre of the table towards him and putting his hand in the flame for several seconds. Will pushed it away again when his brother's skin started to blister and he could smell burning.

'I can't feel heat at all.'

Jack was smiling, putting a brave face on it, but Will could tell he was bewildered. It was the first time he had ever seen his brother looking frightened. Jack grabbed Will's forearm and leaned forward. 'I can't be doing this. What the hell is causing it? You're the doctor. What's happening to me? And don't give me any of your watered-down claptrap. Don't sugar-coat it. And don't dress it up with your fancy euphemisms and medical jargon. I know you too well and I'll see straight through you. So just tell me straight, will you, little brother?'

Will took a sip of his ale. He held up a beer mat and asked Jack to read the words on it.

'Young's Bitter is Better Bitter,' he said. Will saw his brother's pupils constrict as he read the words. Now he held up the candle in front of Jack's face. His pupils did not react at all. Instead of contracting in the bright light as they should, they stayed stubbornly fixed and dilated in the dim light of the pub.

'I'm afraid you're ill.'

'I know that, you daft pillock. You don't need a flaming medical degree to tell me that. But what is it?'

'It's neurosyphilis, Jack.'

His brother nodded almost imperceptibly, as if he'd suspected it. He certainly knew the word 'syphilis', but the 'neuro' prefix was new to him. 'But I had the syphilis over ten years ago. Bradstock treated me for it. He got rid of it with all that malaria stuff and those induced fevers. I left hospital right as rain. Been all right up until now. What's going on?'

'Back then, you had the acute infection. Bradstock was able to deal with that and your initial symptoms all improved. But in some people, the infection becomes dormant. Then, after ten years or more, it can re-emerge in a different form, affecting your blood vessels and nervous system.'

'That's the "neuro" bit?'

Will nodded. 'It affects the nerves in the spinal cord, the nerves that transmit pain, and those which are responsible for temperature sensation and the positional awareness of your joints.'

'Hence the pins and needles and lack of feeling in my hands and feet. Similarly, my floppy todger and my . . . capacity for self-immolation.'

'It's called *tabes dorsalis*, Jack.' He lingered over the syllables *tay-bees*.

'As in rabies?'

Will smiled and adopted a look of feigned exasperation.

'If that's an attempt at Cockney rhyming slang, it's a poor one. But no, it's nothing like rabies. You get that from dogs.'

'To be fair, I have been with a few dogs in my time.' He chuckled despite his predicament. 'Seems they've come back to bite me.'

Jack had asked his brother to be totally candid, but Will did not have the heart to tell him that dementia, paranoia and psychosis would likely follow.

'So what's the treatment?'

Will picked up his glass and sipped. 'It's too late for that. The damage is done, Jack. I'm sorry.'

'What about this new wonder drug you say Grace is working on? Is that worth a go?'

'It can't repair the nerve cells. Nor the blood vessels around the heart. Besides, there's precious little of it to be had, and what we have is reserved exclusively for the military.'

'I'm military.'

'Fighting overseas.'

Jack was silent for a few seconds, weighing it all up. Then he nodded vigorously, stood, shook Will's hand and hugged him. 'Thanks, Will, I appreciate that. Back in the day, you'd have bottled that. Can't have been easy.' Will blinked back a tear.

'Don't be a soppy bastard,' said Jack. 'I'll be all right. Can you do me a favour, though? Don't worry Aunt Clara with it. Or anyone else.'

'Sure.'

Jack turned to go.

'Jack?'

'What?'

'You sure you should still be working? You're defusing bombs, for Christ's sake. Your vision, your coordination, fine hand movements and sensation. Shouldn't you tell someone? It can't be safe.'

'What, and be sent home with no pay? What would I live on? Bugger that. I'll be just fine, you'll see.'

He turned to go again but then turned straight back.

'Give my love to Grace, would you? Danny boy and Emily? And Kitty?'

'I will. But you can pass it on yourself next time you see them.'

'Look forward to it, brother. You take care, now.'

And with that, and a cheeky smile, he was gone.

81

SS Führungshauptamt, Delft

'You are not Margherita Vogel any more than I am Hermann Göring,' said Altmann menacingly. 'Who are you?'

Liese said nothing. This man was repugnant. Despite his sadistic torture, not to mention the burns she'd sustained in the blast, she had revealed nothing.

Now she found herself in a squalid yard behind the town hall the SS were using as their headquarters, her hands tied behind her back and fastened to a rusty metal ring in the brick wall. She had refused a blindfold and faced the six men of the firing squad with serenity.

Altmann stood in front of her, his face inches from her own. She could already feel her burns starting to contract and felt some ironic consolation that she would not live long enough to end up looking like her tormentor.

'Any last requests?' he said with a self-satisfied grin. 'A cigarette, perhaps? No, probably not. As a doctor, you would not approve of such a filthy habit. Some say smoking even causes premature death.'

Liese regarded him with utter disdain.

'A last meal, perhaps? Without pork, of course, Miss Fischl.'

She looked up sharply at this.

'Oh yes. We know who you are. You deceived us for quite a while, didn't you? You are smart.'

Liese remained silent. She would not be goaded.

'So, no last requests, then?'

'I could use a gas mask,' she said defiantly. 'Your breath stinks.'

He took a step back and slapped her with the back of his hand. Her head snapped to the side and her mouth filled with blood.

'Altmann!' yelled another officer behind him. 'Just get on with it.'

He shrugged, stepped back, and stood behind the men holding the rifles.

'*Zielen!*' he commanded.

They raised their guns and aimed. Liese looked up at the azure-blue sky and recalled her idyllic childhood with her parents. She remembered the games she had played with her father in their lovely garden in the leafy suburb of Oranienburg, and swimming in the pond with her mother on hot summer days. Fleetingly, she wondered if she had made any real difference in fighting the fascists. She realised she had always been prepared for this eventuality. Then, as if being woken from a dream, she heard the staccato sound of submachine gunfire roaring loudly in her ears.

82

Sandhurst Road School, Catford

Jack had taken the call at seven o'clock that morning, but arrived at the scene two and a half hours later. He had told the bomb disposal team not to start without him. Huwie saw him shuffling slowly towards him, his shoulders hunched and a look of dejection on his face. Jack had become a shadow of his former self, and however much Huwie had tried, he had not been able to shake his friend out of his decline.

The device was about a yard long and looked as if it weighed about forty stone.

It was a monster. A safety cordon two hundred metres square was already in place, so Jack and Huwie got to work. Huwie noted that Jack's usual bonhomie was still absent and any attempts at conversation were met with a grunt. Perhaps he was just hung-over. After the outer portal cover had been removed and the innards exposed, Jack peered inside and fished about with his fingers for a while. He straightened up, looked at Huwie, and sighed. 'Listen, mate,' he said, 'I've got this. No point in us both being here.'

Huwie was taken aback. Up until now, they had always worked together, but Jack was the boss. 'You sure, Jack?'

'Yeah. Go on, old son. Sod off, would you? And not just

over there in the rubble. Get your sorry arse over there with the other lads, out of harm's way.'

Huwie felt uneasy.

Jack took ten pounds from his top pocket and handed it to him.

'Stick that on the horses for me, would you? I fancy that Belle of the Ball running in the two-thirty at Newmarket. Twenty-to-one on.'

'You can stick it on yourself later, when we go down the bookies. What's the matter with you?'

'I don't know how long this'll take me, and only one of us can get their hands in here anyway. So, hop it. Off you go, mate.'

Reluctantly, Huwie stepped back from the bomb and loped away towards the fire trucks. Just as he reached them, a massive explosion behind him almost lifted him off his feet. Instantly, he realised that Jack had made his first mistake. Whether or not it was deliberate was another matter.

83

Kennemerstrand Beach, Netherlands

Emily and Bembe had broken all the rules. He was an RAF fighter pilot whose services were badly needed. If he failed to return to base for his next duty, he would be considered AWOL and would be court-martialled. Emily had promised her father she would do nothing riskier than the role she was already undertaking for the WAAF, and the RAF had barred women pilots from engaging in any activities involving confrontation with the enemy. Yet Emily was hell-bent on picking up her aunt Kitty. Once Bembe had learned of her plan to fly there alone, he was never going to let that happen.

Now they were only ten minutes away from the beach at Kennemerstrand.

The Westland Lysander was easy enough to fly; the question was whether Emily's repairs on its damaged undercarriage would withstand a safe landing on the soft sand. The plane had been standing idle in the hangar near Oxford since the beginning of the war. They would find out soon enough.

Nor could they be sure Kitty would successfully make the rendezvous, but the message two days previously had sounded positive and the risk of her being captured was too awful to contemplate. It was only because the local

Resistance network had been betrayed that they had become involved at all. SOE had deemed a rescue mission too hazardous, and resources were stretched. But a chance conversation at Duxford aerodrome had led to Emily discovering more information and she had decided to take matters into her own hands. Now they had nearly completed their descent, with only the light of the moon on the water to guide them. Bembe expertly glided the plane on to the sand at stall speed only. The flats and struts had deployed automatically, and although the wheels made deep ruts in the sand, they did not sink into it. Hoping they would not be spotted by enemy patrols likely to be in the area, Bembe turned the plane around and taxied back to where they had landed, ready to take off again, this time into the wind. Then they waited.

After five agonising minutes, there was still no sign of Kitty, and several sets of headlights could be seen snaking over the dunes towards them.

As Bembe opened the throttle to prepare for take-off, a shadowy figure stumbled out from among the grass on top of the sand dunes and started running towards them. Her long, matted hair stuck to the side of her face, her cheeks hollow and her eyes wide and wild, Kitty looked exhausted. Emily threw open the door of the plane and her aunt climbed in, almost out of breath. Bembe pulled back hard on the stick, and the stubby little black-camouflaged aircraft jerked forward. The damp sand hampered its forward momentum initially, but once up to speed, the aircraft seemed to lift out of it and accelerate. At the same time, shots rang out from below them and bullets peppered the wings and the thin Duralumin fuselage. Bembe banked the plane steeply to the left to give the soldiers below less of a target. Seconds later, they were over the sea and in the clear. Bembe's shoulder was bleeding profusely where he had been hit, but he was smiling and giving the thumbs-up to the two women, who were hugging each other affectionately in the back of the plane.

84

Malmedy, Belgium, December 1944

Will ducked as yet another shell exploded near the turret of the chateau that had been transformed into a makeshift hospital. He could hardly believe the number of wounded men being brought in. The maimed man on the stretcher before him was holding loops of his own intestines in both bloodied hands and crying out in pain, begging for morphine. Next in line was an officer with a terrible head wound; part of his brain was exposed, with a cavity the size of a golf ball. He was incoherent and agitated. It was impossible to choose who to attend to first. How could he prioritise the men when so many were in such a critical condition? It was all very well in theory having the medical facilities of the field hospital deployed as near to the fighting as possible, but how could anyone be expected to calmly operate with bombs and air attacks raining down incessantly? Only an hour ago, an ambulance that had drawn up outside had suffered a direct hit, killing all inside, including two nurses and an orderly. Clearly marked as an ambulance with the bold and unmistakable Red Cross symbol emblazoned on its roof and sides, the enemy were demonstrating once again their total disregard for the Geneva Convention. As far as they were concerned, the casualties and the hospital itself were all legitimate targets. In this last desperate throw of the dice, the Ardennes counter-offensive was an all-or-nothing affair for the Nazis. Their plan was to prevent the Allies taking the strategic port of Antwerp, split their lines, and then encircle and destroy four of their opponents' armies. If they could achieve this, so late in the war, they would at least stand a chance of being able to negotiate a peace treaty, offering much more favourable terms. They had already executed 150 American soldiers not far from Malmedy, and the Allied wounded and the medical teams treating them would only hamper their chance of victory: a patched-up soldier returned to the frontline could still claim the lives of German fighters. The scenario was kill-or-be-killed, and this was the environment in which Will was struggling to work.

In one corner of the chaotic mass of patients lying about in the hall was a lieutenant, half his face shot away, his lower jaw and tongue missing. Goodness knows how he was still alive, never mind conscious. He had no prospect of surviving such injuries. Will could only offer carefully chosen words of reassurance and administer morphine for the pain. Speed was of the essence: decisive intervention would save lives. Will could not be in two places at once, and it was a terrible dilemma having to decide which patients to treat and which to leave. One man had already lost an arm because in the chaos of triage, a forgotten ligature had cut off the circulation for too long.

The scene reminded Will of the carnage he had witnessed as a lad all those years ago at the Somme. At least there had been fewer civilians there, and very rarely had there been any children caught up in the bloodshed. Still, it had taken him years to come to terms with the appalling images in his head. The nightmares he would likely experience for the rest of his life. Grace had kept him updated about penicillin over the last few months, and it seemed almost unbelievable that in her letters, she had not exaggerated its potential effects. D-Day had proved penicillin's worth and it truly was a miracle that deep, penetrating wounds could now be treated and cured long before the victims succumbed to infection. The procedure was to surgically debride the cavity, sprinkle in the seemingly magical powder, cutting away all dead tissue and any shrapnel, and then leave the wound open, or leave antiseptic dressings on without agitating them. This protocol was transforming the standard medical approach and bringing remarkable results.

Just then, Will was snapped out of his reverie by an officer barking orders, and the arrival of several Jeeps and armoured vehicles. The town was about to be overrun by advancing Germans, supported by Panzers and a large contingent of heavily armed infantry. Evacuation of those who could physically stand or be carried was imperative. There were many who could not be moved, by dint of their condition, and Will and most of his surgical team of orderlies and nurses could not in all conscience bring themselves to abandon those too sick to leave. These poor souls had been through enough. It was decided that all the nurses would go, and a plan was hastily drawn up that three doctors and five orderlies would stay behind.

Everyone volunteered to remain, but since most were needed to transport the sick, it was agreed that drawing straws seemed to be the fairest way to decide who would and who would not be evacuated. The choice was stark. Either flee with the wounded and disabled, and expect to be strafed and bombed all the way, or stay with the critically injured and dying, and either be taken prisoner for the rest of the war or shot in cold-blooded retribution.

As the medics gathered together, the most senior among them held out his fist. In it, he clutched eight wooden tongue depressors, with only the top parts showing. Three of them had been broken in half. Whoever selected one of these would stay behind with his patients. Six doctors made their selection, four picking an intact tongue depressor and another two pulling out a broken one. It was Will's turn to pick next in this extraordinary game of destiny roulette, and as his colleagues looked on, he made his choice. He felt totally resigned to whatever fate had in store for him, and it all hinged on which of the two remaining wooden sticks he would pick. One intact, one broken. He reached out and plucked the nearest one from the officer's hand.

85

SOE, London

Kitty's debrief at St Ermin's Hotel with Sir Andrew Morrison was almost as fraught as her escape from Delft. 'You were lucky we were able to extract you. Delft was crawling with Nazis, and several of our operatives put their lives on the line to get you out.'

'I realise that, Sir Andrew, and I'm very grateful to them.'

'I hope they live long enough to appreciate it. How exactly your niece and her beau were made aware of your plight is still something of a mystery to me. Information was leaked, and that will need investigation. Heads may roll.'

The SOE director picked up his pipe and sucked on it.

'However, I'm pleased you are safely back home with the job done. Dr Schmidt's factory was totally destroyed, as I believe you are aware, and as far as we know, Liese's actions at her laboratory in Delft prevented the enemy obtaining any materials enabling them to start afresh.' His tone softened. 'I'm sorry to have to inform you that Miss Fischl, Liese, died at the hands of the Nazis exactly a week after she was captured. Our information is that she revealed nothing, even under interrogation.'

Kitty had feared as much but it was still devastating news. Liese had been the closest and dearest friend she had ever had. She would miss her terribly, but was proud in the knowledge of what she had achieved.

Sir Andrew Morrison saw the tears in her eyes and allowed Kitty a few moments to compose herself.

'You have been extremely brave, Mrs San Grefria, and you have served the SOE very satisfactorily. We took a big risk sending you to the Netherlands.'

'Thank you, sir. But there is still work to do, and with my language skills and experience, there is more I can offer.'

'Not anymore, I fear.'

Kitty was disappointed. Were her services no longer required? She had done her very best, but was she no longer to be trusted?

'Your cover is blown. Your name, identity and appearance will have been widely circulated to the Abwehr and their satellite organisations. Returning to the fray would be tantamount to suicide, and I won't allow it.'

Kitty nodded. She knew he was right. 'I understand.'

'I'd like to thank you personally for your services to the country, and I'll do what I can to mitigate any repercussions from your family's breach of protocol.'

'Thank you, sir.'

'The fortunes of war are turning, Mrs San Grefria, and with the help of our allies . . . allies at least for the time being . . . the conflict is reaching its conclusion in our favour. I'm reliably informed your husband's army division is currently stationed south-west of Rennes. He is due some well-earned leave, I believe. I hope you can resume your married life together and catch up on the time you have lost.' He looked up from the papers in front of him and regarded Kitty gravely. 'But you're stood down for now. You have never worked for us. SOE has no record of you, and you will remain bound by the Official Secrets Act for the rest of your life.' He stood, nodded curtly, and shook Kitty's hand.

He pressed his intercom and spoke to his secretary. 'Please see Mrs San Grefria out, would you, Isobel?'

86

314 Chiswick High Road, London

Aunt Clara had taken the news badly. She had known Jack's job was fraught with danger, but she'd always had confidence he would survive. Jack had managed to escape from every scrap he had ever been in – and there had been many. She had cried herself to sleep for several nights, but had not been able to share her grief or seek solace from Will or Kitty, as she did not know where they were, and had no means of reaching them even if she did. They would discover the loss of Jack soon enough, she realised, but she could not bring herself to tell Robbie. News of his eldest son's death could easily send him back into depression. She would give it time.

Clara's hip was playing up badly in the damp chill and she'd had to stop and rub her leg a few times on the way back from the grocer shop in Chiswick High Road. It had not helped that she'd had to queue for over an hour just to use her ration card for the few measly provisions still available. In her basket she carried her weekly allowance: eight ounces of sugar, two ounces of cooking fat, eight ounces of cheese, and two ounces of tea. As usual, all the eggs had already gone by the time she had limped there, and there was no point bringing home any American-made egg powder as Robbie stubbornly refused to stomach it. 'Beggars can't be choosers,'

Clara would always tell him, but at least she had secured the four ounces of ham and bacon she knew he would like for his dinner.

Robbie greeted her cheerfully as she came in. He was having one of his better days. Daniel had worked wonders with him since he had started work at the Maudsley, and his patience and care had enabled Robbie to emerge from the deepest of chronic depressions and return home to live with his sister. He could still be morose and moody at times, but Clara and Daniel were encouraged by his increasing episodes of engagement.

'Thought you'd left home,' he mumbled, sitting forward in his favourite armchair.

'I had to queue as usual. I bought you a lovely bit of ham and bacon for your tea, if you'd like it.'

Robbie considered the offer and nodded. 'I think I would.'

Clara smiled and hobbled off into the little kitchen to prepare his meal. The return of his appetite always seemed to mirror a happier state of mind.

'Thank you, sis.'

She unpacked her basket and felt guilty about keeping her brother in the dark about his eldest son. As she cooked, she continued to talk to him from the other room, maintaining her monologue and imparting any bits of news she thought he might find interesting. She brewed the tea, spread a little lard on to a slice of fried bread, and placed two rashers of streaky bacon on the top, just as her brother liked it. She put the teacup and the plate on a tray for Robbie to perch on his lap, and carried it into the lounge. Careful not to trip over the carpet with her dragging leg, she placed the tray down on the little side table beside him. 'Here we are,' she said, 'your favourite.'

Robbie was sitting right back in the armchair with his head cocked strangely to one side, staring vacantly into the corner. He was a grey colour, the same drab hue as the rainclouds she had seen in the sky earlier. There was no sign of him breathing. She knew. Instantly, she knew. Tears filled her eyes and she dabbed at them with a napkin. But for the first time in as long as she could remember, there seemed to be no trace of that anxiety and infinite sadness on Robbie's face. There was no outward sign of the emotional trauma he had suffered over the last years. Finally, his agony was over and he was at peace; at rest in the same humble little house where, in the bedroom upstairs twenty-five years earlier, Kitty had been given life and his dearest and most beloved wife Evie had had hers cruelly stolen away.

87

Bellevaux-Ligneuville, Near Malmedy, Belgium

When the Germans arrived at the hospital, several of the walking wounded were rounded up and herded into trucks. Will had protested, and had tried to determine where they were being taken and who would be caring for them, but he was unceremoniously pushed aside and threatened by two stony-faced panzergrenadiers armed with rifles. He pushed one of the weapons to one side and got the butt of the other man's rifle across his face for his efforts. The skin split across his cheekbone, and blood sprang out and ran down his cheek and neck into his collar. For a moment, he was completely dazed. Then he was ushered into a waiting canvas-covered truck and driven away at speed with what was left of his hospital staff. Behind him, he heard the unmistakable sound of machine-gun fire coming from inside the hospital. It could not have been a two-way fight as those who had been left behind had either been bedbound or unable to move. Will had heard rumours that this enemy was under strict orders to show no mercy, but this was the first time he had ever witnessed first-hand the truth in the rumour.

The road was bumpy and uneven. As they were jostled about in the back of the truck, an orderly, who had demanded to know where they were being taken, was knocked unconscious. At the end of a muddy, winding farm track they were forced out of the truck and herded into a dilapidated hay barn. Will knew there could only be one explanation. He had heard about the Einsatzgruppen, the death squads comprised of paramilitary personnel from the Schutzstaffel. But he had always imagined the Panzer Division commanders would conduct themselves within the acceptable conventions of warfare. He was wrong.

As he was lined up against the far wall of the barn along with the others, the German officer barked further orders at his men, who threw open the wide barn doors to allow another vehicle to reverse into the opening. The tailgate dropped and the canvas sheeting at the back was swept aside to reveal a man seated behind a machine gun mounted in the rear.

There were many ways in which Will might have imagined confronting his own demise, but it had never involved being murdered in cold blood.

Will thought of Grace, and of Emily and Daniel. Resigned to his fate, he felt no great sadness for himself. But as they were made to wait, he became aware of raised, strident voices outside. A sanitätsoffizier, in his recognisable medical officer's uniform, emerged from behind the barn door and bellowed at the other military official. They yelled at one another, their faces crimson with anger. Eventually, the commanding panzergrenadier backed down, although he was obviously furious about losing face in front of his soldiers. He nodded curtly at the doctor, but not before delivering what appeared to be a threatening message. Will could not understand what was being said, but guessed it might be a threat to report the doctor to a higher authority. The man then stormed out with the soldiers following in his wake, and the truck with the machine gun packed up and drove away. The doctor glanced at Will's RAMC insignia and came forward holding out his hand. Will took it. The doctor had apparently saved their lives.

'Royal Army Medical Corps, I see.'

'That's correct.'

'The German medical corps have been ordered to perform many tasks in the futile prosecution of the war,' he said in perfect English, 'and some have been quite unsavoury. The last order in particular I was not prepared to obey.'

'I'm glad,' Will said. 'Thank you.'

'The outcome of our great leader's masterplan is now inevitable. There is no sense in any more unnecessary slaughter. My name is Christoff.'

'I'm Will.'

'The immediate future is obvious. Long-term, who knows. I studied medicine at Cambridge for five years before the war, Will. I much admired your English traditions and your academic disciplines. Perhaps we will see each other again one day in happier circumstances. Although for me, after today, I fear that may be doubtful.'

Christoff pointed to a bag of medical supplies his men had left in the corner of the barn.

'There are dressings, antiseptic and medicines in there. None of your penicillin, though, which I have heard so much about. You seem to have beaten us there as well.'

The German doctor looked again at the men standing next to Will in their bloodied uniforms, some leaning on crutches. 'Look after your men. I expect your advancing army will be here quite shortly to relieve you. Good luck.'

88

Janowska Concentration Camp

Jürgen Altmann had caught up with the frail, skeletal woman in her striped shirt and trousers. In her chronically weakened state, she had only just managed to reach the outer perimeter of the forest. The roofs of the huts in the camp, from which she had escaped with a handful of others, were still visible through the trees in the distance.

When he shouted at her, she froze. She turned in horror, as she recognised the voice of the man in front of her. Her instinct for survival made her look around frantically, but for what, she did not know. Her breath came in rapid, shallow gasps: little puffs of mist in front of her face as the warm moisture mingled with the cold air.

Altmann stepped in front of her and looked into her expressionless eyes, lingering for several seconds before swearing a few quiet obscenities under his breath. Then he smiled crookedly and emptied the eight-round magazine of his Walther P38 into her body. Her fragile form jerked like a marionette and she fell backwards.

Three of the bullets passed straight through and lodged with a dull slap in the rough bark of the tree behind her. The executioner raised his eyebrows at the sound and a quiet grunt of pleasure came from his throat. He stood over the woman's limp remains, fascinated by the blood spatter pattern on her ripped cotton clothing.

The sudden, sharp click of a weapon being cocked made him spin round. Facing him were five Russian soldiers from Marshal Georgy Zhukov's Red Army Division. In the centre stood a formidable-looking woman wearing a Soviet military officer's NKVD uniform, and brandishing a Tokarev TT-33 semi-automatic aimed straight at him. Altmann had just emptied his own gun. He would not have stood a chance anyway. The four soldiers either side of their leader looked well-armed, and murderous, though the fact that a woman led the group gave him hope. Women were the weaker sex, in his opinion. They were less aggressive and, he assumed, naturally more given to the capture and imprisonment of enemy soldiers rather than their execution. He could hardly believe his luck. He had never had any trouble with women. They had their uses, and he had always taken pleasure in taking what he wanted from them. He was confident he could handle this Russian woman, too, who now stared at the corpse on the ground. His mind was racing. It was unfortunate he had been caught in the act, but he could not imagine the Russian would be too bothered about that. From what he had heard, Stalin's Red Army was busy imprisoning and slaughtering plenty of citizens of their own. Besides, the war was nearly over. If he could bluster his way out of the situation and surrender, he could look forward to a life of freedom.

The woman was several inches taller than any of the four men beside her, and had considerably broader shoulders. Her face was wide, and inscrutable. Her khaki gymnastyorka jacket was adorned with shoulder boards showing her superior rank.

She took her eyes off the dead woman and looked back at

Altmann, stepping directly in front of him. She seemed to be scrutinising the network of scars on his face, his drooping left lower eyelid and the ugly curl of his upper lip.

He turned his empty pistol around in his hands, held on to the muzzle, and offered her the grip. It was a clear expression of surrender. She ignored it. Thinking she might not be sure what to do, Altmann presented it again. Once more, she showed no interest.

'I was following my orders,' he blurted out in German. 'I was just doing my duty.'

'*Ja*,' she said, in his native tongue. 'Every soldier must do their duty.'

Her next words were spoken quietly and calmly in Russian, which meant Altmann failed to understand them. 'Germany had an alliance with my country. First you broke it and then you invaded, destroying my home city. You left half a million people dead or missing. A further million casualties whose lives will never be the same again. I fought with the 51st Army. In Stalingrad.'

Altmann tensed. He recognised that last word: Stalingrad. That had been a bitter fight, but at least it gave him an opportunity to respond. Conversation was good. He knew the longer it continued, the greater the chance of his being spared. He had not been to Stalingrad himself; he had not been sent to the Eastern Front at all. He had always managed to dodge that particular posting. But he knew a lot about it. The Nazi propaganda machine had been very active, convincing the German people of their all-conquering army's crushing victories.

The woman was still talking. 'My two brothers were killed. My father perished on the Frozen Steppe. My husband was tortured, then shot. My sister, raped.'

Altmann tried to speak but the woman was now shouting. 'Murderer! Rapist!' she yelled, her spittle peppering his face. She glanced again at the body on the ground, stepped back from Altmann, and barked instructions to the other soldiers. Two ran over and tied his arms behind his back. Unexpectedly, the woman undid his belt, and his trousers dropped to the top of his boots. In an instant, she took out her serrated NR-40 combat knife and sliced through both sides of his underpants. They fell away, leaving him exposed. Altmann was terrified. The woman looked at his shrivelled manhood and smiled at him mockingly. She turned to the other men. 'Not a Russian-built weapon, is it?'

Two of them shared furtive glances, but took care not to laugh.

'So small?' she said. 'I can't imagine you or anyone else will miss it.'

She gripped the end of his penis, pulled the soft flesh towards her, and sliced the base of the organ away from his groin in one swift movement. Altmann screamed. A crimson spray splashed on the ground and a spreading pool of it collected between his feet. His mouth was open and his jaw was working but he could not seem to make any sound.

'No longer a rapist,' she said, before quietly issuing further commands.

The men took out some rope and tied him firmly to the same tree his own bullets had pockmarked only minutes earlier. If Altmann had understood Russian, he would have been able to translate the words *target practice.*

He assumed the four men lining up in front of him were forming a firing squad. So, he thought, at least a quick death. The first bullet struck his right knee, shattering the joint and the bone adjacent to it. Altmann screamed in agony and leaned to his left to take as much weight off it as he could. The second bullet put a large hole in his other knee and he collapsed against the coarse rope holding him upright. Two more bullets found their target in his shoulders.

'No longer a torturer,' the woman said, in German.

Altmann heard the words. The blood loss was mounting but it was not yet life-threatening. The pain and the shock were beginning to overwhelm him. He mumbled something in German. A curse of some kind.

The Russian officer raised the Tokarev pistol and shot Altmann in the right side of the face. His head jerked sideways and thudded against the tree.

'No longer so ugly,' she said. 'You look . . . better, now. More . . . symmetrical.'

She cocked the gun again and the men under her command looked on as she shot Altmann squarely through the heart. Twice.

'No longer a killer.'

89

Bergen-Belsen Concentration Camp, 15 April 1945

Daniel was driven into the camp in an armoured M3 half-track two hours after the first tank had passed through the gates. He was one of the first medical officers on the scene, but the only psychiatrist. Having witnessed the stark realities of war in the previous year, he had almost become inured to the horrors of the carnage, but nothing could have prepared him for this. Behind the wire fences, silent, emaciated prisoners stood two- or three-deep, their stick-thin arms reaching out towards their liberators, their soulless eyes in their deep sockets peering out from skeletal faces. Some were dressed in dull, striped rags, others were not clothed at all, apparently oblivious to their nakedness and the dirt and grime ingrained in their parchment-like skin. Mouths were open but no words were spoken. Behind them, other bodies shuffled about, their movements laboured and sluggish, their arms hanging limply by their sides, their heads bowed and their gaze fixed directly on the ground in front of them. The stench and pall of death was everywhere.

As the vehicle turned in behind the fence, Daniel saw what lay beyond. Corpses as far as the eye could see. Bodies piled in heaps. Bodies being used by other inmates as furniture. As he stepped down from the vehicle, a woman threw herself on the ground in front of him, held on to the tails of his greatcoat, and kissed his boots. He bent down and gently helped her up. 'You are free,' he said. 'You are all free. And we will look after you now.'

The woman staggered backwards, unable to comprehend his words. How long has she been living in hope? Daniel wondered. There was no mad rush towards the rescuers, no chaotic surge forward in a desperate bid for food, medicines, or clothing. There was hardly any reaction at all. A few seemed to understand that their ordeal might finally be over, but there was no emotional response whatsoever. All sentiment and hope seemed to have died along with the tens of thousands of prisoners who had already perished there.

Around the huts, emaciated shells of human beings moved on hands and knees; others lay in the doorways among the dead, those who had stayed where they had fallen. Daniel could barely believe what he encountered inside. More victims on soiled wooden bunks and floors, where people had been sleeping three-abreast. No sanitation, and human excrement everywhere. Some of those who were still alive would not be for long. The signs of advanced cholera, typhus, colic, diarrhoea, TB and sepsis were unmistakable. A few were suffering from gangrene, and nearly all had skin covered in boils, sores and abscesses.

A lance corporal from the British Army film and photographic unit stepped inside the hut to find Daniel, looked around, and promptly threw up. When he had recovered, he dutifully took the pictures he needed and came over. 'According to my sergeant, there's around forty-five thousand poor souls still here,' he said. 'The Wehrmacht moved many out in the last few weeks – the ones they didn't murder, that is – and left these poor buggers to fend for themselves. No food. No water. Nothing. They left them to die.'

'I'm afraid many still will. We've come too late. But we're here now.'

'But where do we start, mate? Apparently hundreds of them died yesterday, some soon after eating. Most would have died anyway, I guess, from starvation or disease, but this is a challenge.'

Daniel had heard about refeeding syndrome, from the experiences of other liberated camps; Auschwitz-Birkenau in particular. Severely starved inmates had not been able to tolerate the relatively rich British Army rations and had died as a result. A concoction they had been given, Bengal famine mix, was excessively sweet, and something in the make-up of normal feed altered the chemical processes in their emaciated bodies, causing a fatal reaction. The medics had tried intravenous feeding, but that had induced terror and panic.

'It seems diluted, watery soup and glucose drinks are best to start with.'

The lance corporal nodded at Daniel and winced at the sight of a couple lying in a mortal embrace on the floor behind him.

'I'll be getting on then, Doc,' he said. 'They're burning down huts out there and I want to capture it on film. I can't get the volley of shots our chaps will be firing off in salute on my camera, but images of the unfurling of the Union Flag and the flamethrower that will start the blaze should do the trick for our cinema audiences back home.' He turned and left.

Daniel wondered if audiences would be able to stomach such scenes. Churchill's government would want to emphasise the enormity of the deeds of the foe the British people had helped to overcome, but for many ordinary citizens, divorced from the reality of war and unwilling to accept its dreadful human cost, it would likely be a step too far. Easier for sensitive or indifferent folk to turn a blind eye. The immediate medical challenge here would be to treat illness and starvation. They would not be able to save them all, but, physically at least, thousands would be restored to freedom and health in civilian life. The psychological scars, however, would stay with them forever, the sheer scale of the brutality inflicted upon these victims causing them to suffer more fear, anxiety, depression, and, ironically, even guilt.

He heard the crackling of the flames as a hut was razed to the ground outside. There was no celebratory cheering. No cursing of an enemy now fled. Just an eerie silence. The insipid sun above them was shining, but it seemed to shine without warmth.

Daniel's knees went weak and he sat down on the edge of a broken wooden box. As a psychiatrist, he assumed he had known everything there was to know about the complex workings of the human mind. He had thought he had grasped its scope for ambition, its desires and emotions, as well as its capacity for good and evil. He had thought he could rationalise any type of human behaviour. Now, he realised he would need time to recover from an experience that had only just begun. Later, he might very well need to consult a psychiatrist himself.

It was impossible not to feel desolate in this man-made tomb, where it was unclear who was dead or who was still alive. Daniel was a compassionate young man who only wanted to do good in this world, to ease people's anxieties, to find goodness, generosity and love in his own and other people's hearts. But how could that be possible now?

Seconds later, an orderly he knew stepped into the hut and cleared his throat.

'Sorry, sir, but you're needed.'

'Another hut like this?'

'Worse, I'm afraid, sir. Much worse.'

90

Houses of Parliament, London, 3 p.m., 8 May 1945

Fitz and Stephen sat behind their desks at Westminster, having tuned into the BBC on the small Bakelite wireless to listen intently to Churchill's long-awaited broadcast.

'Yesterday morning . . . General Jodl, the representative of the German High Command, and of Grand Admiral Doenitz, the designated head of the German State, signed the act of unconditional surrender . . .'

Fitz jumped up with a huge grin on his face and came over to Stephen, shook his hand vigorously, and gave him a lingering hug.

'It's over,' said his faithful assistant. 'It's finally over.'

'The German war is therefore at an end,' the prime minister continued, '. . . we must now devote all our strength and resources to the completion of our tasks both at home and abroad. Advance, Britannia! Long live the cause of freedom! God save the King!'

Outside, in Parliament Square, Fitz and Stephen could hear the cheering of the gathering masses who were filling the streets from Birdcage Walk and the Mall all the way to the Queen Victoria Monument in front of Buckingham Palace, where Churchill would later stand on the balcony with King George VI and Queen Elizabeth. The two men looked through the window and saw hundreds of people wearing red, white and blue making their way towards Trafalgar Square, embracing, singing and dancing as they went. For a moment Fitz thought he saw his estranged wife walking arm in arm with her newfound literary friends, but then whoever it was became swallowed in the melee and he dismissed the idea.

'You heard him, Stephen. "We must devote our strength and resources to the completion of our tasks, both at home and abroad." He can say that again!'

'I agree. We may have won the war, but we're billions in debt, the economy is in chaos, we've nothing to export, and we can't afford to import anything but the most basic foodstuffs. It looks like it will be the end of Lend-Lease, too, before very long. We're effectively a bankrupt nation.'

'An inevitable consequence of war, I suppose. But looking on the bright side, it gives the Labour party a wonderful opportunity, don't you see?'

'How? We're in such a mess. Churchill's popularity is still soaring. His approval rating in all the polls has never fallen below seventy-eight per cent. In the latest one, it reached eighty-three. What chance has Labour got?'

'Every chance, I believe. Look, I have the greatest admiration for Churchill. He's been an inspirational leader in the war and is a great orator. With his rousing speeches, he single-handedly mobilised the English language and sent it into battle. But these very qualities make him less suited to what's needed next.

'Bevan's plan for a welfare state may be a bit radical, but his heart's in the right place. They genuinely want to repay the working classes for the sacrifices they've made and fulfil a promise to them. Can you imagine it? A health service that is available to everyone, whatever their class or background. A free service based on clinical need, not the individual's ability to pay. Medical care where standards remain high wherever you live, extra beds and social care for our wounded heroes and those left homeless or unemployed after the war. It's a dream come true. We can build on the wartime emergency medical service we provided in adversity and improve on it. We'll have free medicines, and dental and visual services, too. The idea has captured the imagination of the masses and it's what they deserve. What they demand. My brother-in-law, Will, is passionate about it.'

He turned round and looked at Stephen again, who nodded.

'Unfortunately, not everyone else is. Including many Tories,' Stephen warned. 'Or doctors, apart from Will, as I understand it.'

'To hell with them. The people want change, Stephen, and I'd put money on Churchill being beaten. He faced a titanic challenge during the war and the nation owes him a huge debt of gratitude. But now the electorate will want fresh, radical ideas. More equality in both wealth *and* health.'

'And if they don't get it?'

'They will. Otherwise, Churchill and his fellow opponents will risk finding themselves described by the masses in the same way as Bevan has described them.'

'Which is?'

'Lower than vermin.'

'Vermin? He doesn't beat about the bush, does he?'

'He doesn't. And as a proud Welshman, he debates in just the same way they play their rugby. He plays to win.'

91

Bergen-Belsen Concentration Camp

The war in Europe was over but Daniel's struggles were only just beginning. His initial shock at the horror of Bergen-Belsen had given way to a reluctant acceptance of the terrible truth and he had become resigned to the potential moral depravity of his fellow man.

'What is your name?' he gently asked the emaciated shell of a man sitting in front of him. The translator was posing the questions in Polish. The man lifted his forearm and showed Daniel the six-figure number on his skin. 'Four-six-zero-two-seven-one,' he answered.

'No. Your name,' asked Daniel, patiently. 'What is your name?'

The survivor looked back at Daniel suspiciously. He glanced around him as if he were about to be punished.

'It's all right,' Daniel tried to reassure him. 'We are just trying to help.'

Progress with all these poor souls was agonisingly slow. They had experienced a world that others would not understand or share. Some of them expressed guilt and shame at still being alive in the presence of so much death. Others were silent, too physically weak or ill to say anything at all. A few cried continually; others could not cry at all. Some were able to draw on inner strength and a stubborn refusal to be broken. In painstaking detail, their torture was meticulously described. The majority, however, were catatonic – paralysed both physically and emotionally. Many more were dying, already too weak and dispirited to be rehabilitated. Daniel continued to supervise their controlled feeding, had them properly cleaned and clothed, and ensured their sores and infestations were treated. He cared for them with dignity and respect, and, slowly but surely, through his seemingly infinite patience and empathy, he began to see some of his patients improve.

The search would now begin for relatives, and, where possible, a renewal of the lives they had once lived in their own countries and homes.

92

British Medical Association, Tavistock House, London

For the last two years, Fitz had devoted most of his time at Westminster to trying to ensure the establishment of a National Health Service. Yet Churchill, the man he had admired so much during the war, and his Tory party, had now voted against it seventeen consecutive times. On the last occasion, Fitz had collapsed on the floor of the chamber and Stephen had had to revive him. His heart condition had been deteriorating for some time and any kind of excitement or stress could trigger a relapse. Will had personally insisted on taking Fitz back to see his cardiology specialist, Dr Brewin, who finally shared the information about the procedures Dr Robert E. Gross was carrying out in Boston. The medical authorities there still regarded the operation as experimental, but the availability of penicillin had at least made it a great deal safer. Without it, Fitz was going to die of heart failure, and according to Brewin, that time was not far off. As soon as Grace had been told, she'd booked Fitz's passage to New York on the next available transatlantic voyage, and sent a telegram to Amy to do all she could to introduce her little brother to Dr Gross as soon as possible. She knew Amy's senator husband, Donald, could be very persuasive. As far as she was aware, Fitz was now halfway across the ocean, accompanied by Stephen. There was no guarantee of success, and Will and Grace both knew the operation was risky. If he came through it alive, the rehabilitation would be long and arduous – six months, at least – but there was no other solution. The alternative was unthinkable.

In Fitz's absence, it was Will and Grace's turn to agitate for the NHS, and the opportunity had arisen at the annual general meeting of the British Medical Association. They decided to drive up to London in the Riley Nine. It was a bright, sunny day, and they would have a rare chance to do some shopping in the capital and bring the goods home in the boot of the old car. It was a treat to have the opportunity of spending an entire day together, and they were hopeful of a positive outcome of the vote at the BMA later in the day.

Will's recent mood of despondency had lifted since penicillin had made such an impact, and he was more optimistic that outcomes of treatment would continue to improve and that more invasive and innovative procedures would become possible. Most ordinary people were already able to buy the antibiotic from the local pharmacist.

But Will's optimistic mood soon became more muted as they drove through villages scarred and diminished by six long years of war. Memorials to the fallen were bedecked with fresh flowers on every village green, and overgrown gardens and dilapidated houses bore testament to the absence of the men who had never returned. Many of those that had could be seen limping about on crutches, their trousers tied up over the stumps of their knees. They saw children with limbs withered from polio, others malnourished from the privations of rationing, or wheezing and coughing from the effects of whooping cough or bronchitis. Just like the charity patients Will and Grace tended to in their free time, these people had endured years of hardship and anxiety. The menfolk had gone off to war, the women had worked in the factories or tilled the land, and the children had either been evacuated to the safety of a family of strangers or left to their own devices to make do. Now the only thing in plentiful supply was a surfeit of bereaved and impoverished widows and orphans. They deserved better than this, and Will and Grace were adamant the medical profession should help. The Beveridge report had already established the principles, and Aneurin Bevan had published his bill on the health service just last month. The public consensus supporting it was unequivocal, and Labour's landslide election victory the previous year would hopefully guarantee its acceptance. Will and Grace had been discussing the topic excitedly on their journey up.

'For most families, being able to afford to see a doctor is still an impossible luxury,' said Will.

'I know. A single visit can easily cost the equivalent of half a week's wages.' Grace knew that most ordinary workers earned money at no more than subsistence level. 'Clara's neighbours' daughter had TB, and because they couldn't afford to send her to a sanatorium, it spread to her spine and left her an invalid. It's wrong.'

'Children are dying all the time from preventable diseases and lack of treatment. It makes me so angry.'

'Well, let's just hope the rest of our profession has developed a conscience.'

Now, taking their place in the Great Hall of the BMA in Tavistock Square, the debate was in full flow. The discussion had started well enough, with Will confidently addressing the 600-strong audience.

'The establishment of a national health service, which is

available to everyone based on their medical need and not their ability to pay, must be a given in any civilised and socially just country,' he had begun. There were a few quiet murmurs of approval, and loud clapping from Grace.

'All of us should be entitled to the highest standards of excellence and professionalism, and this must revolve around the patients rather than ourselves.' This time, the murmuring was distinctly critical. Cries of 'Shame!' and 'Traitor!' could be heard from the back. Grace turned around to see the outgoing president of the trade union making rude gestures and heckling.

'There will be a cost involved, of course,' Will continued, 'but the service will be publicly accountable and provide the very best value for taxpayers' money.'

'Rubbish!' called a portly gentleman at the front. 'It will bankrupt the country overnight. Every Tom, Dick and Harry will want something for nothing, not to mention their wives, mistresses and children. The system will be abused from the outset and hamper our ability to look after those that actually run the country, and on whom the economy depends.'

Cries of 'Hear, hear' resounded through the chamber, followed by loud demands for Will to shut up and be seated. He tried to continue, but was shouted down. The current chairman of the BMA took his place to great applause. He straightened the waistcoat of his three-piece suit and ostentatiously adjusted the gold fob chain of his Prince Albert pocket watch.

'Let those who say they cannot afford our fees self-medicate as they always have. Why remove the financial incentive to better themselves and care for their own families by asking the rest of us to provide it for them for free? Why remove their motivation to lead healthier lives? The current system provided by insurance companies, local councils and charities has served us well for decades. Why would we want to reinvent the wheel?' Loud cheering filled the auditorium.

'Because it's dysfunctional, failing, and unfair,' shouted Will, to howls of derision.

'Neither charities, nor churches, nor local authorities welcome the revolution you propose, sir,' retorted the chairman. 'This gentleman here, a surgeon, if he is to be believed, is advocating for us to become mere servants of the state. He wants to destroy your private practices, force you to administer to any kind of self-neglected ne'er-do-well or half-wit, and accept the paltry salaries as determined by faceless bureaucrats in government.'

The hall was now erupting in loud protest against the draconian and shocking proposals.

'I have examined the bill outlined by Bevan, a man whose main claim to political authority, I believe, was working in a Welsh colliery and inciting insurgency during the General Strike of 1926. It looks to me uncommonly like the first step towards national socialism, as was practised in Nazi Germany.'

'Are you mad,' yelled Will, feeling hopelessly outnumbered, 'or just exceedingly selfish?' Furore erupted around him.

'Is he actually a paid-up member of the BMA, do you imagine?' asked one consultant doctor within Grace's earshot, looking towards Will. 'If so, he should be struck off.' His neighbour nodded in agreement.

'If you are comparing anything to National Socialism, look at your own ideals, Mr Chairman,' continued Will. 'Are you really prepared to allow a whole underclass of people to perish unnecessarily, simply because they were not born into privilege? Aneurin Bevan is the epitome of why we need an NHS. He lost three of his own brothers and sisters through poverty. He knows what it's like not to be able to access a doctor's skills and services.'

Aware of the growing anger in the room directed at her husband, Grace tried in vain to support him. 'Let him speak,' she cried, but nobody was listening. The chairman smelled blood and continued.

'We will not be dictated to by a newly elected, fledgling Labour government who apparently cannot understand how our health services work. They are not medically qualified, they demean us with their ideas of our worth to society, our profession and status, and risk permanently damaging the fragile status quo, which we ourselves have strived so hard to maintain.'

Will felt like punching the man, but Grace had grabbed his arm and made him sit back down. One or two doctors behind him patted him on the back, but the gesture was half-hearted and unconvincing. Once a relative calm had settled again in the hall, the chairman took his cue. 'Let's put it to the vote,' he said. 'Let's have a show of hands. All in favour of rejecting the proposal for a national health service?' He surveyed the room and the forest of hands that shot up. 'And against?' A mere forty or so of the six hundred delegates raised their arms. In that moment, Will realised that if the NHS was ever going to be established, it was clearly not going to be with the support of the medical profession itself.

An hour later, he drove back to Oxford in silence, simmering with barely controlled fury. He still could not understand the attitude of his colleagues. How could so many self-respecting doctors, whose job was to cure the sick and the dying, not want to treat every human being the same?

Grace understood his mood and sympathised completely, but knew that any attempt to divert him from his current gloom would be useless. The shopping trip, which she had so looked forward to, and dinner at Simpsons, as well, would have to wait.

93

Mill Lane

The following Saturday, Daniel's letter arrived from Germany in the first post. Grace tore it open. It had been three months since the last, and although she knew how important his work was, she could only guess at his awful environment and the toll it must be taking on his sanity. She read the first few lines and became more and more excited as she read on.

Dear Mother,

You will scarcely believe this, but by some incredible chance last week, I experienced something that was most unexpected. It was during one of our routine fortnightly roll-calls outlining who was still here, who had been repatriated, who had entered our camp for psychiatric care and so on. There was a woman, a German lady, about fifty years old. She had been brought to us from a camp further east. She was proud, imperious and eloquent. And so defiant. Quite unlike most other survivors. She had even excised the tattoo on her arm bearing her prisoner number by using a hunting knife and then stitching it up crudely with thread. Her name is Greta. In 1936, she was taken from her home in Oranienburg by the Brownshirts because her mother was Jewish. I checked it all out and there seems to be no doubt: she is Greta Fischl. I seem to have found Liese's mother.

I hope you are all safe and well. I miss you all,
Daniel

Epilogue

Bishop's Cleeve, Gloucestershire, 5 July 1948

The big family reunion to celebrate the inauguration of the NHS had been planned for weeks, and despite the recent dreadful news, everyone who could be there had gathered as promised, in the outside hope of some happy revelation.

Grace's mother, Dorothy, remained unhealthily thin and perpetually anxious, and so on edge that the news received four days ago had only made her worse. The SS *President Coolidge*, the ship on which Fitz was returning to England following his successful operation, had struck a rogue mine and had sunk, with significant loss of life. Survivors in lifeboats were now reaching Ireland, but so far there had been no word from Fitz or Stephen. Dorothy naturally feared the worst, although the others were of the mind that *no news is good news*. Fitz was a natural survivor.

In the afternoon, the mood was distinctly sombre, as they all knew how much Fitz had done to help Aneurin Bevan push through his NHS bill after its second and third readings.

Until six in the evening, when the sun was just beginning to dip below the ridge of the trees at the top of the hill, no one had had much of an appetite for a celebratory dinner, but all that changed in a heartbeat ten minutes later. From the drawing room, they heard a car draw up on the gravel outside, followed by loud, happy voices, and the slamming of doors. Dorothy went to the window and shrieked with delight. 'It's Fitz!' she yelled. 'I can't believe it!'

The others all jumped to their feet and rushed out of the front door. Standing there with Fitz and Stephen were Amy and her husband Donald, their various suitcases all piled on the steps.

'But your ship went down,' said Grace incredulously. 'The newspapers are saying the rescue operation is still continuing. This is impossible.'

'No, it's not,' said Fitz with a grin. 'Because we weren't aboard!'

Grace looked back at him blankly.

'Stephen and I never got on the *President Coolidge*. Amy and Donald were flying to Paris via London for a fashion show and had two spare tickets. Why would you turn down two complementary seats on a Pan-Am Douglas DC-4 taking a few hours to return home when the alternative is a tiresome sea journey taking over a week?'

'So you flew?'

'We flew. We just hope those poor souls on the ship are all safe.'

Grace threw her arms around him and hugged him. 'You look so well, Fitzy,' she said when she finally released him. 'Pink and glowing.'

'I know,' he said, rolling up his trouser leg. 'No fluid here. No breathlessness. I'm a new man.'

'He certainly is,' added Stephen. 'There'll be no stopping him now.'

'God help the Tory party,' said Will, laughing.

Dorothy pushed Grace aside and swamped Fitz in a

smothering maternal embrace. 'You're all just in time for dinner. And now we can really let our hair down and celebrate.'

Dorothy thanked the Lord for returning her other children to her after the war, even though her precious Charles had been tragically taken from her in 1916.

Greta Fischl had discovered she had a lot in common with Dorothy and was settling in nicely to the new life she had been offered at Bishop's Cleeve. She and Kitty would undoubtedly be sharing fond memories of Liese all evening.

Clara had brought Leandro with her and the handsome young teenager was proudly telling everyone about his admission to Oxford University.

Henry, having raided what was left of his father, Arthur's, wine cellar, produced three fine bottles of 1936 Chateau Petrus, which, far from being savoured and sipped as a vintage wine usually demanded, was soon being swilled and swigged as if it might evaporate before they had a chance to enjoy it. It was turning out to be a happy and heartwarming family reunion.

'Look at the size of my scar,' Fitz declared, opening his shirt and proudly displaying the livid vertical scar down the centre of his breastbone. 'Ten inches long and healing nicely.'

'We told you,' said Amy. 'Dr Robert Gross, MD, knows his stuff. He did his first successful operation on your . . . arterial duck thingy or whatever it's called . . . on a little girl aged seven back in 1938. So even though nobody is doing the operation here in England yet, he'd had loads of practice.'

'*Patent ductus arteriosus* is the correct term, dear sister. Let me make that "patently" clear. And the fact that mine never behaved itself and stubbornly stayed patent immediately after birth when it should've closed like everybody else's is the problem that has held me back all these years.'

'Not anymore, though,' Stephen chipped in. 'I can hardly keep up with him myself, and I run marathons!'

'It's true. I'm not breathless anymore. No dizziness, no swollen ankles. No blue lips or palpitations, either, when I get annoyed by dyed-in-the-wool politicians trying to block social welfare reform. Present company excepted, Donald.'

'Well, you've got Amy to thank for your operation,' replied the senator. 'Without her extensive circle of social contacts in Boston, I doubt Dr Gross would even have considered operating on a penniless Limey like you.'

'I don't doubt it, Donald. Sister, I'm in your debt.' Fitz stood and raised his glass theatrically. Since his operation, he seemed to have taken on a new lease of life.

'A toast,' he cried. 'To Amy, and her extensive circle of social contacts.'

'To Amy,' everybody around the table echoed before drinking to her health.

'And what of my favourite nephew?' Fitz continued after sitting down again. 'What have you been up to, Daniel? You do *know* you're my favourite nephew, don't you?'

'You only have one nephew, Fitz,' Daniel replied, smiling, 'but I appreciate the sentiment. I'm back working at the Maudsley. There are so many people traumatised by the war. People have lost their homes. People have lost their jobs, others have lost loved ones, or parts of themselves. The ones physically disabled, military and civilian alike, are visible and people are generally sympathetic. The unfortunate ones with psychological injuries, not so much. Like Robbie, some will never be quite the same again, and it doesn't help when they are shunned and stigmatised. At least they can now access free treatment, thanks to the NHS. Most of the time, anyway.'

'And those poor souls from the concentration camps?' Dorothy asked. 'Do you still have any contact with them?'

'Many of them, yes. It's a work in progress and a task that will never be finished. The important thing is that the world learns from it. Not just how to treat the medical consequences of such horrors, but how to make sure the ideology of eugenics and the practice of genocide never happens again.'

'I'm hoping there will never be another war ever again,' said Donald optimistically. 'Hiroshima and Nagasaki put an end to this one, and the atomic bomb our scientists created, with your British guys helping out as well, of course, should mean a world war on this scale will never conceivably be repeated.'

'I hope so,' added Will's aunt Clara. 'But didn't we think the first war would be the one to end all wars?'

'It will be a different kind of war in the future,' said Kitty, jumping in. 'A geo-political and ideological one. There may not be any direct physical confrontations, not between the superpowers anyway, but there will be regional conflicts, for sure. You'll see. There will still be struggles for global influence, economic advantage and technical advance. I regret to say it's inevitable.'

Will had noticed how passionate his youngest sister had become about such issues. She had never told him about the exact role she had played working for the 'Ministry of Information' in France and the Netherlands, and she had never mentioned an organisation known as the SOE, but nonetheless he wasn't daft and had a very good idea about what she might have been up to. He was inordinately proud of her.

'And you, Ned?' asked Clara, changing the subject. 'How will you keep this feisty young lady under control and stop her setting off to fight yet another war?'

Clara loved Ned almost as much as Kitty did. She loved his quiet strength and resolve, and the thoughtfulness and wisdom that lay beneath – not to mention his athletic physique and stunning good looks. No wonder Kitty had impulsively agreed to marry him three days after their dramatic reunion in London. Ned looked at Kitty and took her hand in his. 'First, I'm whisking her away to Québec. I've persuaded her to come with me when I see my parents for the first time in a decade. Unfortunately, the authorities have not been kind to my mother. But I look forward to seeing what Kitty thinks of the country of my birth. Perhaps she'll like it enough to stay.'

'We haven't decided yet, Auntie,' added Kitty, 'but it's exciting.'

'What will they think of your new name, Mr San Grefria?' asked Bembe. 'Won't they wonder why you changed it from Harding?'

Ned laughed. Bembe had been amused by the story leading to Ned's change of surname and loved teasing him about it. Luckily, Ned was happy to play along.

'Bembe and I are planning to set up a flying school at Kidlington,' Emily said. 'We could call it the Blackbird Flying School. The BFS.'

'A flying school?' asked Dorothy. 'Is there a demand for one?'

'I'm convinced of it. Planes are in plentiful supply. Now the war's over, there's a surplus parked up on airfields just going rusty and collecting mildew. They'll all need ongoing maintenance. Bembe and I are never going to stop flying, and we've already got a contract to tow advertising banners around the skies of Oxford behind our biplanes. We'll set up aerobatic displays, too. Just like you do in America, Donald.' Emily could not help exuding her customary bubbly enthusiasm. 'Besides, the world is changing. Air travel for leisure will become quite the thing. I want to get more women into aviation, too. Why not? Women have got used to doing things that were once the sole province of men. By the end of the war, there were hundreds of women like me delivering planes of all descriptions, whenever and wherever. Look at what Kitty has achieved, as well.' She winked at her aunt and added, 'She's my hero.'

Kitty smiled graciously and raised her eyebrows. 'I don't know why,' she replied dismissively, 'but thanks anyway.' Now it was her turn to propose a toast. 'To the BFS. The Blackbird Flying School.' She stood and lifted her glass, and the others echoed the sentiment.

Emily wasn't finished. 'There'll be hundreds of women wanting to fly now, just you wait and see. And Bembe and I are going to teach them.'

'And this time, I'll back you, Emily,' said Will. 'As you know, I did once have my reservations. Now, my former concerns have all but evaporated.'

'I'd like to propose a toast myself,' said Henry, finally. 'A more sombre one, this time. So please charge your glasses again and raise them. To my brothers: Fitz, who is finally himself again, Rupert, who will be returning from sea within a few months and who should be demobbed next year, and James, who is just about to launch the Ford Motor company's latest model. To my wonderful mother Dorothy, and beloved sisters, Grace and Amy. And finally, to our dear departed father, Arthur, and our brother Charles. And, Clara, to your brother Robbie, and to yours, Will and Kitty. To Jack.'

Whenever Jack's name was mentioned, Will felt conflicted. Despite the differences between him and his brother in personality and behaviour, he had loved Jack and his enormous capacity for living life to the full. He had lived on the edge, and had flirted with danger just as naturally and frequently as he had flirted with women. Will had no doubt that when the end came, it had been entirely Jack's decision. There was no way he could have tolerated living with his worsening condition, not with his physical powers and cognitive function slowing, his job under threat, and his sexual adventurism curtailed.

Will caught Daniel's eye across the table and suspected his son was thinking exactly the same thing. He felt Kitty kick him under the table and realised Henry was continuing to propose his toast. 'Kitty and Grace, I know you were very close to Liese. And Greta, your beloved daughter was a true heroine of our times. We hold her dear to us and shall never forget her.' He raised his glass above his head. 'To those that have gone, but who will live forever in our hearts.'

'To those that have gone,' murmured everyone around the table, 'but who will live forever in our hearts.'

A few moments passed in silence before Kitty picked up the conversation. 'What about you, Will, and you, Grace? What are you planning next?'

'More of the same, I guess,' said Will. 'There'll be plenty of orthopaedic and other surgical work for me, especially now that everybody in the land has equal access to excellent healthcare.'

'And surgery will be so much safer and more practical now we have access to significant amounts of penicillin,' added

Grace. 'That will keep me occupied. No more collecting urine from patients and riding off to the lab on a bicycle to extract what remains of the antibiotic!'

'And thanks to the Labour party and its wonderful and much-vaunted National Health Service, nobody will have to pay for it,' Fitz said.

'That's just as well,' Clara replied. 'Because I'm having this tiresome, arthritic hip of mine replaced with an artificial one, apparently made of stainless steel and attached by bolts.'

'That's marvellous, Auntie,' added Kitty, knowing how much pain Clara had been in recently. 'And good to know that penicillin will be on hand should you need it.'

'Yes, and thanks to my lovely nephew Will, here, I'll be one of the very first NHS patients on the famous surgeon's list. Ideally, I'd have Will perform the operation, but he says because I'm family, he's not allowed to do it.'

'And I'm not familiar enough with the new procedure anyway. You're in very good hands though. You've probably got the best hip surgeon in the world carrying out a revolutionary new procedure and it won't cost you a single penny. So it's my turn to propose a toast.' Will stood up.

'To free treatment at the point of delivery for everybody, independent of their means. To our new NHS.'

'To our new NHS,' everybody joined in enthusiastically.

'It's incredible, really,' Grace continued after everybody had sat back down again. 'Not so long ago, we had barely enough penicillin to treat a single patient. Every fraction of a microgram was more precious than gold dust.'

'But once we in the United States entered the war after Pearl Harbor,' added Donald, 'we soon regarded its production as second only in importance to the development of the atom bomb. Dozens of companies started producing it.'

'Howard Florey was brilliant,' Grace said. 'And I do believe he was right. The production of penicillin really was, as he put it . . . something of a miracle.'

'A toast, then, to penicillin,' said Henry, taking the floor once more.

'To penicillin,' they all rejoined in unison.

Acknowledgements

First and foremost, to Kerr McRae for contacting me out of the blue and inviting me during that first year of the COVID-19 pandemic to consider writing a novel in the first place. At the time I was caught up in the dramatic maelstrom of up-to-the-minute TV reporting on breaking medical news about the virus, and it turned out to be a wonderful departure during those turbulent and challenging times. For me personally, this work of fiction and imagination was a welcome and therapeutic antidote to the cold hard science and reality of it all.

To my wife Dee, for doing most other things whilst I was writing the book.

To Imogen Taylor, Executive Publisher at Headline and Mountain Leopard Press, for taking over the mantle so that I could complete the trilogy and for her expert input and guidance from the outset and to Beth Wickington, Publisher at Mountain Leopard Press. Also to Laura McCallen, who must surely be one of the best copyeditors ever and to Jenni Edgecombe for her eagle-eyed editorial guidance.

To Judy Leverchain, Ernst Chain's daughter for welcoming me into her home and sharing insights about her famous father.

To the Dunn School of Pathology in Oxford, who pointed me in the direction of the BBC's production 'Breaking the Mould' starring Dominic West. The Dunn School is an integral part of the book and 2027 will mark the centenary of this famous institution.

To Eric Lax, who authored 'The Mould in Dr Florey's Coat', (Little, Brown and Company 2004) a comprehensive and detailed analysis of the entire penicillin story.

Under Darkening Skies is based on true events and accurate timelines but the fictional characters epitomise the dedication, courage, sacrifice and sheer bloody-mindedness of all those involved in resisting the rise of fascism during the last century, and the incredible scientific endeavour required to investigate, test and produce the revolutionary and life-saving medicine that came to be known as penicillin. We owe them.

About the Author

DR HILARY JONES is a General Practitioner and regular contributor to multiple newspapers and television shows. He is a well-known and trusted face to millions in the UK.

@DrHilaryJones

www.drhilaryjones.com